MISS TERRY

MISS TERRY

for Pat –
Great to meet you

liza

Liza Cody

liza Cody

iUniverse, Inc.
Bloomington

MISS TERRY

iUniverse books may be ordered through booksellers or by contacting:

iUniverse
1663 Liberty Drive
Bloomington, IN 47403
www.iuniverse.com
1-800-Authors (1-800-288-4677)

ISBN: 978-1-4759-3243-0 (sc)
ISBN: 978-1-4759-3244-7 (hc)
ISBN: 978-1-4759-3245-4 (ebk)

Printed in the United States of America

iUniverse rev. date: 08/28/2012

Cover picture by Elsie and Emzel
Author picture by Emzel

Contents

Other books by Liza Cody

Anna Lee series:

DUPE
BAD COMPANY
STALKER
HEADCASE
BACKHAND
UNDER CONTRACT

Bucket Nut Trilogy:

BUCKET NUT
MONKEY WRENCH
MUSCLEBOUND

Other novels:

RIFT
GIMME MORE
BALLAD OF A DEAD NOBODY

Short stories:

LUCKY DIP and Other Stories

1

Sweet Nita

//

If you could watch Nita Tehri while she was sleeping you'd probably get the wrong impression. She looks dishevelled and mellow, an independent modern woman alone in her double bed, in her own flat. Her hair fans out on the pillow like an open crow's wing. Her mouth is sweet with dreams—she's almost smiling. Relaxed, her arm is naked to the elbow because the sleeve of her Snoopy pyjama top is rucked up. With her hand curled near her face and she looks almost young enough to suck her thumb.

But sometimes the fates decide to play games with smiling young women, and one morning, while it was still dark, Galloway Waste delivered a skip and left it outside number 14, almost opposite Nita's house. It was dented yellow on the exterior, blackened with age and rust on the interior. It remained empty for only three and a half minutes. Then Harris Searle, on his way home to number 6 from his nightshift at the hospital, threw in his breakfast burger wrapper instead of taking it home to his own waste bin.

At 7.30 workmen turned up in a white van and sat, drinking coffee and eating sandwiches until the owner arrived to let them into number 15. They, too, threw their rubbish in the skip but that was legitimate because the new owner of number 15, Bret West, was the one who hired it.

That morning all the people who lived at the top end of Guscott Road had their lives disturbed by the building work at number 15. Jen Brown met Nita at the corner outside Women's Aid and said, 'They've only just begun but noise's driving me crazy already—like, they're tearing the place apart.'

With cold fingers, Nita tweaked nervously at her tidy hair, now safely controlled by a hair band and clip. 'That's developers for you. They don't care about the neighbours. But I'm glad weirdy-boy with the blue hair's gone. He stared.'

'You should've given him something to stare at.' Jen, dressed to be stared at in long boots and short skirt, made no concessions to the cold weather apart from a fluffy pink scarf. 'If you ask me it was his father was the weird one. Dragging a dirty old canvas bag around everywhere. And that car of his—the guys downstairs used to do stuff to put him off parking outside.'

'What?' Nita was shocked.

Jen tossed blonde hair. 'They just snapped off a few windscreen wipers and the odd wing mirror. They couldn't stand having that heap of crap out by the front door.'

'I never knew they were so fussy. It's not like they're fastidious when it comes to rubbish day, is it?'

'Rubbish is only rubbish,' Jen said. 'But you gotta respect a car. Craigie's late for playschool, so tar-rah now.'

Nita watched her bounce away—a night-clubber with a pushchair. She was late now herself so she ran to the bus-stop.

On her way back home that night she glanced into the skip and saw that along with a crumbly mess of plaster and rotting floorboards there were three interior doors and a brittle, brown Christmas tree. It was mid February and Nita wondered why blue-haired weirdy-boy and his dad had kept their tree for so long.

Later still when she looked out of her top floor window at the crescent moon and the deserted street, she noticed that one of the interior doors had been removed but two black garbage bags and a second Christmas tree had taken its place. A weary thought about the ever-changing status of rubbish crossed her mind like a thin cloud in front of the moon. She went back to bed.

In the morning, chewing toast at her sitting-room window, she noticed that someone had dumped half a dozen empty cardboard boxes in the skip and another interior door was missing. The workmen turned up and one of them threw a bulging black bin-bag in before going to number 15. The noise began, and Nita left for work.

She met Stu and Diane at the bus stop. Diane said, 'I heard they're gutting number 15 and turning it into three flats. Student accommodation. You know what happens when students take over a street, don't you? You might as well move right out. You own your flat, don't you? Well, there go property prices, straight down the pan.'

Stu looked at his watch. 'Bleeding bus. Late again. Diane, you should send them another email.'

Nita said, 'The guys downstairs from me are students.'

'Medical students.' Diane sniffed. 'Gay medical students. And they own their own. Could there *be* better neighbours?'

That night, tired and lonely, Nita stood by her window and looked down at two filthy ovens which had arrived, it seemed, without human intervention. Why did she never see anyone deposit anything? It was as if the skip were spontaneously generating its contents, like a huge yellow metal pig endlessly farrowing. Nita's weary brain pictured a monstrous modern fertility goddess perpetually giving birth to Christmas trees, doors and ovens.

Two days later, full to overflowing, the skip was replaced with an empty one and the process began again.

Diane, Jen and Nita met outside Women's Aid on their separate ways back home. Jen said, 'They're knocking down walls in number 15. I got a headache like a right bastard. My Dave won't stop overnight no more. He says he needs his lie-in. He says what with our Craigie kicking off in the middle of the night an' all, he's got no shuteye whatsoever. My sex-life sucks and it's all number 15's fault. Think I can sue the developer?'

Diane said, 'What're those two police cars doing down the end of our street?'

'That'll be those twats next to old Daphne again.' Jen said. 'She called the cops out last summer cos the boys were using her roof as their private patio and dancing round in the nuddy to the Kaiser Chiefs and chucking beer bottles down her chimney. She's no fucking fun is Daphne.'

'Stu says you shouldn't swear so much in front of the baby,' Diane said, sniffing loudly. 'He'll pick it up.'

'Stu can kiss my arse,' Jen said, 'and you can go fuck yourself.' She stormed away at such a speed that Craig started yelling in protest.

Diane watched her go with a relieved expression on her face. 'I wish the council would put her somewhere else. You know Dave isn't Craig's father, don't you?'

'All the same, she really looks after that baby,' Nita said.

'He's at the child minder's all day and she gets income support but she's working at the discount furniture place. My taxes pay for her. I'm thinking of reporting her.'

'Reporting who?' asked Harris Searle, on his way out to start his shift at the hospital. 'Now's the time to do it with all the cops knocking at doors.'

'What do they want?' Nita liked Harris. She'd hardly ever spoken to him, but she thought he looked dependable.

'Search me,' Harris said. 'I left while they were talking to the old bat in the basement. I didn't want to wait around. I was already late.' He walked away quickly.

Diane watched him go. 'He's married,' she said, 'So don't look at him like that.'

'I wasn't.'

'She left him after their dog died. Daphne says he's still bitter but he never got a divorce. He doesn't like women much.'

Nita didn't question Diane's knowledge or opinion. She'd only lived on Guscott Road for six months. It was a dead-end street that stopped at the river. With only one way in and out neighbours passed to and fro all day, and it gave a false sense of intimacy. She said, 'Well, I'd better be going now.' But Diane was in no hurry. She said, 'You teach, don't you?'

'Midford Junior.' Nita felt uncomfortable. Personal questions did that to her.

'Yes, they said you didn't have anything to do over the holidays. Tigs and Joe go to your school, don't they? Noisy little beggars. They call you Miss Terry.'

'Teh'ri.' Nita spelled it for her.

'Well it had to be something foreign, didn't it? No disrespect, mind. Aren't you a bit scared the police'll talk to *you*?'

'No. Why?'

'Oh I don't know. Immigration. Terrorism.' Her pale blue eyes stared at Nita innocently.

'I was born here.' Nita said patiently. 'Now excuse me please. I've books to mark.' She walked away to her own front door, promising herself to avoid Diane in future. As she passed the skip she noticed, under a heap of torn-up plasterboard and five wall units, another dead Christmas tree. There were coils of threadbare stair carpet stained with nameless spillages. How long had blue-haired weirdy-boy and his dad lived there without a wife or mother? The dead artefacts from their old house murmured to Nita of neglect and decay, of things falling apart without a caring witness. She knew she was constitutionally unable to live with a stair carpet so worn and filthy. But she knew too that all around her nature and entropy were working without cease to pull apart the material world and turn it to dust. She let herself in through the front door and ran upstairs to her own newly decorated flat.

The tiles in her bathroom gleamed with care. She showered and washed the day's frustrations out of her hair. Now she could watch the evening news, make supper and mark school work feeling fresh and in control. Spotlessness and control were somehow linked in Nita's mind. She wasn't quite sure why, but as usual she blamed her mother. It seemed to her that it was what her mother was for: to be blamed for things Nita didn't understand.

2

Local Enquiries

///

The doorbell rang while she was in the kitchen chopping vegetables to combine with rice that was already cooking. A man's voice over the speakerphone said, 'Miss Terry? PC Reed here. Could I come up for a chat, please?'

'Tehri,' Nita said. 'Can you tell me what it's about? I'm making supper.'

'Just some local enquiries,' the tinny voice said. 'It won't take long.'

Nita pressed the entry button and heard the front door open and close down below. She went to her flat door and put the chain on. It wasn't as if she had any doubt about PC Reed's authenticity. She just wanted to demonstrate that she was careful and nobody's fool.

He sat on her small sofa, his long legs stretched out on her woven rug, looking as out of place as a lawn-mower on a dance floor. Not many men sat on Nita's sofa except for the guys downstairs who didn't really count. She felt unnerved and offered him tea, not knowing what rules of hospitality applied to big men she hadn't invited.

'No thank you,' he said. 'You have a really good view of the street from here. How about the building opposite—does the noise bother you at all?'

'I'm at work during the day. And I get up early so I don't mind much.'

'What about the skip? Does it interfere with parking? You've got a good view of that too.'

'I don't own a car.'

'You don't?'

'I'm a teacher,' Nita explained. 'I can't really afford a car, and it isn't necessary in a city like this.'

The policeman looked as uncomprehending as any guy who had automobiles stamped in his DNA. He shook his head, and brought himself back to business. 'But I suppose you can see people putting stuff in the skip, can't you? I mean people not authorised to use it.'

'Fly-tippers, you mean?' Nita was accustomed to people presuming she didn't know the common terms, but it made her feel tired. 'You aren't here about fly-tipping, are you?'

'Not really.' PC Reed looked embarrassed. 'Er, one of your neighbours mentioned that you've lost a lot of weight recently.'

'I beg your pardon! Who told you that? What business is it of yours?' She stood up with her hands on her hips as if she were in front of a class of rowdy eight-year-olds. Happy to see the policeman's face redden.

He said, 'Look, this is coming out the wrong way. I was just meant to ask you about what you could see from your window. Someone said they saw you sometimes, late at night, you know, looking out, watching the street.'

'I watch the moon and I mind my own business.' Nita was furious. 'You'd better leave now, my rice is burning.' She turned and walked away into the kitchen. The rice wasn't burning but it was ready and she took it off the hob. Her hands were shaking. She never told off grown men. It was a cultural relic, she supposed. For the second time that evening she blamed her mother.

She heard her flat door close and Reed's heavy tread on the stairs, and she realised she had been holding her breath.

7

Bad things happen to women who stand up to big men, she thought, and then was horrified at how automatic her reaction was. 'I'm a teacher,' she said out loud to her knife and chopping board. 'It's a respected profession. He can't just walk into my flat and say any old thing.' She finished cutting up chilli, ginger, mushrooms, pak-choi and coriander, trying to steady herself. The vegetables hissed in the hot oil, smelling delicious, but she was no longer hungry. Nevertheless she filled a plate and took it into the sitting room hoping that the last of the evening news would bring her back to her own sense of reality. But the TV picture was of a dusty place where big men in turbans screamed in rage and fired guns into the air.

She looked out of the window and saw two pigeons on the roof of number 15. The male was strutting in circles around the female who crouched immobile. Suddenly the male jumped onto the female's back, flattening her against the slates, his wings raised and beating triumphantly. It was over in seconds. Then he flew away leaving her, a grey sad shape, sitting alone on grey sad slate.

Nita got up and closed the blinds. She hoped no one on the other side of the road was watching her watching pigeons. Someone had already told the police about her standing at her window late at night. Who on earth was watching her? Why was anything she did worth reporting? She remembered Diane's remark about terrorism. But Diane lived on the same side of the street as Nita and therefore couldn't see her when she looked out. And what did her weight matter to anyone except herself?

Nita took her plate out to the kitchen. She covered it with foil and put it in the fridge. Perhaps she'd feel hungry later. She filled the kettle for a cup of tea, and the doorbell rang.

A man said, 'Sergeant Cutler here. Might we have a word?'

'What about, Sergeant Cutler?' Nita swung her head to loosen the tightness in her neck. 'I was just talking to Constable Reed, and he wasn't very polite.'

'Would you let me in Miss Terry? Perhaps we could have a little chat about that.'

Sergeant Cutler looked tough and tired. He said, 'Do you mind if I raise the blind? I'd like to be able to see out.'

'Would you like to rearrange the furniture too?' Nita said without thinking. 'Look, why don't you just tell me what you want? I can't help you if you don't ask direct questions.'

'Would you mind if I raised the blind?' Sergeant Cutler sounded like a machine. He didn't wait for her permission, but opened the blind and peered out at the rapidly darkening street.

Nita turned and marched out to the kitchen. She switched on the kettle again with sweating fingers. Sergeant Cutler followed her in. He said, 'Reed told me you were touchy.' He watched her warm the pot and go methodically through the steps for making proper tea.

'Two sugars for me,' he said when she'd finished. 'And only a dash of milk.'

'Are you having me on?'

'Maybe we got off to a bad start,' he said, running blunt fingers along her cream coloured counter. He picked up the chopping knife and tested the point. 'Sharp,' he said, and licked blood off his thumb. Nita opened a drawer and handed him a tin of plasters. Having seen the colour of his blood she felt she probably owed him a cup of tea. She filled a mug and added two sugars and a dash of milk before silently handing it to him.

He followed her back to the sitting-room and watched while she lowered the blind once more. She sat down opposite him and waited, determined to force him into making himself clear before rushing in with responses.

'What we're interested in is the night before last,' he said eventually.

Nita said nothing.

'I mean the night before they took the skip away to empty it.'

Nita remained silent.

Sergeant Cutler sighed and said, 'When you were looking out the window that night, Miss Terry, did you happen to see anyone placing anything in the skip, and maybe trying to conceal it?'

'No, I didn't,' Nita said. 'Why?'

'Did you yourself put anything into the skip late that night and try to conceal it?'

'No, of course not. Why're you asking me this? What have you found?'

'Who said we'd found anything?'

'I'm just following the drift of your questions.'

'Well don't,' Sergeant Cutler said. 'Just answer the questions honestly and we'll get along fine.'

'I am,' Nita said. She folded her hands and waited for the next one but Cutler got to his feet and said, 'Well, that's all for now. If you remember anything you might've wanted to tell me, give me a bell at the Wallace Street nick.'

He left and Nita went to the kitchen to put the tea mugs into the dishwasher. She opened the kitchen window. With Sergeant Cutler inside, her flat had felt tiny and short of oxygen. She breathed deeply. The evening air chilled her but did nothing to open up more space. She took her thick coat from its hook in the hall and went out. She stopped and listened at Toby and Leo's door but there was no sound. Sometimes they went to the university sport facility after work to tone and tighten in the gym, and didn't come home till late.

Outside the front door she paused, looking right and left. The police cars were gone. She thought about walking down to the river to see if any of the other Guscott Road residents were around, wanting a chat. But she didn't feel she knew anyone well enough to ring their bell or knock on their door. With Diane and Jen it was a bus-stop acquaintanceship. She'd never been inside their homes and they'd never been in hers. Daphne lived with her two grown up sons and Nita had chatted with her regularly about the pot-plants she grew outside her house in the summer. She hadn't seen much of her since the weather turned cold and the plants either died or were moved indoors. She'd never met the old bat who lived in Harris's basement.

In a street of thirty terraced houses, Nita suddenly realised she wasn't acquainted with many people. She didn't know how to find out if the police had been rude or intrusive to anyone else. Had she been the only one? Or did any of her neighbours know what the police wanted? That was what annoyed Nita most: the way the two policemen refused to tell her what she felt she had a right to know.

She turned towards the main road. There was a pub close by called The Green Man which she'd been to with Toby and Leo. Maybe a couple of Guscott Road residents would be in there discussing the police inquiry and she could just casually join them, buy a round of drinks and find out what they knew. She barely hesitated at the pub door, but walked briskly past as if the thought hadn't entered her head. Another cultural relic, she supposed, irritated with herself. She never went to pubs on her own.

Pretending she had somewhere to go, Nita walked on for nearly half a mile until she found herself outside the all-night supermarket. She went in and bought a packet of chocolate biscuits. It'd be alright, she promised herself. She'd eat them on the move, and in the morning she'd get up early and walk to school instead of catching the bus. In fact, she could start right now: she would walk a long circuit home—across the bridge, along the river walk. Chocolate biscuits couldn't harm her if she took her punishment at the same time as doing the crime.

She walked briskly in the cold night air, feeding herself with gloved hands, breathing white into the dark, and thought about the sensible plate of rice and veg she had no appetite for. Some of life's emergencies, it seemed, responded only to chocolate. But it would be better to start yoga again or find a meditation group, than to re-awaken an old addiction.

It took Nita half an hour to complete the walk. She was proud of herself. Proud too of the way she'd thrown the last two biscuits in a bin. She turned left into Guscott Road, and as she passed the skip she saw that a mattress that hadn't been there when she went out was now lying on top of yet another

Christmas tree. Outside her own house a Toyota four-by-four was parked with the driver, who was wearing a sleeveless T-shirt and some very exotic tattoos, appearing to be asleep.

There were no lights on in the house so her downstairs neighbours had not yet come home. She let herself into her silent flat and checked both phone and computer for messages. There were none, so she took another shower and got ready for bed hoping the walk had made her tired enough to sleep quickly.

Maybe it was a drunk leaving the pub shouting that woke her. She turned on her bedside lamp and saw that it wasn't yet midnight. She got up, as she always did, and went to the window. The moon was older by one more night, and dimmer. Orange street lamps warmed the chilly road below her. She wanted to know if the man in the Toyota was still there but it was too cold to open the window. Her night-stained brain told her he was a police spy watching her door. If he could see her bedroom window he would think *she* was the spy, spying on him, waiting for him to sleep so that she could place her dark-skinned bomb in the skip and blow up Guscott Road. He was on to her. She was busted. He'd been warned. Everyone knew: by day she was a butter-wouldn't-melt teacher of little kids, but by night she was an evil thing who should be watched and restrained. Sooner or later someone would have to take preventive action. Which of course they would, as soon as they discovered that she'd forgotten to mark the books she'd brought home.

Judges and juries would surely be appeased if they could see her now, in her enormous Snoopy pyjamas, sitting in her study, hunched against the cold, dutifully doing the right thing. But could she suffer enough to propitiate the gods who doled out sleep and peace? It was rare but not impossible.

Before going back to bed, Nita took one more look out of her bedroom window. As far as she could see no one else had sacrificed at the altar of the yellow skip goddess. But a moving light caught her eye—on the other side of the road, at the end closest to the river, she saw a figure wrapped up against the cold move from door to door examining by torchlight the names, if any, next to the door bells. Then the muffled figure crossed to her side and she could no longer see him.

The plate next to her own bell simply and accurately said, Flat 2. No one looking at that would guess that Nita Tehri hid behind a little number. No one, that is, who hadn't talked to the police and neighbours who apparently knew far more about her than she did about them. With midnight certainty she understood that the man examining nameplates was also the police spy in the Toyota. She went to the bathroom and popped a pill out of a bubble card. She swallowed it with water from her tooth mug. Ersatz, plastic, sleep was the best she could expect tonight.

3

Creepy Insights

//

I n the morning, early, while frost still dignified the dead
Christmas tree, Nita left her house to walk to work. There
was no Toyota outside her door. It was too early for Jen or
Diane and the road was deserted. In spite of the cold Nita was
glad to be out and walking. It helped drain the sleeping-pill soup
that was sloshing around in her head and ease the uneasiness of
the night before.

She walked steadily, feeling younger and stronger the further
she got from home and by the time she reached the school she
was sure she had managed to expiate yesterday's sin of chocolate.
She was early—only a few children and their parents called out
a greeting as she pushed through the glass doors into the hall.
On her way to the staff cloakroom she met the Deputy Head
coming in the opposite direction. He looked at his watch and
then said, 'Miss Terry, the Head has asked me to tell you to go
to his office at first break. He's at a meeting so I'll be taking
assembly.'

'Okay,' Nita said. 'Do you know what it's about?'

'I wouldn't dream of asking.' The Deputy Head frowned
icily, and went out to supervise the school gate.

The first lessons would've been calm and orderly if it weren't
for Ryan. Everyone in the staffroom, except Nita, always referred
to him as 'the little shit'. He was a bully and a cry-baby who,

Nita was convinced, had a food allergy or at very least a violent reaction to sugar. She could always tell when he'd had sweets and fizzy drinks for breakfast. And he was most likely to have a bad breakfast when his father was around to upset his mother.

Today he began by stabbing Poppy with a pencil and tearing up Sam's poem about a snail—which was a pity because it was a very good poem for an eight-year-old, yet it didn't bear the trace of a parental hand. When Nita tried to persuade Ryan to sit on the Naughty Chair he kicked her ankle and screamed, 'My dad'll hit you. He'll whack, whack, whack you and fuck you.' It was a creepy insight into Ryan's family life, she thought, struggling to separate him from the rest of the kids as gently as she could.

When break came she went straight to the Head's office. It was a narrow room with a desk in front of the window. Mr Hughes always sat with his back to the light where he could see Nita's expression but she couldn't see his.

'Come in, come in,' he boomed. 'Sit, sit.' He began as usual as if she were twenty kids with hearing difficulties. 'Now what's all this about a police enquiry? I said, "Not our Miss Tehri, surely you can't mean our sweet young Miss Tehri?" But the inspector or whoever he was was quite adamant.'

A sudden trickle of sweat crawled down Nita's ribs to her waist.

'What on earth do they want?' Her voice shook and even to herself she sounded like one of the children in her class.

'That's precisely what I brought you here to find out.'

'Something seems to have happened in the street where I live, but they wouldn't tell me what it was. They were knocking on doors when I got home last night. I think they questioned everyone.'

'Is that so?' Mr Hughes gave a sceptical flick of his eyebrows. 'Because they gave me the distinct impression that this was an immigration query.'

'I beg your pardon?'

'Exactly what I said, Miss Tehri. But they wanted to know if I had seen your passport or your birth certificate, which is of course absurd: anyone employed to work with children has to undergo police vetting, so they should have all the relevant details at their own fingertips instead of calling me in the middle of supper. I was less than ecstatic, as you can well imagine.'

'I'm sorry,' Nita said.

'They had the gall to ask if you'd married recently and how did it feel for someone like me to attend a Hindu wedding. You haven't married someone without telling any of your colleagues, have you, Miss Tehri? The police seemed to think it might have happened without your consent and that therefore you might have been reluctant to share the information.'

'I can assure you, Mr Hughes...'

'No secret marriages, then? Because, as you must know, the school board has an interest in any change of status in its employees.'

'I don't understand...'

'That's a pity, Miss Tehri: I was hoping you would enlighten me.'

'I can assure you that I haven't got married. But I don't understand why it's any business of the police.'

'Nor do I,' Mr Hughes said, staring at her with no discernable expression.

'Was it a Sergeant Cutler?' Nita asked trying hard not to sound scared.

'I can't remember the name, but that's neither here nor there. What concerns me is the notion that you might be involved in something that might affect our school's reputation.'

'Well I'm not,' Nita told him, mimicking firmness. 'I promise.'

'So there's nothing more you want to tell me?'

'There is something actually.' She sat up straighter and unfolded her arms. 'Is there anything we can do about Ryan? I'm worried about him.'

'I suppose I'd better have another word with his mother,' Mr Hughes said without any interest at all. 'Can it wait for the next PTA? Then you could talk to her yourself.'

On her way to the staffroom Nita found Poppy crying in a corner. 'It's Ryan, Miss. He says he's going to cut Sam's eye with a knife.'

'No he isn't.' Nita took the little girl by the hand and led her towards the playground.

'But he's got a knife,' Poppy said, still sobbing. 'I saw it.'

'Oh my goodness.' Nita started to run.

'Now where would the little shit find a knife like that?' Miss Whitby asked the room. 'Eight years old and already he's armed and dangerous.' She was tall and fair and smoked cigarettes. She wouldn't put up with any nonsense from Mr Hughes, Nita thought. If Ryan had been in her class she'd have forced Mr Hughes to act after her first complaint. Now Miss Whitby looked at the plateful of rice and spicy vegetables Nita had just warmed in the staffroom microwave and said, 'That looks nice. Today's lunch smells like halitosis.'

'Do have some,' Nita said, flattered. 'There's too much here for me.' She divided the food and handed it to her colleague.

The Deputy Head said, 'Mr Hughes will have to exclude Ryan now. It won't do our reputation much good.'

'And how much good would it have done if Ryan had stabbed Sam?' Miss Whitby said, taking a mouthful of Nita's lunch. 'This is delicious, really delicious.'

'Some teachers keep a tighter grip on what's going on in their class,' the Deputy Head said.

'Unfair,' Miss Whitby said with her mouth full. 'We all know what Ryan's like.'

'I've asked for help or action on four separate occasions,' Nita said, emboldened by Miss Whitby's support. Normally Miss Whitby barely noticed her enough to say 'good morning'.

In spite of everything she felt as if this was turning out to be a good day. Maybe Miss Whitby would become a friend and some of her confidence would rub off on Nita. She knew that people thought of her as a bit of a wuss. It wasn't true, but perhaps a tall, fair, confident friend would give her some credibility.

She began the afternoon lessons with more bezaz than usual. Ryan's mother came to pick him up and even the furious looks she directed at Nita failed to discourage her. Without Ryan the class was more responsive and less distracted.

Her good mood sustained itself until she got off the bus and saw Jen and Diane talking together outside the Women's Aid shop. They looked up and saw her crossing the road towards them. Without a word they both turned and hurried away. Nita walked to her own house feeling queasy and almost failing to notice the police car parked two doors down. As soon as she saw it she backed away and returned to the corner. There was nowhere to go except Women's Aid. Nita very rarely went inside because she hated the smell of unwashed second hand clothes. But the two old women who worked there were sweet and friendly and often greeted her with a smile and a wave.

This afternoon the little one with the curly white hair said, 'This winter seems to be going on for ever. I expect you wish you were back somewhere warm again.'

'I expect you do too,' Nita said politely.

'What can we do for you today?' the little woman asked, looking confused.

'Just browsing.' Nita pretended to look at the rail closest to the window which gave the best view of the police car.

'We've got some lovely Indian fabrics in the back.' The little woman hovered behind her.

'I need a jacket for work.' If she peered past the posters stuck to the inside of the window Nita could see, further down from the police car, the sinister Toyota parked outside number 21.

'But you're so tiny,' the woman said, 'you could almost wear Junior Miss sizes and I'm afraid we don't have any very small jackets in stock just now.'

Nita turned round to face her and said, 'Do you know what's going on, why the police are here?'

'Well they did come in yesterday morning to ask if any of us worked late which we don't. We've all got families and homes to go to. So whatever it was happened after 6.30. But you know the man who lives upstairs? The one who marches and plays Wagner very loudly when he's off his medication? And tears up his utility bills and throws them out of the window? Well he came in this lunchtime for a paperback about the war we'd just put in the window display, and he said they were digging up bodies in the basement of number 15. You know, bodies of people the government doesn't like. But I take everything he says with a pinch of salt because he thinks Hitler's alive and well and living in St John's home for the elderly. It's just round the corner, dear, only a few steps from the bus stop. He thinks Hitler is an unrecognised saint. Can you believe that? Maybe you should try our children's section, dear, although children don't go in much for tailored jackets.'

'Digging up bodies?'

'I know, dear, that's silly, isn't it? There's no one in there digging except the workmen. I don't know where he gets his ideas from.'

'Maybe he thinks they've been there since the war,' Nita said. 'I'm sorry you haven't any jackets to fit me. Bye-bye.'

The old lady opened the door to let her out. As she walked away, Nita could feel eyes like pins in the back of her head. She turned just in time to see the door closing so she faked a friendly wave of the hand. Oddly cheered she looked into the skip as she passed. Bodies, she thought, were better than bombs. Suppose the police had found a packet of ammonium nitrate or aluminium powder, and hers was the only suspicious face in Guscott Road?

The idea that anyone could be a mass murderer but only she could make a bomb amused her, and she pictured herself engaged in some inexplicable alchemy where ammonium nitrate and aluminium powder, which were the only ingredients she could think of, went into her tagine along with eye of newt and mandrake root to be stirred and simmered until ready for detonation by cell phone. She would live up to expectations and explode Guscott Road, and with it, her own home, her hard won refuge, privacy and independence.

There were rotting window frames and broken glass covering the latest still-born Christmas tree in the skip. Nita shuddered at the sight of a filthy, cracked hand basin before she turned away and let herself into her own house. Today she sat down and marked her children's homework straight away. There would be no repeat of yesterday's forgetfulness, and with homework done, the weekend could begin. Nita remembered acting exactly that same way as a student. Sometimes it seemed that her metamorphosis from student to teacher was incomplete.

Only after the neatly marked books were stowed safely in her book bag and the bag was placed by the door ready for Monday morning, did she allow herself to check her phone and computer for messages.

Her brother, Ash, only ever rang when he knew she wouldn't be there. He never used email because he was afraid their father would trace the records. This evening his remote voice said, 'Hey, Neets, just to tell you Mina's pregnant again. Thought you'd like to know. Ma's planning another trip across the dark water. You can imagine...' He broke off and then rang off. There wasn't much privacy, even for a son, in the Tehri family home; and not much forgiveness if you left it without permission or the protection of marriage.

A message on email gave the same 'joyous' news. Mina seemed tired: this would be her fourth pregnancy in five years, and she'd already aborted a female foetus. Sometimes, in the dead of night, Mina would ring and the sisters would talk about it. The memory still made both of them cry. Such conversations always ended with Mina saying, 'Of course I love my family. I love all of them to bits. But darling Nita, stick to your guns. They'll come round in the end. I'm sure they will.'

Nita showered, but before she'd had time to dry her hair there was a knock on the door. Toby called, 'Sweeter Nita, let me in. I'm hiding from Leo.' He came bustling in carrying a bagful of gaudily wrapped parcels decked with pink bows and sparkly stars. 'The nosey boy found my hiding place. Nita, you've got to put these under your bed till his birthday or he'll spoil the surprises. He has the self-restraint of a three-year-old for which I usually thank God but when it's this time of year I could kill him.'

'Why wasn't he just as bad at Christmas?' Nita asked, finding a space at the bottom of her wardrobe.

'Too many distractions. He says Christmas is everybody's but his birthday is only about him, him, him.' Toby stacked everything neatly. 'You're such a disappointment when it comes to shoes. Where are all the spiky dangerous heels and the jewelled slippers? Can I brush your hair? It's so fabulous when it's drying. Promise you'll never cut it. You should leave it loose instead of exerting your iron will on it. It's exotic.'

'That's what I'm afraid of.' Nita handed him the hairbrush. 'Toby, what did you do with your tree after Christmas?'

Toby brushed with long firm strokes as if she were a horse and he a groom. 'We took it to the dump, of course.'

'Dead ones keep turning up in that skip and it's over a month since Christmas.'

Toby stopped brushing. He said, 'Did the police talk to you?'

'They were so rude. I came to look for you afterwards but you weren't there.' She met his eyes in the mirror. 'And they rang up my Headmaster at supper to ask about me.'

'They caught up with me after ward rounds.' He put the hairbrush down. 'Come out for a drink with us. Cheer yourself up.'

'I haven't eaten yet.'

'Ooh, are you making your spicy chicken thing?'

'It'll be ready in half an hour.'

'I'll tell Leo. He loves your chicken.'

It wasn't hard. Nita had a lot of spicy chicken in the freezer. All she'd have to do was make the rice, which she'd been intending to do anyway. Now she'd have company. And she'd discovered that Leo really liked her cooking. Without warning she felt her eyes sting with tears. She said, 'Bring your own beer and don't be late.'

'Yes, Miss,' Toby said from the door and scampered away downstairs.

4

Dead Baby

//

They ate like small boys—elbows on the kitchen table, hardly looking up until their plates were empty. Nita stood, dishing out more when required, feeling like her own mother who never sat with the family but grew fat, fatter, fattest, sampling her own cooking in the kitchen. They looked like brothers, fair-brown in colouring, preppie in dress, eager disguised as cynical in demeanour.

This is so modern, Nita thought proudly, two gay boys in my kitchen; two men in my kitchen. I'm cooking for two non-familial guys. It's normal. Maybe hospital canteen food is like school lunch and smells, as Miss Whitby said, of halitosis. So I'm not good, I'm just better than institutional.

'That was wonderful,' Leo said, looking up at last with bright eyes.

'We could have tea or coffee in the sitting room,' Nita said. 'It's more comfortable.' She made herself tea while the guys took their beer to the other room. The kettle boiled and she could hear them talking together. It was better than having the radio on.

'I'm telling her,' Toby said when she came in with her mug.

'I don't know,' Leo said, taking a swig from the bottle.

'Telling me what?' Nita asked. She sat opposite them on the small armchair.

'It's about what the police wanted to know,' Toby said. 'They told us not to say.'

Leo said, 'So we might be getting ourselves into the brown stinky stuff.'

'But the cops don't make gorgeous spicy chicken like you do or take turns cleaning the hall and stairs.'

'On the other hand,' Leo said, 'it's weird and I don't want to upset you.'

'Oh for goodness sake!'

'Okay,' Toby said in a rush, 'Sergeant Cutler wanted to know how long you'd lived here? Had we met your husband? And did we help deliver your baby?'

'*What?*'

'I told you it was weird,' Leo said. 'Of course we said, Six mouths, No, and What the fuck're you talking about? Are you married Nita? I haven't even had a sniff of a feller round here.'

'And believe me, Leo can sniff out a feller at a distance of a hundred miles.'

'I don't understand,' Nita said. 'I've never been married or had a baby. Is this about immigration? Because I was born here. I've got a passport and everything.'

'I don't think it's about immigration,' Leo said. 'The sergeant kept asking if you were pregnant when you moved in, and what happened to the baby.'

'He was fixated on weight loss. Someone in the street told him you'd lost a lot.'

'It wasn't us,' Leo said, 'I swear.'

'But you were, well, sort of chunkier when we first met you. Fabulous of course, but just a little wider. But I didn't tell Cutler that. I wouldn't, would I, Leo? And now you're sweeter petitter Nita. Right?'

'But the only trouble is,' Leo said, 'we're med students, right? So the big hairy sergeant obviously thinks we're putting ourselves through school by performing unlicensed medical procedures.'

'You should've told him about the trust fund.'

'He didn't ask about the trust fund, and I didn't catch on till later.'

'But why?' Nita cried. 'Why do they think I'm married and have a baby? Why didn't they ask outright? I could've told them. And what business is it of theirs anyway? I'm not an illegal alien. It shouldn't matter what I do.'

Leo and Toby glanced at each other. They sipped from their beer bottles.

'What?' Nita said.

'We think,' Toby said reluctantly, 'but don't quote us, cos no one's said anything for sure. We think it might have something to do with a dead baby the police brought in to the morgue early yesterday morning.'

'We think,' Leo added, hushed and excited, 'that someone found a dead baby in the skip when it was emptied. They were all talking about it in the Green Man last night.'

'Well there were a lot of stories—one about mass murder...'

'And one about an unexploded bomb left over from the blitz.'

'But there's only one dead baby in the morgue at the Royal, so we put two and two together, didn't we Leo?'

'We did. But we can't say for sure cos the cops are playing it very close to their manly bosoms. So you mustn't say anything.'

'But why me?' Nita asked hopelessly.

'We don't know.' Toby looked very uncomfortable. 'If I had to bet it would be on Sally Slapper—she's already got one little mistake.'

'You mean Jen Brown?'

'Is that what she's called?' Leo said. 'Or the uptight one with the boring boyfriend.'

'Diane?'

'We're just thinking of other women of child-bearing age, Nita dear. Don't panic.'

Nita said, 'Why just in this street? It isn't only the people in this street who've been fly-tipping. It can't be.'

'No, you're right,' Leo said. 'But the police are only asking about people here.'

'Like maybe they know something?' Toby said.

'Well they don't know anything about me,' Nita said. 'How could anyone possibly think I'd fly-tip a baby?'

'Anyway,' Toby said, 'all they have to do is take blood samples and compare DNA.'

'What about that woman in the basement of number 6?'

'Really Leo! Call yourself a med-student? She's menopausal if ever I saw it. She's just an old urban hippy who goes to the gym.'

'There's Tigs and Joe's mother down by the river.' Nita felt as if they were playing a game. 'Except I don't see how a woman can be pregnant and have a baby without two curious kids like those catching on.'

'Besides, she's married,' Toby said. 'We're looking for someone who can't cope, wracked with guilt and loneliness whose life'd be ruined by an unwanted baby.'

'Or a teenager who didn't even know she was pregnant until she started having stomach cramps on her way back from Club X.'

'Are you sure it's a neonate, Leo? No one said it was newborn.'

'I just assumed... '

'If it's newborn it can't be mine, can it?' Nita felt disgusted at herself for joining in their guessing games.

'It could've been kept in the freezer for a few months.' Toby seemed to be enjoying himself. 'That's the sort of thing they find out at an autopsy.'

'Shush, Tobes.' Leo had caught the expression on Nita's face.

'Well honestly,' Toby said, 'we can't take this seriously.'

'We might have to. Just think—we've already been interrogated as if we could be implicated in something illegal. We can't ask too many questions. The powers that be would get suspicious and we'd be struck off before we're even qualified.'

'Only if the baby has something to do with Nita,' Toby said. They both turned towards her and fixed her with sea-grey eyes as big as spoons.

—∞∞∞—

At a quarter to four in the morning Nita woke to the sound of a powerful car racing down the main road, tearing great holes in the shrink-wrapped silence. With the jagged fragment of a dream about a sea-grey baby lodged like shrapnel in her brain Nita got up and went to the window. The sky seemed to begin just above the roof tops and tiny flakes of snow trickled slowly, slowly down dragging her mesmerised eyes to the skip. A wrecked fridge-freezer lay on its side on top of the builder's waste. The snow vanished into wetness leaving the road looking slippery and treacherous.

Nita let the curtain fall and went to the bathroom for a sleeping pill. Why a fridge-freezer, she thought. Maybe the police had bugged her flat for last night's conversation and had left it there to frighten her into confession. But perhaps they could DNA test the freezer to see if a dead baby had been incubated in its chilly womb; just as the yellow metal goddess now sheltering the freezer had spontaneously generated the still-born white box.

But why me, she thought as she skidded falsely into sleep. What do they know?

5

Unnerved by Nipples

//

I t was ten o'clock when she woke. She calmed her racing heart by making a cup of tea, reminding herself that it was Saturday and she was not late for work. Nothing remained of the snow although the day was grey and cold. The fridge-freezer was where she'd seen it last night but now it was partially obscured by what looked like filthy torn army blankets. Nita dressed in gym clothes and went out to buy a paper and go to the Pilates class at the YMCA.

She took her gym mat to the back of the studio where no one could stand behind her and notice the size of her bum. She hadn't been to a class since just before Christmas and she was stiff and unsteady. Her breathing didn't match her movements making her feel as if she were starting from scratch. Nevertheless, after twenty minutes she began to settle into the routine and ignore feelings of inferiority every time she watched the willowy blonde teacher demonstrate with grace and ease movements which nearly tore Nita's thigh bones out of their sockets.

After another twenty minutes she was relaxed enough to notice that one of the women in the front row looked familiar. Toby's description of her as a menopausal urban hippy who went to the gym was bitchy enough to make her smile. Actually the woman who lived below Harris at Number 6 was sturdy, muscular and competent. Her greying hair was caught up in a child's plastic clasp which, Nita thought, made her look raffish and original.

As they put their mats away after the class Nita said, 'You live in Guscott Road too, don't you?'

The woman turned to look at her. She had sharp brown eyes that crinkled at the corners.

Nita went on, 'I talk to Harris Searle sometimes. He seems to leave for work just as I'm coming home.'

'I think I've seen you.' The woman turned to walk away.

'Nita Tehri,' Nita said, sticking out her hand so that she couldn't be ignored.

The woman said, 'Rose Peters.' She clasped Nita's hand briefly, and they walked down to the changing room. Their lockers were close together.

Nita said, 'Have the police talked to you?' She opened the door of her locker as she spoke so that she didn't have to look directly at Rose who had stripped off her T-shirt. She was wearing a black sports bra but to Nita she looked shockingly naked.

'A couple of days ago,' Rose said, starting to remove her trousers. 'But they didn't stay long. They seemed to be more interested in the view from the upstairs windows.' She was wearing a black thong. 'But of course it's Harris who lives upstairs and he'd already left for work.'

Nita grabbed her sweater and pulled it on over her head. It wasn't unusual in a changing room to be surrounded by women in varying stages of undress, but normally she left before anyone could talk to her. She was appalled by the thought that she had initiated a conversation with a soon to be naked woman old enough to be her mother. It simply hadn't occurred to her that Rose, in spite of living nearby, might want to shower at the gym. She turned her back and began to wash her hands and face in one of the basins.

Rose said, 'I don't suppose you know what all the fuss is about?'

This was exactly what Nita had been hoping to ask. She said, 'I think someone found something in the skip.' She looked up and saw in the mirror that Rose had removed her bra. She dried her hands hurriedly and snatched her coat out of the locker.

'Who found what?' Rose asked, eyes and nipples turning to face Nita.

It was too much for Nita. 'Got to go,' she mumbled and rushed out of the locker room, out of the gym and into the cold, dirty, city air.

She showered in her own bathroom, a place so guarded against intrusion that it had two locks on the door and no window. The sea-green tiles showed only her own dusky shadow and the mirror was too high to reflect nipples. She stayed under the hot water long enough for the extractor to lose its battle against the steam, so even her teeth looked soft and fuzzy as she brushed them. Her body was protesting about the stretch and exercise of Pilates. She took an aspirin before drying her hair.

The phone rang and a woman's voice said, 'This is Sergeant Eavers of the Wallace Street police station. Sorry to bother you at the weekend, but would you have a minute to come down here?'

'What for?' Nita felt sudden pin-pricks of sweat break out under her towelling robe.

'We were hoping you might agree to donate a sample of your DNA,' the sergeant said, as if she were asking for a biscuit. 'It's a simple, non-invasive procedure which won't take even five minutes.'

'Why?' Nita gripped the phone and sat down on the end of her bed.

'To help us with our enquiries,' the bland voice said.

Nita took a deep breath. 'What enquiries?'

'It's a local matter, and your cooperation would be greatly appreciated.'

'I'd love to cooperate,' Nita said, slowly and carefully, 'but first I need a little more information. I've already had two visits and neither PC Reed nor Sergeant Cutler explained. Is yours a related enquiry? And if so, please would you tell me what it's all about and why you want a sample of my DNA.'

'As I've already said.' Eavers' voice took on a tone of weary patience. 'This is a local enquiry of some importance, and we'd like to see you today.'

Looking down, Nita noticed a small place, about six inches above her knee which was red and swollen. She ran her forefinger over it but felt nothing. She wrapped her robe more securely round her legs and said, 'That doesn't constitute an explanation. Who else are you asking for samples?'

After a few seconds silence Eavers said, 'I'm afraid that is confidential information.'

'Okay,' Nita said, 'but I still want to know what your enquiry is all about and why you want a sample of my DNA.'

'Your attitude disappoints me.' Sergeant Eavers said, and rang off.

'And your attitude scares me to death,' Nita said aloud to the unlistening handset.

It couldn't just be the Pilates. Her whole body felt as if it had tried to carry far too heavy a load. She lay down on her plain white duvet and closed her eyes. The only solicitor she knew was her uncle Jag. He was her father's brother and almost as dangerous as her father.

She got up and dragged herself to the living room where she took the directory from its place on the shelves and looked up the Citizens Advice Bureau. After a few minutes, the message that kicked in said, 'The office is open Monday, Wednesday and Friday. You can drop in between the hours of 9.30 and 12.30.'

Nita went back to the bedroom and dressed in jeans and a thick sweater. She would go out—to the movies for instance, or the library—somewhere that she would not be available to police officers and their intimidating behaviour.

On her own doorstep she met Rose Peters who said, 'You left your Weekend Guardian in your locker. Are you okay? You ran off in such a rush.'

'It was awfully crowded,' Nita said, accepting her newspaper. 'Sometimes, you know, claustrophobia?'

'Never suffered from that myself.'

'But thanks so much for bringing my paper.' Ancient laws of hospitality asserted themselves in Nita's mind and she added, 'Do come up and have a cup of tea.'

'But you're just going out.'

'Only to buy another paper.'

'Well, if you're quite sure,' Rose said, and followed Nita as she climbed back up the stairs. 'Nice,' she added when she saw the living room. 'You know, the guy who had this flat before you was a naval officer.'

'I wondered,' Nita said. 'There was a lot of manly blue below the dado rails. Did you know him well?'

'He was away a lot. But my niece went out with him a few times.'

'Have you lived in Guscott Street long? Do you know everyone?'

'About six years,' Rose said, 'since my divorce. No I don't know everyone—this is England after all.'

Nita smiled and went to the kitchen to fill the kettle. Rose followed her.

'God, you're really organised.' Rose said. 'I won't show you my kitchen. I dye wool there. It's a messy activity.'

'Is that your job?'

'Part of it. I hand-dye wool, silk and cotton samples for knitwear designers. I knit for them too.'

'How interesting,' Nita said, but she was thinking—Oh my god, I've got a divorced woman in my kitchen. What on earth would my mother say? Rose didn't even look ordinary. She wore a black embroidered top over layers of multi-coloured skirts. Her hair was now loose with freshly washed tendrils coiling round her face. The style didn't seem appropriate to her age—which Nita put at over fifty. And she wore a little makeup. Nita's mother, who disapproved of cosmetics under any circumstances, absolutely vilified older women who used them.

Rose said, 'I gathered, from what you said at the gym, that you had a visit from the police too?'

'Two, actually.' Nita decided suddenly to be frank. 'And a request just now to give a sample of my DNA. I don't understand. They won't give a reason. Did they ask you too?'

'They did not.' Rose looked shocked.

'Can they do that?' Nita poured boiling water onto tea leaves. She concentrated on keeping her hands steady.

'I think they can ask,' Rose said uncertainly. 'But I don't think they can force you to.'

'So it isn't like being breathalysed? I always wondered about that—English law being built around people not having to give incriminating evidence against themselves. But boozy breath is definably incriminating evidence and if you won't give breath the police can forcibly take blood, can't they?'

'I don't know,' Rose said. 'I've never been pulled over for drunk driving.'

'Nor have I.' Nita put teapot, cups, milk and sugar on a tray and led the way back to the living room.

Rose settled herself and her many skirts in a chair with her back to the window. She said, 'The more I think about it, the more outrageous it seems.'

Nita lowered her head and concentrated on pouring tea. Her throat tightened and she was afraid she might cry.

Rose went on, 'Have you talked to a lawyer? I'm no expert but I don't think you should do anything without talking to a lawyer.'

Nita said, 'I called the Citizen's Advice Bureau but they don't open till Monday. By which time I'll be back at work.'

'You see, that's typical.' Rose accepted a cup and sipped from it absent-mindedly. 'The police make an outrageous demand when they know all the solicitors will be on the bloody golf course.' She frowned and drank some more tea. 'You know, I truly suspect this is a civil rights issue.'

'What?' Nita said alarmed.

Rose drained her cup quickly and looked as if she'd burnt her tongue. 'I'll make some enquiries. Leave this with me. In the mean time, keep your head down and don't go to the police station alone, or do anything they ask just because they ask it. They may be taking all kinds of liberties because they don't think you have any friends.' She got up, handed back her cup, planted a quick kiss on Nita's surprised cheek and departed in a rustle of textures and fabrics.

Nita rushed after her but was too late. 'Why would the police think I haven't got any friends?' she said to the door. She heard Rose's footsteps on the stairs and then the street door slam.

6

The Rottweiler

D aphne was tiny. She was the only one to make Nita feel tall. She wore long snow-white hair in a tight knot at the back of her head. She was frail but according to Leo and Toby, had the heart of a lion and the tongue of a viper.

'She's the Guscott Road Rottweiler,' Toby told Nita when she first moved in. 'Don't fight it. Just tell her anything she wants to know and mind your p's and q's. She'll be a good friend, sort of, but you don't want her as an enemy.'

'There were some louts peeing on our doorstep after closing time last summer,' Leo said, 'and she steamed out of her house like Mighty Mouse in a night-gown and told them they had bladders smaller than their brains and dicks smaller than their bladders and they ought to be ashamed.'

'She did not,' Toby said.

'But she did take their pictures with her son's digital camera,' Leo said, 'which we thought was a really good idea.'

'She also restored the purity of our doorstep with a bucket of bleach.'

After a description like that, Nita treated Daphne with the utmost respect. So far their only conversations had been horticultural when Nita complimented her on the display of pots and hanging baskets outside her house. But she gathered from the boys that she was the only one left in Guscott Street who had been born and brought up there.

Now, hurrying down the main road towards the supermarket, she met Daphne coming in the opposite direction. Daphne planted herself in Nita's path, forcing her to stop. She said, 'What you been adoing of to annoy everyone? Why's everyone asking about you?'

'I don't know, Daphne,' Nita said humbly. 'I'm really worried. What did the police tell you?'

'Bleeding cops don't tell nobody sod all.' Daphne jutted her jaw. 'Useless lot, don't know their arse from a hole in the ground no more. You stop out their way, my girl.'

'I'm trying. But Daphne?'

'What?'

'Did anyone say anything about a baby?'

'Bombs and babies,' Daphne said. 'What a world. The tarty one said you was up the duff when you moved in. The snotty one said you was illegal, and the barmy twat above Women's Aid said you was an Arab bomber. I said you wasn't the type, but the bleedin' cops said there wasn't no type and we all had to keep our eyes open all the time these days.' She stared up at Nita with blue eyes so faded she seemed to be peering through milk. 'Like the bleeding war if you ask me, which you didn't. No one remembers but me. It's a lonely old life when there ain't no one to share me memories with. They all moved away, see, to them high-rise projects out of town, and then they died. That's what happens when you cut off roots—you die. You listening, girl? Cos I'm talking to you.'

'I'm listening, 'Nita said. 'But you've got your two sons, haven't you? Don't they remember too?'

'Number one, they're boys. So they got their heads stuffed full of fancy pants facts. Facts ain't memories. Number two, they wasn't born till years after the war. I was only a girl then. You may laugh but I didn't always look like this.'

'I'm not laughing.' Nita was uncomfortably aware that they were standing stock still in the middle of the pavement, in the way of every pedestrian in either direction. Although she didn't want to go back to Guscott Road she said, 'Let me carry your shopping back home.'

Daphne promptly handed over three plastic bags but kept a tight grip on her huge black handbag. 'One thing I can say for your lot,' she said, 'you still got some respect for your elders. Not the English kids, oh no. Them little bleeders knock you down to get at your pension. Or they dance on your roof in the middle of the night and shout obscenities down your chimney. And there's no one to tell them "no". My generation just gave up on them. Shouldn't have. But did.' She walked slowly but with such determination that everyone moved aside to let her through.

Nita said, 'The man and his son, who used to live at number 15? Hadn't he been there a long time?' They were passing the skip, and Nita couldn't help noticing that the dirty army blankets had disappeared and that the vile fridge-freezer now lay under a pile of broken mirrors and splintered picture frames.

'Only about fifteen years,' Daphne said. 'They came here when the boy was just a toddler. Most of the street was derelict then. The council wanted to tear us all down and rebuild. As they always bleedin' do. But we survive—as we always bleedin' do. Anyway rents was nothing in them days and he had the whole sodding house for a spit and a handshake. He was supposed to keep up the repairs. Fat chance. Lazy bugger. No wonder he couldn't keep a woman. Never did a hand's turn, argumentative with everyone. Whatever happened it was always someone else's bleedin' fault.'

'Do you know why he left or where he's gone?'

'Why d'you want to know?' Daphne narrowed her milky eyes.

'It's just that if the police found something suspicious in the skip, it'd make sense to me if it came out of number 15.'

'I know you called the kid, "blue-haired weirdy-boy", but it wasn't his fault if he was growing up with that waste of space for a father.'

'You certainly can't help who you've got for a father,' Nita agreed, feeling bad for the kid.

'But why he wanted to dye his hair blue, I'll never know. Kids! He was always tormented at school too. Still can't read. No, the landlord put them out when they couldn't afford the rent no more. Then he sold. In case you hadn't noticed, this road's gone all gentrified. I'd be a bleedin' millionaire if I sold now. I kept my house in good nick. Well, I would, wouldn't I? I own it. I'm not some bleedin' don't-care tenant.'

'Your house looks beautiful,' Nita said, 'especially when you put all the pots out in the spring.'

'Wish I had a proper garden.' Daphne fished for keys in her vast handbag. 'Still, I wouldn't of had even the pots if I'd moved out to them poxy high-rises. P'raps that's why they had to stuff the poor little baby in the skip. Nowhere to bury it, see.' She opened her front door onto a narrow hall. 'Stick the bags in the hall, dearie.'

Nita obeyed, suddenly overwhelmed because Daphne had never called her 'dearie' before.

'Ta for the help,' she said now, and closed the door softly in Nita's face.

As she turned away, Nita noticed Jen watching from an upstairs window with Craig in her arms. She waved. Jen's mouth moved in a way that Nita read as saying, 'Suck up.' Nita walked away, down to the river. It could have been 'stuck up', she thought as she stood at the iron railings and watched the river roll lazily by. Then she thought, why put the baby in the skip when there was a river so close? Maybe whoever it was didn't know about the river, and therefore wasn't local.

The wind blew cold off the water and Nita shuddered. Or maybe, she thought, the unknown person was scared of the water and on a cold dark night couldn't bear to throw even an unwanted dead baby into it. Maybe who ever it was, like Nita, had never learned to swim and watched the river with atavistic dread.

She bought a sandwich at the supermarket for lunch and then went to the Odeon Multiplex looking for a movie that didn't cast brown-skinned people as terrorists and villains. Instead she found one that cast a cigarette-smoking Frenchman as the villain, and quite enjoyed it. Two hours in the dark calmed her. Movie explosions were fun; movie death was instantaneous and clean. Men died. Babies did not.

In the cinema lobby she saw a few of the children in her class who had been to see a block-buster cartoon. They grinned and waved to her. Their parents did too. She was Nita Tehri, popular schoolteacher. The cinema felt like home. She joined the queue for an American high school movie based on the myth of Dido and Aeneas. There was safety in fiction; safety in the dark. Nothing much matters while you are watching a movie. Often the movie doesn't matter either.

It mattered so little that Nita fell asleep halfway through. She woke with a crick in her neck to find a cleaning crew clearing up the spilled popcorn and drinks cups. Sheepishly she grabbed her coat and bag and scuttled out into the cold night.

It wasn't late. The city was only just getting ready for the Saturday night invasion of students, stag-parties and hen-parties. Anyone over thirty-five scampered home and left the pubs and clubs to the various tribes of the young, the drunk, the stoned and the stupid.

Nita was the right age but the wrong temperament. She walked home avoiding the gangs of squealing girls and shouting guys who roamed the streets searching for the cheapest drinks and the loudest music. Instead, she went to the all night supermarket. Her normal Saturday of laundry and weekly shopping had been disrupted and she wanted to make up for lost time, to reassert her own rhythm on the disjointed day.

She pushed her trolley to the fresh fruit and vegetable section, steadfastly ignoring the snacks, sweets and fizzy drinks aisle. She could see the security cameras watching her. It was time to be publicly virtuous. Under the harsh light she felt like an actor in a bad movie; tracked and observed until she made her move at the cash-desk.

Another trolley crashed into hers in front of the grapes and kiwi fruit. Harris Searle said, 'I thought it was you. Unusual. I never see anyone I know shopping at this time of night.'

'The lonely life of a shift-worker,' Nita said, smiling at him.

'Don't joke about it,' he said. 'I spend all weekend trying to adjust to normal life and catching up with normal people and by the time I go back to work on Monday I'm exhausted.'

He had nice hazel eyes, Nita thought, and broad shoulders under his thick coat.

'Forget the fruit and veg,' he said suddenly. 'Come and have a drink with me.'

'But it's Saturday,' she said stupidly, thinking, is he asking me out? Is this a date? 'I mean, it's all kids getting drunk.'

'I know somewhere very untrendy, where they still play cards.'

'Okay,' Nita said, 'why not?' It's not a date, she thought. It's just two acquaintances meeting by chance. It's alright.

'We'll take my car,' he said, abandoning his trolley and walking her firmly to the underground car park.

7

Harvard Slut

///

He drove leaning back, one arm almost straight, one hand on the wheel, looking casual and commanding. Nita noted the regular profile and the curling hair just beginning to grey above his ears. She didn't know much about cars, but this one seemed reassuringly clean and well cared for. It smelled of pine and glass cleaner.

Harris said, 'I didn't think you'd be a drinker.' He was driving them safely and steadily out of the city centre, leaving the roaming bands of teenagers far behind. Here the roads were darker and deserted. He leaned forward to punch a button on the dashboard and Marvin Gaye sang 'What's Going On' very softly. The heater blew hot air onto Nita's hands and feet and she realised that she had been cold all day. How, she wondered, did you manage to walk around clenched against the cold for hours on end without registering it? As soon as she realised she was warm she relaxed and began to feel drowsy.

Harris said, 'You're quite a surprise altogether.'

'Am I?'

'Yeah, not half. I mean, you look like a little kid but you're a school teacher. You look like you wouldn't hurt a fly, but word is you're... ' He broke off and pointed to a sign which said, Holyfield Industrial Park. 'No one knows, unless they're told, or unless they're on the mailing list, but there's a Thai massage

41

parlour plying its trade in there. When the regular businesses shut up shop, all the little girls come out to play. That's what you remind me of. Want to take a look?' He slowed the car to a crawl. Walking towards them was a blonde woman in mile-high heels and a pink fleece with Harvard Slut appliquéd to the bosom. Harris stopped the car and watched her intently through half closed eyes.

Nita said, 'I thought we were going for a drink.'

'Tell you what,' he said, 'I think you're scared of me. Tell you what else—I think you like it.'

With astonishment, Nita realised that he was right. This is what sex is, after all, she thought: threatening and painful. She said, 'Diane warned me. She said you don't like women.'

'Diane's wrong. I love women but I don't like Diane. Who's Diane?'

Nita said, 'I need to go home now.' She was worried because she still wanted him to like her.

He laughed and turned in his seat to watch the woman in the pink fleece walk away. 'I could pick her up,' he said, almost to himself. 'Would you like that? She's already told us she's a slut and I believe her. You do too.'

Nita said, 'Please take me home.' Still saying please at a time like this, she thought. Should I feel pride or shame?

'Now you,' Harris said, 'you don't advertise. Have you noticed? Classy goods don't advertise, do they? Only a select few appreciate them. You make us guess, don't you? You force us to take the time and trouble to find out if you're bad to the bone.'

Nita found the door handle but he leaned across her, gripping her hand with such strength she feared her fingers would break.

His breath swamped her ear. He said, 'You modern girls. No one wants to look after the baby, do they? You're too busy with your little jobs, your stupid clothes, and your fucking holidays in Ibiza. Cramp your style, wouldn't it?'

Nita swung her elbow, hitting him just below the ribcage. He crowded in tighter giving her no room for another blow.

'She looks like you,' he whispered. 'Brown skin smooth as a licked toffee. Ice crystals in the heart. She'd been frozen too long, see. Just like you.'

She could've asked, but she already knew he was talking about the baby in the morgue.

He thrust his free hand between her thighs and with a tough hard fingernail scratched at the central seam of her jeans. She could feel the vibration with every atom of the skin and hair under his finger.

Yesterday morning, she thought, I took a knife away from a boy. 'Ryan,' she'd said, not loudly but with force. 'Give me the knife and come indoors.'

'My dad give it me,' he said. 'It's mine.'

'Harris Searle,' she said now, using his name as a weapon against him. 'Behave yourself and let me go.'

'Or what?' His breath on her cheek was as fresh and minty as early morning. 'What you gonna do, school teacher?'

With an effort she said, 'I know you, I know where you live, I know your neighbours.'

'You think they care about you? They talk about you but they don't care. You're the dark stranger come into town. That's what makes you interesting.'

Nita sat very still. She was almost comfortable. There's no point in resisting, she thought. They like resistance: it's exciting. I've been here before, she realised; maybe in a dream, maybe in a memory. This is familiar.

She said, 'Your neighbour, Rose Peters, says she'll find me a lawyer.'

'Dried up old bitch,' he said with surprising fury, and released her.

Reluctantly, she opened the car door and got out. She walked away slowly on legs that wobbled like a newborn foal's. The road was frozen and deserted.

I won't run, she thought, hardly able to walk—pursuit excites them. Behind her she heard him start his car. He'll turn round and come after me, she thought. He'll leap out of the car and overpower me. I'm just not strong enough. She turned a corner into the road that led to the Holyfield Industrial Park. A car revved up and sped away without stopping.

With shaking hands she took her phone out of her bag. The only number she could remember was made up of fives and fours. She pressed buttons and waited till a tired voice said, 'City Cabs.'

She looked around and oriented herself, saying clearly, 'I need to go to Guscott Road. I'm at the corner of Elm Road and Millbury Avenue. Please send a cab.'

The tired voice said, 'That's near the Holyfield Industrial Park, innit? I can get a car to you in forty minutes.'

'Can't you come quicker?' Nita spoke through chattering teeth.

'Saturday night, innit?' the voice said as if that explained everything. And of course it did.

Nita couldn't remember any more numbers of cab companies. She dialled again and heard, 'Toby and Leo are out. When you leave a message, make it amusing.' She couldn't think of a single thing that might amuse anyone so she hung up and started walking. She imagined tall, fair Miss Whitby from school in a similar situation and thought that she must have an address book stuffed with the phone numbers of lots of friends eager to come and rescue her.

She walked briskly towards the city centre, not sure of the way, never having been to this district before. She knew it must be downhill because the river ran through the middle of town and the river was at the lowest point. In Harris Searle's car, warm and drowsy, she hadn't paid attention to directions. The passivity of the passenger, she thought; oh, the passivity of me—happy to sit in a good-looking man's car and be driven goodness knows where. Whatever is it that makes me think older men are dependable?

That was only one of the questions Nita didn't want to address just then. She plodded on into the cold and dark, always turning downhill when faced with a choice of direction. Her gloves were too thin, and the cold wind that bit into her cheeks and brought tears to her eyes stiffened her fingers.

The road she was on finally brought her to a bridge about a mile from where she lived and she crossed the river avoiding the sight of the black water beneath her. On the other side she was engulfed by the light, the screams of intoxication and aggression, the pools of urine and vomit which were the signs and symbols of Saturday night in the city centre. Home, she thought with huge relief, and ducked into the warmth and brilliance of a fish and chip shop called Good Cod Almighty. She had been walking for over an hour in the freezing cold and it didn't put her off at all that there had clearly been a fight in the shop—there was blood on the doorstep, and the safety glass was crazed. What looked like a fishcake was smeared all over the lens of the security camera.

She warmed her hands on the glass display counter and her fingers throbbed and tingled painfully. As she waited, a spasm of anger against Harris Searle clenched her guts and made her, for an instant, feel sick. But she was too hungry to pay attention. She took her food and left the shop. Chunks of hot battered fish scorched her mouth and slid down a throat lubricated by the grease on the chips. She ate as she walked, the paper packet warming her frozen hands, fish and chips, salt and vinegar, filling the emptiness inside.

The wind came in arctic gusts rattling the paper against her coat and whipping up the rubbish in the street into a frenzy. Girls ran past on legs blue with cold, shrieking, chased by boys wearing only tattoos and pride. Nita scarcely noticed. What mattered was the heat and completeness of food. Just food, food, food.

At the corner of Guscott Road all that was left was greasy paper and fingers, a mouth smeared with chip fat, and a feeling of self disgust. She crumpled the paper into a ball and threw it into the skip noticing as she did so that there was now a pair of indescribably filthy red velvet curtains on top of the fridge-freezer. Down the road at number 6 she saw Harris Searle's car smugly parked outside. She turned away and was fumbling for her key when she noticed the Toyota. The streetlight glared off the windscreen so she couldn't see if anyone was inside watching. She glanced from the Toyota back to number 6, wondering if the road was full of men safely, warmly, behind glass watching her stagger home drunk on cold and fatty food. At the corner, close to Women's Aid, another drunk undid his flies and pissed on the wall, so oblivious to eyes and spies that he turned his head and grinned at her.

She opened the door and ran inside—to escape from the cold wind and the gaze of men; to escape from the cold gaze of men. She closed it behind her and switched on the hall light. There, on the doormat, under the letterbox, lay a little rubber doll no bigger than a man's hand.

It was a baby doll without hair or clothes. Its skin was the colour of chocolate and it clutched a tiny bottle of milk in one fist. Someone had hammered a nail through the mouth.

Nita picked it off the floor, delicately, between finger and thumb. She carried it upstairs. Without understanding why, she realised that she would be ashamed to let Toby and Leo see she had been sent such a brutal message. She was ashamed to admit, even to herself, that she was hated this much.

Home welcomed her quietly. She turned on the TV for company and ran a deep bath, soaking herself in hot water and jasmine scented oil until her teeth stopped chattering. Then she wrapped herself in her thick white towelling robe and sat with a cupful of warm milk and honey.

The little doll lay on the mantelshelf wearing its mutilation like a piece of contemporary art. Every now and then Nita imagined a title like, Silence or Scream. She could accept it as an exhibit, even cherish it. On her mantelshelf it was an artefact; she could deconstruct it. Wouldn't it have been more logical or more usual to drive the nail through the heart? Or was her tormentor, who she supposed must be Harris, afraid of clichés? And where would he have found a little doll after ten at night? Of course he might have had it in stock, waiting for the right occasion. Had they really run into each other by chance at the supermarket?

She wondered at last if the nail through the mouth might be a literal representation of the way the real baby died. It was too grotesque to contemplate. But Harris worked at the hospital, so he might know things no one else in the street knew.

Nita hadn't asked him what his job was. He could be a nurse, or a porter, or a manager, even a security officer. He might even be an assistant in the morgue.

She pictured the kind of evening she'd been expecting when he invited her for a drink at an out of town pub where people played cards: they would have sat at a small table in a quiet corner, their knees almost, but not quite, touching. There would have been no thumping music to drown conversation, just the crackle of an open fire. He would drink, at most, a pint of bitter because he was driving. She would toy with a glass of orange juice and ask him about himself and his work. Slowly, they would get to know each other.

She got up, suddenly propelled to her feet by another gust of rage. 'I am not a masochist,' she said out loud to the doll, who lay on her back, uncomplaining, with a nail through her mouth. But the awful truth was that she didn't know who to complain to. She thought about the police who had been so impolite and wanted a sample of her DNA. Then she thought about the woman who lived downstairs from Harris, Rose Peters, and how she'd said, 'Leave this with me,' as if she were going to solve all Nita's problems. She had also said, 'I truly suspect this is a civil rights issue.' What on earth did that mean? Had Rose meant civil liberties? That would've made more sense. Or had she meant it was an issue of racism? Either way, Nita felt she couldn't rely on someone who didn't seem to know the difference between civil rights, civil liberties and racism.

Rose, though, must know a lot more about Harris than Nita did. Maybe he had supper in Rose's flat the way Toby and Leo did in Nita's. Or maybe not. Nita remembered his unexplained anger when she mentioned Rose's name.

In spite of the cold, Nita opened the living room window and leaned out. The Toyota which had been so close to her front door was gone, and no lights showed at Rose and Harris's house. Guys and girls still shouted drunkenly from the main road, but Guscott Road was quiet, seemingly bedded down for the night.

Dressed in a thick black pullover and cords, Nita took a nail and a hammer from the little tool box she kept in the kitchen, and crept downstairs without turning on the hall light. Silently she slipped out into the street. The wind whipped her hair and lashed her face as she scampered down to number 6. She crouched behind Harris Searle's car, protected from accusing eyes by the Honda parked close to his back wheels. She covered the head of the nail with her woollen sleeve so that it would make no sound, and then hammered it quickly and efficiently into his tyre. It took five seconds and then she was running back to the shelter of her own house.

8

Partially Clad

///

In the morning, with a brain like mashed potato, Nita sat at her kitchen table with a cup of coffee and a pair of scissors, cutting sheets of coloured paper into small squares. Tomorrow she would teach the children about mosaic and show them pictures. Then they would make their own and cover the classroom walls with a riot of colour.

Just to be sure she knew what she was doing she made one herself: a dolphin playing in a Caribbean blue sea with orange starfish and a smiling yellow sun. She wouldn't show it to the kids or they'd all want to do dolphins, but she was pleased: her picture looked joyful and summery. If it had been done by a child she would've given it a gold star. If it had been done by *her* child she would've attached it to the fridge with a magnet.

Her fridge door was gleaming and unadorned. The inside was clean and empty too. Soon she would have to go back to the supermarket to buy food for next week. Maybe she should change supermarkets. Or she could order online. Then she wouldn't bump into anyone who knew her.

The washing machine hummed and grumbled in the background and Nita began another mosaic picture, this time of a bird of paradise with a huge swirling tail. When it was finished she carefully put all the paper away and opened a can of vegetable soup. She took her bowl through to the living room to watch the local news while she ate.

The first item reported a murder. With her spoon arrested between bowl and mouth Nita watched the local reporter, a blonde woman in a sensible sheepskin coat, turn and point to a street sign for Millbury Avenue. She was saying, 'In the early hours of this morning a teenage boy returning home from a party found the partially clad body of a woman. Police say she had been strangled and an attempt had been made to conceal the body under a hedge. Residents of this otherwise quiet suburban street are understandably concerned.'

The picture showed a low brick wall with a tall privet hedge growing behind it. Blue and white police tape danced in the hectic wind, and further down the road a trio of men in overalls appeared to be searching the pavement.

The woman in the sheepskin coat was replaced by a man in uniform who said, 'This is mainly a residential area which experiences little or no crime. The victim does not seem to have lived here although my officers are presently conducting house-to-house interviews in the hope that someone either knew the victim, or saw or heard anything suspicious.'

The policemen's image was overtaken by two women who appeared to live nearby. 'This is a friendly little community,' one of them said. 'We're all really shaken up. Nothing like it's ever happened here before.'

'I said there'd be trouble as soon as they opened that massage place on the industrial estate,' the other one chipped in. 'It's barely a stone's throw from where families live.'

'We complained to Environmental Health,' the first woman said, 'and they told us they were "monitoring the situation" whatever that means.'

'So, uproar in an otherwise crime-free suburban neighbourhood,' said the blonde in the sheepskin. 'We'll keep you posted as this story unfolds, but now we're returning you to the studio for an update on United's bid for Cup glory...'

Nita switched off The TV. 'Yes, but *when* did it happen?' she asked the blank screen. They said the teenager found the body in 'the early hours' but the murder must've happened a lot earlier. Because, she reasoned, in the early hours there was a puncture in Harris's offside rear tyre and he couldn't go anywhere. Her mind had fixed, like paint to a wall, on the certainty that the victim was the woman in the pink Harvard Slut fleece. And the killer was Harris Searle who had turned and watched with eyes like razor blades as she walked away down a dark residential street.

She tried to work out what time she'd met Harris in the supermarket, what time she'd left him, how long it had taken to walk home. But her mind and heart skipped away from serious thought, so enchanted was she by the idea that she had escaped death. That could've been me, that should've been me, but it wasn't. I'm alive.

Then it struck her that if this were true, the woman in impossibly high heels who labelled herself a slut had died for Nita. Nita's escape was Harvard Slut's death sentence. Nita, the good little school teacher, responded to danger by running away and thus left a killer with nothing to do—a killer who had casually offered to pick a girl up for Nita. He said, 'She's told us she's a slut and I believe her.' Where was Nita's voice screaming at him, 'You cannot possibly believe an appliquéd slogan; not in the twenty-first century. No one goes around believing sweat-shirts.'

Fear had silenced Nita's voice. And fear was what made Harris think she agreed with him. Good girls don't argue. Bad men take silence for consent. Very bad men intimidate those who want to be good into silence and take fear as consent.

Nita went to the window and looked down towards number 6. Harris Searle's car seemed not to have moved: it was outside his door, and the white Honda was still parked close behind. She couldn't see if there was a flat tyre because the one she'd vandalised was on the opposite side.

Before stepping back from the window she noticed that the velvet curtains had been removed from the skip and several planks of rotting wood and a broken swivel chair lay tumbled in their place. The loathsome fridge-freezer seemed to be a fixture now. No one wanted to touch it. Nita turned away and picked up the bowl of cold soup to take back to the kitchen. The phone rang.

Rose Peters said, 'I've asked around, and I think they'll have to arrest you.'

Nita's heart was already racing from the news of the murder in Millbury Avenue. Now she felt sick. 'I'm sorry? Arrest... ?'

Rose said, 'Yes, I believe, from what I've been told, that the police cannot force you to give them a sample of your DNA unless they arrest you.'

'Oh dear,' Nita said. 'That's terrible.' The DNA crisis seemed a long time ago now.

'I don't know,' Rose said. 'It might actually be a blessing. Then you could sue them for wrongful arrest and discrimination. You know, create a real stink. We could get a petition together, and really shake up the system. The authorities have been taking way too many liberties since 9/11 and the London Bombings. Arrests, imprisonment without trial—there are some poor buggers who've been in prison for years.'

Nita wanted to ask how it would help the poor buggers if she were to be arrested too, but she said, 'They'd still be allowed to take samples of my DNA though, wouldn't they?'

'Unfortunately, yes. That *is* the fly in the ointment.'

'Did you talk to a lawyer about this?'

'I talked to my friend Keen. He works with lawyers a lot. He's heavily into direct action up in Bradford.'

'You know, it's incredibly kind of you to take all this trouble.' Nita felt resentful. She could've found out the same thing far more quickly and accurately on the internet; then she wouldn't have had the added burden of gratitude.

'I haven't actually *done* anything yet,' Rose said, disarmingly.

Nita instantly felt guilty. She said, 'But you've thought about it, and I can talk to you.'

'Of course you can.'

'So, I... this is embarrassing, but I ran into your neighbour, Harris Searle, yesterday and he was a bit weird with me, so I wondered what you knew about him. I mean, he works at the hospital, doesn't he?'

'Mmm,' Rose said. 'Harris. I'm not sure. I think it's something to do with the Accident and Emergency department. He isn't a doctor. He's lived in the upstairs flat for nearly a year now, but I can't say I know much more about him than I did when he first moved in. Actually, I might've offended him—unwittingly of course.'

'How?'

'Well, when he first moved in, I went up to his flat to say, you know, welcome and to tell him what days to put his rubbish out etcetera, and his wife opened the door.'

'Oh yes, Diane said he was married.'

'Well, I didn't know that, and what happened was that when I started to tell her about rubbish and recycling a dog pushed past her and started to growl at me. Then Harris appeared and said, "Don't talk to her, she'll forget everything. Talk to me." But I was so worried about the dog, you see, because there's a clause in the lease which says you can't keep pets in the house without the prior agreement of other residents in the building. You might have a similar clause.'

'I think we do.'

'And the damn animal was growling at me, so I might have blurted out something tactless. He said, "You're not going to tell me what to do in my own home." And I said it was in the lease and I was going to take legal advice.'

'Not a good beginning.'

'The worst. And then before I could do anything about it the poor dog was run over by a truck outside the Green Man. First Harris blamed his wife, and then when she left, he blamed me.'

'How could he possibly do that?'

'He didn't actually say. But things quieted down after a month or so. We don't talk much but at least he's civil now.'

'It can't be comfortable.'

'There are some people you don't want to be comfortable with,' Rose said.

All the time she was talking, Nita was aware of two things: the first was that she felt easier when Rose was speaking of her own difficulties with Harris rather than Nita's difficulties with the police; the second was the growing pressure to warn Rose that she was living below a murderer. She said, 'Aren't you scared, living in a house with someone so hostile?'

'You know what; I think he's more afraid of me than I am of him. He could've bought himself another dog if he really wanted to annoy me. But I seem to have knocked him into shape about those silly things that mean a lot when you're sharing a hall—like picking up the mail from the floor and keeping it tidy. I just had to be tough with him at the beginning.'

'Because, last night,' Nita began, 'I thought he might be quite violent, and he'd driven us up to where that murder happened, and I had to walk home.'

'Well, I certainly wouldn't want to go on a *date* with him.' Rose's voice took on a guarded tone as if she were thinking critical thoughts but didn't want to sound judgmental.

'It wasn't a date,' Nita protested. 'I met him by chance in the supermarket and he suggested a drink.'

'You have to be careful of your reputation,' Rose said. 'In cases like these, when you're dealing with police prejudice, you must know they'll use anything against you, including sexuality. It's wrong, I know, but it's a fact of life.' She stopped for a moment and then added, quite brusquely, 'I'm sorry, I have to go now. I'll call you back.'

9

Immigrant Paranoia
or Folk Art?

//

Nita wandered numbly through to the kitchen where she dumped the cold soup and washed the bowl and saucepan. She'd thought about reheating the soup, but memories of last night's fish and chips came back to haunt her. She should go to the gym, pound the treadmill and sweat all the fatty poison out of her system. Then she'd feel cleaner and clearer, and better able to look the world in the eye. As she walked to the bedroom her doorbell rang.

'Sergeant Cutler here,' a man's voice said over the entry-phone. 'We had a chat a couple of nights ago. Remember?'

Nita's heart back-flipped. 'What can I do for you today?'

'More than you did Friday night,' he said. 'You could begin by letting us in.'

'What's it about?' she asked without much hope of an answer.

But he surprised her. 'It's about the murder that took place in the Holyfield area last night.'

She pressed the button which let him into the hall and then went to open her flat door. Sergeant Cutler was accompanied by PC Reed who nodded to her as if he'd never seen her before in his life. They walked past her and went straight to the sitting-room where they sat side by side on her small sofa like two vultures on a branch. Cutler said, 'You were in the Holyfield area at about 10.45 last night.'

'Was I?' Nita was astounded that he knew more accurately than she had been able to calculate where she was and when.

'Let's not fanny around, eh?' he said wearily, as if she'd done nothing but mess him up just for the fun of it. 'You called for a cab from there at the aforementioned time. We had the dispatcher from City Cabs show us his log-sheet.'

'They couldn't send a cab, so I walked home.' Her mind raced. What could she say about Harris that wouldn't ruin her own reputation?

Cutler broke in and said, 'I'm not interested in your travel arrangements, Ms Tehri. What I want to know is what you were doing up there on the hill, and why, and what you saw.'

'I was going for a drink with a neighbour I'd met by chance in the supermarket.' Nita said uncertainly. 'Only he seemed to have the wrong idea so I got out of the car and made my own way home.'

'Who was the neighbour? And what was the idea he was so wrong about?'

'Harris Searle from number 6.' He was a killer after all. She wasn't going to protect him. She added stiffly, 'His behaviour was quite inappropriate.'

'And you didn't think it "appropriate" to come and tell us?'

'I didn't know anything had happened till I saw it on the news just now.'

'Okay, suppose I accept that,' Cutler said, looking at Reed who seemed quite detached from the proceedings.

Nita hurried on, 'And I don't know what time it was, or what time she was killed. I was cold and upset and I didn't look at my watch.'

'It was pretty cold last night,' Reed said eventually.

'Not many people out walking,' Cutler said. 'See anyone, did you?'

'Just her, the blonde in the pink fleece. It was her, wasn't it?'

'What makes you think that?'

'Harris was interested in her. She had "Harvard Slut" on her jacket and he thought it meant something.'

'Oh I get it,' Cutler said, 'your boyfriend saw another chick he fancied and you decided that made him a murderer.'

Nita jumped to her feet. 'Harris is absolutely not and never has been my boyfriend. The reason I'm telling you this, apart from the fact that you asked me, is that he seemed to be irrationally angry, almost violent. And I'm also worried about the woman who lives in the same house as him. She *is* a friend.'

'You speak awfully good English,' Reed said, in a tone that was supposed to sound placatory.

'I *am* English.' Nita was so angry she almost stuttered. 'Now please would you both leave.'

Cutler didn't move a muscle. 'We have two enquiries into very serious crimes on the go at the moment, and you are involved in both. Would you care to comment?'

'I'll comment when you treat me like a decent human being.'

'I'm treating you like I treat everyone else. As to how decent you are—that remains to be seen. I gather Sergeant Eavers invited you to give us a DNA sample and you refused.'

'I didn't refuse. I asked her for a reason and *she* refused.'

'You're splitting hairs,' Cutler said with a curl of his poorly shaven upper lip. 'See, that's what I object to—it's my taxes pay for your superior education which you then proceed to use against me.'

'I paid for my own education,' Nita said furiously. 'I'm still paying for it. That's why I can't afford a car.' She stared directly at Reed who did not acknowledge that the subject had ever been referred to before. 'I can't believe you treat *everyone* like this,' she went on. 'Don't you get tired of people complaining to your superiors? Because that's what I plan to do first thing Monday morning.'

'You don't want to do that,' Cutler said. 'You might get yourself put on my black-list.' He suddenly roared with laughter and Reed grinned sheepishly. 'Why don't you make us all a cup of tea? She makes a lovely cup of tea,' he added to Reed, 'warms the pot and everything.'

Nita couldn't believe what she was hearing.

'Go on, ducks,' Cutler said, 'then we can stop scoring points off of each other and start again.'

It was to disguise the fact that she was shaking all over that Nita went to the kitchen and mechanically filled the kettle. I asked them to leave, she thought. I even said please. Yet here they are, demanding tea. My home doesn't protect me. I have no back-up. I need to be able to say, 'I'm calling my solicitor.' But I haven't got one, and they know it. They seem to know without being told that I'm an outcast from my family. They're no different than Harris Searle. I had no defence against him either, except to run away. But running away invites pursuit, and is always interpreted as cowardice, weakness or guilt.

She'd been brought up to think of the police as the strong arm of the establishment: the force who didn't understand outsiders at all. But like teachers, police officers were supposed to recognise effort and honesty when they saw it. So, according to Nita's family you had to try harder than everyone else and behave blamelessly. If you failed to prove your worth you would let down your entire family, your entire race.

It was not enough to want to be British. You had to earn it every day of your life. For this reason Nita had always tried as hard as she possibly could, and conducted her private life as if it were a public performance that would face criticism and judgement. She was often exhausted.

As if to demonstrate this point, she warmed the pot and resisted the urge to spit into it or to lace the infusion with laxatives. In fact the mechanical, orderly actions calmed her. She laid out a tray with cups, milk jug and sugar bowl and carried it through to the sitting room.

'What did I tell you?' Cutler said to Reed. 'When did you last see a milk jug on a tray when you were conducting an interview? I'm telling you, my son, this girl likes to do things proper.' He stared at Nita as if challenging her to correct his

English. She was jolted by the sudden fear that they had been nosing through her private things. Her laptop lay on a low shelf and she thought it had been moved.

Reed said, 'How long have you been here?'

'About nine months.'

'No, I mean how long have you lived in this country?'

Nita could quite easily have dumped scalding tea in his lap. Instead she continued to pour it into cups. When she'd finished she stood back and said, 'Help yourselves to milk and sugar. May I add that I was born in this country, and that if anyone had bothered to do their jobs correctly when I was first considered for employment at Midford Junior School they would have checked my records including my birth certificate and you wouldn't be asking such insulting questions.'

'He's young,' Cutler said. 'He doesn't do "good cop" very well. Alan, you've offended the lady. Go down and sit in the car.'

'But I...'

'Go on, lad, I won't be long.'

Reed put down his teacup and left. Cutler calmly added sugar to his own cup and sat down again. He said, 'You know, you really don't want to be so touchy.'

'Why not? You don't listen to a word I say. I asked you to leave and yet you're still here.'

'Reed's gone. That's a fifty percent success rate. What more do you want? Where's your sense of humour?' He drank his tea and sighed with pleasure. His face looked as if it had been hacked from a gravestone. 'I don't understand what it is about you, but when I'm here I seem to act like one of those bloody awful cops you see on TV. Maybe it's because your standards are so high. That's why I brought Reed—to iron me out. But there you go—he's even more tactless than me.'

Nita said, 'Yes.' But she said it with less conviction than she intended.

'I do listen,' he said. 'You were in the Holyfield vicinity, calling City Cabs because Harris Searle was taking liberties and you didn't want to stay in a car with him. But it was Saturday night and they couldn't send a cab so you hoofed it home. Right? You saw a blonde girl in a pink jacket. Right? But did anyone see you?'

'I don't think so—not that I can recall. Oh, but I bought fish and chips at Good Cod Almighty when I got back to the city centre. I can't think why anyone else would remember seeing me.' She paused. 'Except there's that plainclothes guy you've got who seems to do nothing but sit outside my door in a four-by-four Toyota.'

'Pardon me?' Cutler looked puzzled.

'He's got tattoos on his driver's side arm—Maori ones—and the car's white. You must know him.'

'He's not a cop,' Cutler said, so decisively that Nita decided he must be lying. 'Are you saying now you've got a stalker? They're not fashion accessories, you know.'

She bit her lip.

'Sorry,' he said hurriedly. 'We are not having you followed, believe me. Immigrant paranoia's got to stop somewhere.'

Nita swallowed a retort about the word 'immigrant' and pointed to the mutilated doll which still lay on her mantle-shelf. 'Okay,' she said, 'what do you call this then—folk art?'

Cutler heaved himself out of his chair and examined the little brown baby through half closed eyes. Then he fumbled in his pocket for a bent pair of reading glasses and examined it again. 'Sweet,' he said in the end. 'Where did you find it?'

'It was on the doormat when I got home last night.'

'In the communal hall?'

'Are you suggesting it might be for Toby or Leo?'

'Don't bristle, Ms Tehri, you're always bristling. And going too fast for an old copper. What time did you get home last night?'

'Oh dear,' Nita said, 'I really don't know. It was after midnight, I'm sure. I seemed to have been walking for hours.'

'You didn't come the most direct way if you crossed the river by the bridge near the fish shop. Walking round in circles, were you?'

'Not exactly. But I've never been to the Holyfield area before. I didn't know the way.'

'And this is what you found when you got home? Who do you think delivered it?'

'Harris Searle,' Nita said promptly; and then, 'I don't know.'

'This same Harris Searle who murdered... no, don't try to kick me out again—you haven't got the heft. Just tell me why you think he sent you the effigy.'

'He said the dead baby looked like me.'

'Ah,' Cutler said, 'the dead baby.'

'I only have local gossip for information. Thanks to you. But Harris works at the hospital and seems to know more than everyone else. So perhaps now you'd like to tell me why you want a sample of my DNA. And perhaps you'll tell me if you've also asked the other women in the road. And if not, why not?'

'Local gossip,' Cutler said almost to himself, 'don't you just love it? Well, Thursday, Galloway Waste took the full skip away to empty it. Which they did legally at a council site. But you always get bunches of scavengers picking over builder's rubbish, and someone found a dead baby all rolled up in the local paper and duct tape. It was a baby girl not more than a few days old, although we're still waiting for the forensic report to be sure. And as you've guessed the baby was of mixed race.'

'Which races?'

Sergeant Cutler looked uncomfortable.

'You don't know, do you?' Nita felt something like triumph. 'So you pick on the only woman of any colour in Guscott Road. The mother could be white—or is abandoning a dead baby something white women simply don't do? Why are you interested only in a woman? The colour might be the man's. Not everything is a woman's fault.'

'I can't tell you how the investigation is proceeding,' he said stiffly.

'But it sounds to me as if the local constabulary is suffering from a lapse of logic.'

Cutler put down his teacup and grinned icily at Nita. 'I'll bring our "lapse" to the attention of the Chief Constable, shall I? Thanks so much for pointing it out.'

She'd gone too far. Another big man was angry with her. There would be consequences. Why couldn't she keep her mouth shut and smile and nod the way she'd been trained to do? Was that so difficult?

When he'd gone, taking with him the mutilated doll, and she was washing up and putting away the tea things, she thought about Cutler. He might be ten or fifteen years younger than her father but he showed some of the same traits: withdrawing when offended, threatening future punishment, sarcasm. They both demonstrated similar mistrust of educated women: a mixture of ridicule and envy. They both won every argument with strong-arm techniques rather than reason. They both used push-pull tactics.

Nita examined her own reaction. There was no doubt she was scared of Cutler and angry; but there was something familiar and tauntingly seductive about him as well. If I could learn to please Sergeant Cutler I'd be safe, she thought.

The cup he had been drinking from crashed to the floor splitting into hundreds of sharp, wounding fragments. Nita stared at them and recognised with horror that she had experienced the same emotions last night on the hill with Harris Searle.

10

The Ghost of Blood

//

Nita pushed her trolley up and down aisles, filling it with fruit and veg, rice, bread and milk; everything she'd need for next week. Resolutely she ignored the CCTV camera which would have recorded her meeting with Harris Searle last night and her embarrassingly eager response. She was glad that today she could be seen, an ordinary, innocent woman, doing something ordinary and innocent. But no one she knew saw her and she took her shopping home without witnesses.

In the kitchen she made more spicy chicken to replace what she'd taken out of the freezer on Friday. It surprised her that she'd seen or heard nothing from Toby and Leo since then. But sometimes they worked on weekends. Sometimes they went away and stayed with friends or family.

Nita was waiting for a call from Mina. It was a regular thing for the sisters to speak to each other on a Sunday evening. To while away the time she cooked a vegetable dish based on dhal and bahmia. She'd never made it before so she invented as she went along. Cooking delicious food was the one way she knew to please people without bringing injury upon herself; unless, of course, you counted excess weight as injury. She caught herself planning to take extra to school tomorrow just in case Miss Whitby wanted some, and she stopped, staring at her knife.

She didn't even know Miss Whitby's first name. Now was she planning to feed her? Why? To please her? To become her new best friend?

All Nita wanted from Miss Whitby, or from any of her colleagues on Monday was the name and number of a good solicitor. She didn't need to grovel to get that.

The point of her knife glinted and she was reminded that it had cut Sergeant Cutler's thumb. The ghost of his blood stained her blade. She put it down and walked away to the sitting-room trying to dismiss the thought. If she couldn't get over herself she'd have to buy a new knife. Good kitchen knives were expensive.

Mina rang and when the greetings were done, Nita couldn't help blurting out, 'Someone I don't like cut himself on my knife. He bled on my knife.'

Instantly Mina said, 'Get rid of it. It's no good for cutting food you put in your mouth. What was a man you don't like doing in your kitchen? Did Dad send him?'

'Dad still doesn't know where I am. Unless you've told him.'

'Of course not,' Mina said huffily. 'I haven't even told my husband. But men feel loyalty to each other. Two fathers now. Two fathers together. They talk on the phone, you know.'

Well they would, wouldn't they? Nita thought. Rolam ran the business in M'bai. She was most disconcerted to hear Mina calling him 'my husband' rather than his name. And she was picking up traces of his family's lilting accent in Mina's speech.

Mina said, 'He's a wonderful father. Not like our dad at all. I just thought you might've been lonely one night and rung Mum or Ash.'

'That would be asking for trouble.' Nita guessed that Rolam was now in the room with Mina.

'You should try to make it up with them,' Mina said, sounding close to tears. 'A girl can't survive alone without her family.'

Yes, Rolam was definitely there, and Nita's chance of a confidential talk with her sister vanished. She changed the subject and asked how Mina was feeling.

'Sick,' Mina said resignedly. 'Feeling the heat.'

'It's freezing here.'

'I miss winter.'

'I miss *you*.'

'Only cos you can't throw far enough,' Mina said, sounding sad and more like herself. In the background Nita heard a child begin to cry and Rolam said something loudly.

There wasn't anything left to talk about. Nita couldn't tell Mina her troubles, and Mina couldn't share with Nita her fear of the scan which would tell her whether or not she could keep this pregnancy. Nita said furiously, 'When can I call you for a private chat?' She was suddenly bursting with pent up rage at their father for giving away her sister, her best friend, to a man, another family, halfway across the world.

'I'll call you,' Mina said. The crying was coming closer. Misery was on its way to Mina's lap, her arms, and her hands, expecting comfort. Exactly what Nita wished to do with her own problem but was prevented. She hung up knowing that Mina too was left with a weight she'd wanted to halve. To talk to her sister Nita needed the permission of a husband, three children, and a host of in-laws. Her very own sister who, it turned out, had simply been a disposable asset belonging to their father to be awarded to the most useful male who put in a bid.

Her rage blew scorching in Mina's direction too. She had accepted. She had allowed them to remove her from college after only a year on the grounds that half an education made her 'educated', but a complete education would make her arrogant and less marketable.

She returned to the kitchen and stared hard at the knife. Her sister's reaction to Sergeant Cutler's blood on its point had been instant and supported with extreme force her own atavistic feeling. It was the reaction of a half-educated woman, a disposable asset.

Nita picked up the knife and selected a plump mushroom to chop. But the hand holding the knife refused to cut. The ghost of Sergeant Cutler's blood, once imagined, would not go away. Reason bowed its noble head before superstition. Nita sighed and consigned the knife to the back of a drawer, picking out her little paring knife instead.

She made a separate mushroom dish, paying great attention to balancing the spices. Mushrooms have a delicate flavour all of their own, but they pick up surrounding flavours very readily, so they can be easily overwhelmed if the spices are too lively. If on the other hand the spices are too weak, the mushroom may be dismissed as nothing. Poor little mushroom, Nita thought, spending most of its short life in the dark, and then usually just added as bulk or background to a more exotic concoction.

What she was studiously shoving to the back of her mind was the thought that even her cooking was being affected by Sergeant Cutler and his stupidity. Who asked him to test the point of her knife in the first place? It was his own nosiness and intrusiveness that hurt him.

She cleaned the kitchen and started the dish-washer. Enough food for a week was sitting, cooling, next to the freezer. The air was filled with the scent of spice and herbs.

Nita knew she could eat all of it at a single sitting. She wanted to eat. She was hungry and angry, anxious and sad. It was a very dangerous combination. She left the dish-washer purring and put on her coat.

Outside, wet snow was drifting sluggishly to earth and melting. A dented black metal filing cabinet had joined the swivel chair in the skip. Its drawers were gaping, empty. Nita hurried by. Tonight, to be unwanted, even if you were only an old filing cabinet, struck her as tragic.

She glanced towards number 6. There was no police car nearby, no sign that Sergeant Cutler had even thought about visiting Harris Searle. He had taken the doll, but she had no guarantee that he wouldn't simply give it to his kids or his dog to play with. Somehow she managed to annoy him without ever being listened to. Maybe her voice was like a crying seagull in his ears: a grating sound with no message.

Unthinking, she stepped off the kerb to cross the road. Brakes squealed, a horn blared. Bull-bars hit her shoulder. She sat down abruptly on the wet tarmac.

A man's voice shouted, 'What the fuck do you think you're doing?' A car door slammed.

Nita struggled to her feet. She felt no pain. In fact she felt nothing at all except her heart beating in her throat.

She looked up and saw, standing near her, a tall man with blond hair and big arms. He wore a thick padded gilet over his white t-shirt. There were Maori tattoos decorating his driver's side arm.

He said, 'You fucking idiot, why don't you look where you're going? I could've killed you.' Then he faded out and all she could hear was a soft roaring sound in her ears. She sat down again.

A hand pressed down on the back of her neck and a voice that seemed to come from a long way off said, 'You got up too quick.'

Fainting felt like a wonderful thing to do—a warm and comfortable thing with no painful choices to be made. The hand on her neck was a protecting blanket. But the voice said, 'You ain't hurt, right? Please tell me you ain't hurt.'

'I know you,' Nita said. 'You're the police spy. Sergeant Cutler won't like this at all.'

'What?' he said. 'Look, get in the car, I'm taking you to the hospital—you're raving.'

Nita sat up and pushed his hand away. 'I'm not getting into any more cars with strange men.'

'Then I'm taking you home. You can't sue me—it was your fault—but I ain't leaving you here in the snow not knowing if you're hurt. Come on, where do you live?'

'You know very well where I live,' Nita said, climbing unsteadily to her feet again. 'You've been sitting outside in that gas-guzzler for the last three nights. It's harassment and I'm going to complain about you and Sergeant Cutler to the Police Commission.'

'Don't do that,' he said, 'you'll embarrass us both. I'm not a cop, I swear.'

'Then why are you spying on me?'

'I'm not,' he said. 'I'm watching number 15. I'm a private investigator.'

Nita almost sat down again but he caught her arm and drew her towards the car door. Pain punched her shoulder and she winced, but he opened the passenger door and said, 'At least get in and warm up while I park. I can't sit in the middle of the road all night just so some dumb girl can play silly buggers.'

She got in. He'd left the motor running so it was warm and smelled of tobacco and Juicy Fruit gum. The ashtray was full. Gum and toffee wrappers littered the floor.

He parked quickly and efficiently. Sunday night left the streets empty and dead. Even on the main road nothing was happening and other vehicles passed only rarely. Up high in the front seat Nita felt isolated and invulnerable. Pedestrians were taller than normal cars which was perhaps why they had a false sense of equality. But only a giant could bang on the roof of a monster like this one. It was, however, a somewhat indiscreet car for a private detective to drive.

She said, 'Who are you, and why are you watching number 15?'

He turned towards her, and in the amber street light she got the impression of symmetry—of straight brows darker than the hair, of a straight nose and straight teeth.

'I'm not supposed to say,' he said. 'You must know confidentiality's the name of the game. But I'm Zachary Eastwood. And you?' He stuck out a big, well-shaped hand, and Nita had no option but to put her own hand in it.

'Nita Tehri,' she said although she wasn't yet sure she wanted him to know her name. She was, she felt, always paying a high price for her own good manners.

He released her hand and said, 'Call me Zach. Look, it's dead around here. Come for a drink at the Green Man and we can have a natter.'

'I don't drink,' Nita said, remembering last night. But even the smell of Zach's car told her that tonight was as unlike last night as two nights could be. Besides the Green Man was just round the corner so she couldn't be stranded miles from home.

Last night there had been live music at the pub and it had been the fixed point at the centre of a lot of noise and drunkenness. Now a few regulars propped up the bar while a few more played billiards in the back room.

Zach brought drinks to their table: a pint for himself, an orange juice and a packet of crisps for her. Nita looked around but there was no one there she recognised. She tested her shoulder. It felt like nothing more than a bad bruise. The seat of her jeans was wet and uncomfortable but the warmth of the pub quickly made her feel sleepy.

Zach watched her, his handsome forehead creased with concern. 'You ain't really hurt, are you?' he said. 'Nothing broken? You could have a, whatchamacallit, soft tissue injury. We can get you checked out at the hospital if you like.'

Harris worked in the A&E department. She shook her head. 'Why am I supposed to believe you? You turn up just when the police are beginning to hassle me. No one lives at number 15 yet, so what're you watching?'

He gazed at her for a moment as if gauging her reliability, then said, 'Well it ain't like it's proper confidential, so I don't suppose it matters if I tell you. But you got to swear not to tell anyone else. I got my professional rep to consider.'

'Okay.'

'Well see, my... client, who I can't name, wants me to check out the neighbourhood. He's spent a lot of money on the property already, and he's going to spend a shit-load more, so he wants to know what the area's like so he can pitch to the right sort of buyers.'

'How very sensible!'

'Think so? It's about noise and pubs and clubs. Also nuisance neighbours—like does the council have any halfway houses for junkies and nut-jobs? I can do a lot of the research from my office of course. But nothing beats the information you collect by being there.'

'And I suppose you need to know if anyone has any plans to build an extension, say?'

'Why? Do you know something?'

'Don't worry,' Nita said. 'I haven't heard anything. There's a madman who lives above Women's Aid—he throws his utility bills out of the window when the moon's full and he thinks Hitler's still alive. You have a family on one side of you with two teenage daughters, but they keep horses out of town so I hardly ever see them. On the other side there's a retired couple who go to Spain a lot and I hardly ever see them either.'

'And you live opposite,' Zach said, smiling. 'I won't introduce you to my client or you'll do me out of a job. What sort of hassle have you had with the cops, then? Anything to do with the baby in the skip?'

'I think so,' Nita said. 'No one's accused me of anything outright but I'm quite worried.' She was relieved he'd asked so straightforwardly. He was a detective after all so of course he would have heard about it. And he looked at her and smiled as if he were listening just for information's sake, and not as if he were judging.

She said, almost without thinking, 'But what worries me most is Harris Searle at number 6 because I think he's violent and my friend Rose Peters lives underneath him. She's quite arty and I think she's miscalculated what he's like.'

Zach stopped smiling and said, 'Tell me about it?'

Warmth and exhaustion loosened Nita's tongue and she found herself relating almost the full story of how she found herself abandoned in the area where a murder was about to take place. She told him about the doll, about trying to warn Rose, and about Sergeant Cutler's attitude.

It didn't occur to her until she woke up on Monday morning that she might have been so relaxed because Zach put something in her drink. At the time all she felt was the huge relief of unburdening herself to a sympathetic stranger.

He walked her home with his hand on her elbow like a perfect gentleman, and took the keys out of her fumbling hands to let her into the hall. But what she remembered most vividly was how he'd brushed a wet snowflake off her hair and said, 'Sleep well. Don't worry; I'll be watching your door tonight.'

And she did sleep well. She slept better than she had all week.

11

Monsters in the River

///

In the morning Nita examined the huge black bruise which had developed on her right shoulder overnight. It hurt. She drank her early morning tea by the window looking down on half a dozen bald car tyres which had appeared mysteriously in the skip and hidden the vile fridge-freezer. Zach probably knew who'd tipped them there. She wondered if, as a private investigator, he kept a log of all the comings and goings in Guscott Road, all the registration plate numbers of fly-tippers, for instance. What was a mystery to Nita was probably an open book to him. It was too bad he'd begun his surveillance the night after the dead baby was found instead of the night before.

As usual Nita's mind lurched away from tough subjects like the secret despair of women and the bleak disposal of a dead baby. In fact, her mind felt cushioned and blunted by an unaccustomed amount of sleep. It was then that she wondered if Zach might've slipped vodka into her orange juice. She could remember talking to him as if he were her best friend whom she'd known for years. She'd told him almost everything she'd been hoping to tell Mina. She cringed. But maybe he was used to it because he had the kind of face people confided in. Or perhaps it was his skill as a private detective—the talent for making people tell their secrets.

She put on her coat and gloves and collected her workbag at the door. Emerging into the cold road she saw Galloway Waste's truck reversing round the corner from the main road with an empty skip hanging between two stanchions. She would never have to look at the fridge-freezer again—it would soon be on its way to the council tip to be picked over by scavengers. It was amazing to think that even a revolting reject like that might have parts that someone else could use.

Zach's huge car was gone. He never stayed all night, he'd told her, just long enough to observe the action. After a complete week he would submit his report to the client and then probably move on to another job.

Nita politely said, 'Good morning,' to Diane and Stu at the bus stop. She was going to keep her distance but Diane said, 'They haven't arrested you then?'

Stu gave a snort of laughter as if Diane were being funny.

Nita smiled coldly and said, 'Not yet.'

Diane said, 'You had so many visits from the police I'm quite surprised to see you here this morning.'

'They just can't get enough of my cooking,' Nita said, keeping her voice neutral.

Stu said, 'Oh yeah, I heard cops fancy the spicy stuff.' And this time Diane snorted with laughter.

Nita kept the polite smile pinned to her face and saw with relief that the bus was coming.

When it arrived, Stu and Diane got on first and took a seat at the front. Without hesitation, Nita went to the back. A few days ago, as a neighbour, she would have taken a seat close to theirs. Not any more.

As usual they got off two stops before hers, but this time they didn't wave or say, 'Goodbye.'

At the school gate Nita met Ryan's mother towing Ryan by the hand. Ryan had a balloon of snot in his left nostril and looked as if he'd been crying. She checked quickly but didn't notice any bruising.

Ryan's mum stopped as soon as she saw Nita. 'You fucking cow,' she said, 'this is all your fault. Listen you dirty Pakki bitch, how'm I supposed to keep my job when I got to look after this little bleeder all day? Tell me that, eh? You never think how us working women are supposed to cope, do you? You with your long holidays and half-terms and every fucking bank-holiday ever invented. You never think how we're supposed to earn enough to put food on the table, do you?'

'I'm sorry,' Nita said, edging past, blushing. Ryan's mum was beginning to collect an audience.

'You're *sorry*,' Ryan's mum shouted. 'You *should* be fucking sorry. You *will* be fucking sorry by the time I've finished with you.'

Nita hurried across the playground leaving Ryan's mum with the sympathetic murmurs of all the other working mothers—all the working mothers on the planet, she supposed.

'You got off lightly,' the Deputy Head said, as she passed him on the school steps. 'She threatened to chuck Mr Hughes out of the window unless he agreed to reinstate Ryan immediately. You don't have to look far to see who Ryan gets it from.'

'Maybe she's desperate,' Nita said. 'Ryan's dad is worse than useless.'

'Seeing things from her distorted point of view won't save you if she decides to get physical. She'll take it as weakness. Believe me, I've seen her type before.'

In the staffroom Nita made coffee and wrapped her hands round the mug for warmth. Everyone was wondering if the boiler was knackered again or whether Mr Hughes had turned down the thermostat to save more pennies in the latest budget cut. Miss Whitby came in last, rosy from the cold. She approached Nita and said, 'Mr Hughes asks if you'll see him first break. Wow—I had a superb weekend—spent Saturday in Paris. Can you believe that? Oh, the shoes! How did you get on?'

'Er, interesting,' Nita said. 'I wanted to ask—do you know a good solicitor I could get in touch with?'

'As interesting as that?' Miss Whitby laughed. 'If you're serious I can give you details of the firm my family's dealt with for years.'

'Thank you, I'm serious.'

The bell for assembly rang and Miss Whitby said, 'I'll write the details on a post-it and stick it to your locker door in case I miss you at break.'

She showed the children pictures of Roman mosaics and then organised them into working groups to share paste and paper. The results were messy and lively. Nita pinned the best ones up on the wall with Sam's red, green and yellow stegosaurus in gold star position. There were houses, pop stars, dragons and creatures no one could identify. She was so pleased with them she thought she might make it a class project and get the kids to collaborate on a frieze. Maybe sea monsters, she thought, remembering her own dolphin. But she knew in the end she'd let the children decide.

At break she meant to go to Mr Hughes' office but he came to her classroom instead. He walked slowly round the room looking at the work while Nita cleared up the paper and set the desks and chairs in order. Then he said, 'Some colourful work here Miss Tehri; although I was going to have a chat with you about sticking more closely to the core curriculum, but something more serious has come up.' He came over to her desk and sat down on the only full-size chair in the room. He took off his glasses and violently massaged the bridge of his nose.

Nita perched on the edge of a table and waited.

He said, 'There have been complaints, serious allegations, in fact.'

Nita began to say, 'Ryan's mother... ' but he held his hand up. 'You can't expect anything different from her. No, what I'm talking about is the allegation that you are somehow involved in the death and disposal of a new born baby. Many of the allegations have been, of course, anonymous, but some have come from parents I would not normally associate with the rumour mill.' He held up his hand again to prevent her from interrupting.

She noticed that he had not put his glasses back on. It was as if he didn't want to see her.

He went on, 'Allegations are meaningless if not backed up by evidence and fact—which I hasten to assure you, they are not—and in any other profession I would ignore them. However, Miss Tehri, we are teachers. The care and education of the very young is our duty. We must be seen to be beyond reproach.

'I have just come off the phone with one of the parent governors and we are in complete agreement: it's with great regret that we must ask you to go straight home.'

'I'm sorry?' Nita said, shock making her whisper. 'Are you sacking me?'

'No, no, Miss Tehri,' Hughes said looking relieved. 'Nor am I suspending you. Those would be official actions. I'm quite unwilling to take any official action at this juncture. I have every confidence you will clear your name and no such steps will be necessary. What I'm asking you to do is simply to go home—as you would if, for instance, you were too ill to carry on. Mrs Cartwright will take your children in with hers until lunch when the agency will send a supply teacher. You mustn't worry about us, Miss Tehri, we'll manage.'

'But,' Nita whispered, 'but. What will you say? What will I say? Everyone will *assume* you're sacking me.'

'I will say nothing, Miss Tehri, and I must ask you to do the same. We are all agreed that a dignified silence... '

'But if I can't defend myself... '

'They are threatening to take the story to the local press... '

'Oh,' Nita said, 'and you need to be able to say the problem's solved because the offending teacher is no longer here?'

'Have you any conception of the forces that will be unleashed by a headline incorporating the words "Baby Killer" and "Junior School Teacher"? *Have* you, Miss Tehri?'

'But I haven't done anything, Mr Hughes. A baby was found in a skip close to my home and somehow the whole thing has snowballed. I don't understand.'

'Nor do I, Miss Tehri, and I'm very sorry for you. But you must understand that this school cannot continue to employ a teacher against whom such allegations have been made. Of course we will institute an enquiry immediately and support you any way we can. But in the meantime you must not come to work. We cannot be seen to be putting you in charge of children. We cannot, you see, ignore the culture of blame which dominates the lives of those of us who work with children.'

Sitting at the back of the bus on her way home, Nita really did feel ill. She felt as if she'd been shot in the heart and was dying. I am no longer a teacher, she thought. I have no job and no identity because I'm no longer allowed to teach. When Sergeant Cutler and PC Reed insult me I cannot stand up straight and say I am a teacher—respect me. When Harris Searle hits on me I can't put him down as if he's a school kid because I'm not allowed to treat anyone as if they're school kids, especially school kids.

There was a real pain in Nita's heart and she pressed on it with her hand as if to stop her life's blood gushing out all over the bus. She would not be able to tell Mina that all the sacrifice had been for nothing because now she wasn't allowed to teach children. How could she tell Mina that this had happened because people—neighbours, parents, other teachers—suspected her of killing a little girl child?

My life is over, Nita thought, hand on heart, sitting dying at the back of the bus.

Instead of getting down outside the Green Man as she usually did, Nita stayed where she was till the end of the line at Coldharbour, a part of the city where the river and the canal met—a place the locals called The Cut. Three locks about half a mile apart brought the canal down to river level.

Dockers used to live in the tiny cramped terraces surrounding The Cut. Now the waterfront houses were highly prized and further back were the delicatessens and bijoux shops and galleries that serviced their owners.

On bright warm days tourists came to take pictures of the locks, the great turning circle for barges and narrow boats, the prettily painted houses. Today, under an iron grey sky which threatened sleet, everyone was sheltering behind double glazing.

Nita walked along the towpath with a cold north wind pushing at her back. She couldn't think what to do. In fact every time she tried to think her brain shut down as if it were on a trip switch. Eventually she stopped trying and allowed her eyes to drift with the freezing current of the river. Under the silver grey sheen on the surface the water was black and opaque. Monsters could lurk there, undetected—creatures unknown to man. Nita pictured them as the mosaics her children might have made with their pixels of coloured paper. She pictured them, huge and slow, scavenging the riverbed, manoeuvring around rusting, encrusted supermarket trolleys. She imagined the supermarket trolleys as a robot tribe, feebleminded, with a poor sense of direction and as irresistibly attracted to water as lemmings are to cliff-tops.

If I jumped now, she thought, weighed down by my coat, unable to swim, maybe the monsters would carry me downstream and out to sea. Or maybe, now that I'm not a teacher, I'll write children's books about water monsters and supermarket trolleys and ask the children to illustrate them.

But she knew she didn't have enough courage to jump or enough imagination to write, so she walked on, dazed and stunned by the morning's events. Not just one person, but many people had rung Mr Hughes. Tigs and Joe's parents would certainly have heard all the rumours because they too lived in Guscott Road. They could be forgiven because naturally they would react violently to any perceived threat to children. That was one probable phone call. Harris Searle unquestionably would have been one of the anonymous callers. That made two. But Mr Hughes talked as if there had been an avalanche of calls; which meant that in a little street of only thirty terraced houses, Nita must have a high proportion of ill-wishers. What had she done to make so many people believe she had killed a baby?

She wondered if Sergeant Cutler had rung Midford Junior to warn them. Would the police do that? It occurred to Nita that they might. Clearly, from the stupid questions they'd asked her, they had not looked for the results of their own CRB and background checks they were supposed to have made. It was possible therefore that they might be making a pre-emptive strike against her, covering their backsides in case she turned out to be guilty.

On the other hand, Mr Hughes did not appear to know about the death of Harvard Slut. Surely if Sergeant Cutler was going to inform the school about Nita's involvement in the dead baby enquiry he'd mention that too.

Nita, skinned alive by her own questions as well as by the freezing wind, turned away from the water and went off uncertainly in search of a place to sit quietly and eat her lunch. She couldn't find one: any place she might've found expected her to buy food and drink. There was no library where she could hide behind a stack and eat. In the end she decided with amazement that she wasn't hungry. Her problem was so huge, she realised, that she wasn't even tempted to solve it by eating. She needed to take action, proper action, and stuffing her face with gooey comfort just wouldn't cut it.

She felt as if she were sitting in the middle of a road where one truck after another bore down on her at eighty miles an hour, hit her and drove on. Anyone with any sense would get out of the road. Nita didn't know how. Normal young women, when in trouble, go back to their families. They ring up their mothers. They go home, have a long chat, maybe a cry, and leave comforted, with advice they've no intention of taking ringing in their ears. At least that's what they did in college, she remembered.

Nita took her phone out of her bag and looked at it. She might text Ash and ask him to ring her after school. But how could an ex-teacher ask a schoolboy for advice? He was in his last year, and if he achieved good enough grades he would go to university. But even so, he was just a kid. She was the older sister. When they were children, Mina had been expected to look after Nita, and both Nita and Mina had been charged with the care of Ash, the little lord of the Tehri household. It was a situation many boys in his position took advantage of. But Ash had been a sweet-natured kid with an innate sense of fairness; for which Nita was extremely grateful. When, eighteen months ago, she was disowned by the older generation, he said, 'They told me to think of you as dead. I can miss you and mourn you, I can remember you with pity, but you don't exist. How stupid is that?'

'I can explain,' she said, her heart breaking.

'You don't have to,' he said. 'The way I see it, those dinosaurs tried to take over your life. They made two incredibly stupid choices, and you're trying to get your life back. Am I right?'

'Yes.'

'Well. I don't think I can be hurt quite the way you've been hurt, but all the same, can I come to you if I ever need a place to hide?'

'Only if you stay in touch,' Nita said.

'All I need is a phone number,' Ash said quickly. 'Don't give me an address—they might force me to tell them.'

'I don't have an address yet, 'she said. 'Dead women don't need houses.'

'Bollocks,' he said cheerfully. 'No self pity—that's what you're always telling me. And of the three of us, Mina says, you're the cleverest and the strongest. I agree with Mina.'

'Oh Ash,' Nita said aloud, the wind whipping the words out of her mouth and sending them flying with the seagulls. 'That doesn't actually make me clever or strong enough for the real world when it turns nasty.'

She was walking through a tunnel that ran under the main road. On the other side she hoped she'd find her way to a bus stop or a book shop. Instead, she saw the silhouette of a tall man blocking her way. She was faced once again with what was, in her life, a familiar dilemma: should she turn round and leave, thus inviting pursuit; or should she carry on and risk confrontation? She gripped her book bag firmly and carried on.

The tall man stood aside, almost politely, and let her leave the underpass. But as soon as her back was turned he said, 'Can you spare a little change? I don't have enough for the Shelter tonight?'

She swung round to face him. He had a ginger beard hiding half his face and making him look demented, but his eyes were pale grey and watering from the cold. His clothes looked like the rags that should have been left in the skip on Guscott Road.

She didn't want to open her bag to search for her change-purse in such an isolated spot so she said, 'Are you hungry?' and kept walking briskly towards the main road. Something inside her drew strength from the fact that, beaten down as she was, a big tall guy had asked her for help.

He said suspiciously, 'I suppose I am a bit hungry, lassie,' and followed her up the ramp to a place where shops were open and traffic was passing by.

She found the entrance to an abandoned building, out of the wind, and rummaged in her bag. First she handed him the plastic container of spicy vegetables and rice with a plastic fork, and only when his hands were full did she look for a pound coin to give him.

The money vanished instantly into his many layers of clothing. He said, 'D'ye expect me to eat this?' But he lifted the lid and sniffed cautiously. 'Ooh, I love a curry,' he said, and dug the plastic fork into the food.

Nita said, 'Can you tell me the way to the nearest book shop?'

'I could,' he said, chewing and gulping rapidly, afraid she'd snatch the food back. 'But I don't like it there. They won't even let me in to use the toilet. What d'ye want a book shop for anyways?'

'I need a book to tell me about DNA and the law,' she told him, as usual blurting out the truth without thinking.

'Save yer money, lassie. Wha' d'ye want to know?'

She stared at him in surprise.

He said, 'I haven't always looked like this. But I was once mistaken for a murderer.'

Nita believed him: she too had just made that mistake. She said, 'So did the police want a sample of your DNA?'

'They did, lassie. And I gave it to them willingly. I fitted a description, see, and I wanted to clear meself, so I said, Take what you want and let me go.'

'Is it true that they have to arrest you?'

'Only if you don't give it voluntary. It's like fingerprints, see, in the end you don't have no choice.'

'And is it true that they can keep the sample in their database forever, even if you gave it voluntarily?'

'That's the catch, girlie, they got me for always. When it happened I was happy I could prove the cops wrong. They take your sample, see, and then they give you a week's bail. You got to appear again in a week's time. But then they said, You're in the clear, we're sorry we bothered you. And I was chuffed to hear the cops say sorry.'

'But what about your human rights?'

'I'm in two minds about that.' He scraped the bottom of the plastic box for every last grain of rice. 'I don't want to be in their poxy database, but when it comes to rapists and paedos, especially paedos—I do hate them—I'm glad they got a database.' He sucked the plastic fork loudly and forcefully. 'You're a right good little cook, lassie.'

'Thank you,' Nita said. 'Do they take blood?'

'Just a wee swab around the inside of your cheek. No needles—nothing like that. Are you scared of needles?'

'It isn't that,' she said. 'It's just I'm outraged that I was the only one in my road the police want a sample from.'

He stared at her. 'I'm homeless. I get hassled twenty times a week. I used to be outraged. Now I'm just tired. Being outraged is a waste of your energy. If it's the sodding cops, girl, do what they want. They always win in the end, believe me.'

'Even if they're wrong and prejudiced?'

'Maybe you can afford a good lawyer. I never can. Anyways, a night in the cell's a night out of the cold. There's compensations, see.'

'You're an amazing man to run into just at this moment of my life,' Nita said.

'No I'm not. You didna run into me. I stopped you cos you look like a soft touch. And I was right. But anyone homeless will know more about the police and the law than you want to imagine. I'm not the only undiscovered genius in this city.' Carefully he placed the plastic fork in the box and hid the box in a pocket. He stared at Nita, challenging her to ask for it back. When she didn't he turned away and limped back towards the underpass.

12

A Bloody Vest

///

A t the post office Nita bought a plain white writing pad
and a packet of envelopes. She stood at an empty place at
the counter and wrote, 'Dear Sergeant Cutler.' Then she
stopped and examined her handwriting for signs of weakness. It
was neat and legible; that was all anyone could say about it. Dear
Sergeant Cutler, she thought, how inappropriate. Who on earth
decided that even formal communications between strangers
should begin with the word 'Dear'? It was very un-English and
had probably been copied from the French.

She crumpled up the page and started again: 'Sergeant
Cutler, Today I was sent home from my job at Midford Junior
School because the rumours about my supposed connection
with the baby in the skip reached my head master and the board
of governors. In my opinion the police are at least partially
responsible for these rumours. So please would you...'

That word 'please' again. Please what? I humbly request that
you get off your backsides and clear my name? Do your job?
Did the word 'please' show her up as a soft touch? Please, dear...
oh dear, please, I'm in trouble, only you can save me because
you put me there in the first place.

Trembling with frustration, Nita went on: 'So please would
you make it a priority to find out who the poor baby really did
belong to.'

Did a sentence ending with a preposition show her up as an ignorant soft touch? Sergeant Cutler was hardly a world expert where prepositions were concerned, but he *could* smell weakness.

'To that end,' Nita wrote, with dwindling hope that her writing looked decisive, powerful, intelligent, and above all, innocent, 'I will, as soon as I can, arrange for the presence of a solicitor, and come to the police station to give you a sample of my DNA. This will surely remove me from your enquiry.'

Her use of commas, she decided, was fussy and not at all impressive but she continued: 'However, I must add that I find it outrageous and an abuse of my human rights that mine is the only sample you have requested. Further...' she liked 'further': it seemed to counteract the softness of 'dear' and 'please'.

'Further,' she wrote, 'I consider it to be a violation of civil liberty that the police keep the samples of those proved innocent on their permanent database.'

Was that going too far? She didn't want to make them angry. And what could she say about Harris Searle and Harvard Slut? Maybe it would be less muddling to keep this a single issue letter.

She knew she should end, 'Yours sincerely', but although she was sincere, she certainly did not belong to Sergeant Cutler, so she finished simply with, 'Sincerely, Nita Tehri.'

She addressed the envelope to Sergeant Cutler at the Wallace Street Police Station. She'd bought self adhesive envelopes because she didn't want him to use a licked flap to steal the DNA she'd just offered to donate.

Was this the immigrant paranoia he'd once accused her of, or simply caution? He could have stolen her teacup while he was at her flat, or bugged her phone or hacked into her emails. He could see her any time he cared to look at any of the CCTV footage from the cameras dotted around town. For all she knew her private life might already be a public performance.

Certainly there were CCTV cameras covering the entrance to and lobby of the police station, and if he was interested

Sergeant Cutler could check the time to the last second that she handed the letter over to the desk officer before hurrying away.

She looked at her watch. It was almost the time when she usually went home. She knew she couldn't keep up a pretence that she was still working because Tigs and Joe would tell their parents, and by the time the news hit Guscott Road it would be amplified to the point where she'd been fired and drummed out of school in shame and ignominy. She would have to hide, only go out at night, speak to no one. All the same she felt lighter now that she'd written the letter that took into her own hands the work of clearing her name.

At the Women's Aid corner she almost tripped over Craig's pushchair. 'Oops, sorry,' Jen said, before she saw it was Nita she'd nearly run over. Then she said, 'You stay away from my Craigie. Dave says I'm not to go near you.'

'That's a pity,' Nita said, 'I was going to offer to do a spot of baby-sitting for you. Diane and Stu say you don't go out clubbing nearly enough.' She rushed away before Jen could reply, thinking, oh well done, Nita. Do you really need *more* enemies?

The new skip was already nearly a third filled with rubble and cracked slabs of concrete. It looked as if the builders were digging up the basement floor of number 15. On top of the rubble was a broken-backed, eviscerated armchair. The stained fabric cover was split like hacked skin and springs crawled out of the seat as if from a disembowelling. Nita turned away in disgust and opened her front door.

The post and one small parcel lay on the doormat. This meant that Leo and Toby were not yet home from their weekend away. Nita felt the beginnings of abandonment. As she'd left the school building before Miss Whitby'd had a chance to give her the name of a solicitor, she'd been pinning her hopes on Toby and Leo. She didn't know which one of them had a trust fund, but it stood to reason that anyone with a trust fund must also know a lawyer.

It was only as she sorted the mail that she noticed the parcel was really a badly taped up brown paper bag. 'How Now Brown Cow' was written on it in black marker pen, which meant, she supposed, that it was not for Toby or Leo. She took it upstairs with her letters and put it in a washing up bowl while she forced herself to hang up her coat and deal with the rest of the post as she normally would. But it pulsated with evil possibilities and she didn't want to open it.

She could, she thought, put it in a plastic bag, take it to the police station and dump it on Sergeant Cutler's desk. Or she could just chuck it in the skip. Then whoever it was who'd pushed it through her letterbox would see it there, unopened, and know she was untouched by the contents.

Of course the 'whoever' was Harris Searle, and there was a small, despicable corner of her brain that wanted to know what he'd sent her this time. For a moment she stood wavering. Then she picked up the package and ran downstairs with it before she could change her mind.

Zach Eastwood was on the doorstep looking surprised. He said, 'You're quick. I didn't even ring the bell yet. What you got there?'

Instinctively, as soon as she saw him, Nita hid the package behind her back. It was a silly, childish gesture which just screamed, Look at me, I'm hiding something! She mumbled, 'Just something I'm throwing out.'

'Give it here,' Zach said, snatching it away from her. 'What the bleeding hell does this mean? How Now...?'

'I think it's referring to me,' she said stiffly.

'Oh, I get it,' he said cheerfully. 'I never thought of you as a cow. You shouldn't just bin it you know. There's valuable forensic evidence on everything a perp touches.'

'If there were anyone interested.'

'I'm interested. What's in it?'

'I don't know. I just don't want it in the house, that's all. It may be vile.'

'Usually is. So what?' Tobacco coloured eyes gazed at her and the wind ruffled his blond hair.

'So...' she hesitated and then blurted out, 'You're a private investigator—I want to hire you.'

'Well fuck a duck,' he said, grinning from ear to ear. 'In that case, *I'll* open the sodding parcel.'

'Don't we have to have a contract?' Nita said, terrified by the absence of planning. 'Shouldn't I pay you a retainer first?'

'Well, yeah,' he said, 'of course you should, but seeing as we already know each other, why don't we let that ride while you put the kettle on and I see what that arsehole sent you this time.'

Now that Zach was holding the parcel Nita felt as if she had handed him all the troubles of the world.

'I'll do it out here,' he said. 'In case of explosives, see. You go indoors—I wouldn't want to blow up a new client, would I?'

'Explosives?'

'Probably not.' He weighed the package judiciously. 'But you never know.'

'Oh for goodness sake,' Nita said, taking it back. 'I want to hire you, not explode you in your first five minutes on the job.'

He started to laugh. 'We're a dynamite pair, ain't we?'

Nita was so completely beguiled by the notion that she was half of a dynamite pair that all her cowardice drained away and she ripped the brown paper off the package.

Inside was a copy of the local evening newspaper neatly folded and duct taped.

'Hold on,' Zach said, 'don't... bloody hell, gimme that. You're tearing everything. You don't know nothing about handling evidence, do you? Don't you even watch CSI on TV? Go indoors! That's an order. It ain't a fuckin bomb so I'll be alright. But I'm doing the rest of this proper, in the car. Okay?'

Nita was suddenly aware that she'd come out coatless and she was shaking with cold. She was aware too of all the windows in Guscott Road, like unblinking eyes, staring at her, watching while she opened the shameful package, observing her transaction with Zach. Blushing with embarrassment she retreated back to her flat.

He came up ten minutes later, his arms bare as usual, glowing with self-generated heat as if the boiler had kicked up two notches all by itself.

'You own or rent?' he asked, prowling, looking at pictures, books and CDs, checking the view from the window. Nita noticed that he stood well away from the glass so as not to be seen from the outside.

'Own.' She lowered the blinds before pouring the tea.

'Nice,' he said settling on her sofa. 'But you got one sick puppy for a neighbour. The headline in the newspaper was about that murder up on the hill. And there was a little bit, also on the front page, about a dead baby. But, like, it was hardly anything—cops releasing the bare minimum.' He took a gulp from his teacup and wiped his mouth on his wrist. 'But inside, what was all wrapped up, was a tiny baby's vest, stained red. Animal blood, I hope. Or ketchup. I bagged everything for testing. I could bung the lot over to the cops, or we could do the forensic work private. It depends how serious you was about hiring me.'

Nita said, 'I'm serious. But there's one thing Sergeant Cutler told me that's really creepy: did you know when they found the dead baby it was wrapped in the local paper and duct tape?'

'No shit! No one ever mentioned that little detail before.'

'So don't you think we ought to give the package to Sergeant Cutler?'

'Okay,' he said. 'You know they'll test for fingerprints, don't you? I was wearing gloves but yours are going to be all over it.'

'Of course I handled it—it was addressed to me.'

'Well, so long as you're prepared for the hassle, seeing as they already got you and the baby linked together in their minds.'

'I offered them a DNA sample today.'

'I thought you was against all that.'

'I am. But if they won't do anything to prove me innocent, I'll have to.'

'They still might say you're sending stuff to yourself cos you want to act the victim. You know? The moral high ground and all that bollocks? Or cos you need the attention.'

'Is that what you think?' Indignation hit Nita in the chest and knocked the breath out of her lungs.

'I just know the way them saddos think.' He seemed oblivious to her outrage. 'The point is, do you want to give them the parcel knowing that's how their tiny little minds work? If they think you sent it to yourself they ain't gonna do nothing except bury it.'

'Even if it was sent to me by the same person who wrapped up the real baby?'

'But, see, you're just about the only one Cutler told about the duct tape and the newspaper—they didn't tell the media. And then suddenly, by magic, you get one similar. What's he gonna say, eh? Tell me that.'

'But, don't you see,' Nita cried, 'this means Harris Searle knows something that wasn't in the media. It means...'

'It means you're obsessed by Harris Searle and you'd do anything to fit him up.'

'You can't think that. I mean, Sergeant Cutler can't.'

'Look at it this way,' Zach said, draining his cup and gazing hopefully at the teapot, 'you keep going on about this blonde bird with Slut written on her boobs, but if you'd read the paper you'd know the dead girl's from the Philippines, like, somewhere out East, and she got black hair like...'

'Like me?'

'I was going to say, like they knew you was talking bollocks right from the beginning, but did they put you straight? Did they? No, cos they'd rather sit around laughing at your obsession with Harris Searle.'

Nita sat crushed by the weight of humiliation. She said, 'Where would you send the package for forensic testing? What exactly would they test for?'

'It's a good lab,' Zach said, getting up and pouring his own tea. 'They work for the cops too. They can run a whole battery of tests. And if you're worried, we can send the results to the cops as well. It's just, the way things are going, I'd of thought you'd *welcome* an independent analysis.'

'Yes. You're right. Of course you're right.'

'Only trouble is, it doesn't come cheap.'

'Oh dear,' Nita said, 'how much?'

'Can be as much as five grand,' Zach said, looking worried.

Nita felt the blood draining from her face. She said, 'That might be a problem.'

Zach wisely said nothing while Nita panicked about money. Mortgage, utilities, tax and her student debt jostled each other in her brain. Added to her regular expenses, she had just hired Zach without asking him what he charged, and she would have to pay a solicitor as well when she finally got to meet one. She had not yet been fired so she still had a regular income, but a junior school teacher's pay wouldn't cover a mortgage *and* a five grand lab charge plus hire of a private detective and a solicitor.

Zach said quietly, 'Ain't this the kind of thing your family'd want to help with?'

'My family,' Nita began, but the lump in her throat stopped her. Of course she couldn't go to her family, but thinking of them suddenly reminded her that she had an insurance policy and a pension plan. Members of her family might never have trendy clothes or computer games but they practically came out of the womb waving policies in their tiny fists. By the age of three she had been better provided for in her old age than most sixty-year-olds.

'I've got something I can sell,' she told Zach. 'But it might take a little time. A few days.' She could also remortgage her flat, she thought, feeling dizzy. She was not without resources, she realised. She sat up straighter and thought, I've got the stuff to fight back. She looked over at Zach and tried to meet his eyes calmly.

'I been thinking,' he said. 'Maybe it's a mistake trying to keep control of this. Maybe you was right in the first place and we should trust the cops to do a proper job.'

'Presumably the lab would charge them the same as me?' Nita suggested. 'Are the cops going to sanction expensive lab work? They're working to a budget, aren't they, so they're going to spend as little as possible.'

'I never thought of it like that. But it sounds right. I usually think they're just lazy.'

'How much would it take to get this process moving?' Nita was enjoying a sudden burst of energy.

He stared at her, smiling. 'When you take charge, you're really strong, aren't you?'

'I'm not being too bossy, am I?' Nita started to worry again.

'Shit, no,' Zach said. 'I like strong women, but I wouldn't of blamed you if you'd wimped out.'

'I'm just so tired of being the victim,' Nita said. 'Being the victim is exhausting.'

Zach took a notebook out of an inside pocket, a pen from Nita's coffee table and scribbled some notes. 'Right—I figure we can get the ball rolling for about five hundred quid. I got a friend at the lab, and if he can shepherd this job through and let us know what things cost before we have to pay for them we won't have to waste a penny. The five is up front for my friend Woody, to keep him interested. It may seem like a lot but it's actually a saving, because he'll make sure they don't pad the bill or do unnecessary work. Okay?'

Nita nodded. Five hundred was a lot more manageable than five thousand.

'Then there's me. Normally you'd pay me a five hundred quid retainer, and come to the office to sign on the dotted line. But if you want me to start right now all I need is a piece of paper signed by you saying I represent you. And seeing as this is out of sight more interesting than doing surveillance on an empty property, and seeing as I trust you, I won't ask for...'

'Oh no,' Nita said, 'you're a professional—I've got to pay you.'

'Well, alright,' he said, giving her his crinkly warm smile again. 'But I'm only charging you half for now. Unfortunately it'll have to be cash and it'll have to be now. It ain't the sort of job my mate Woody can put through the books. I can wait, but he can't.'

'I do need a guarantee, though,' Nita said. 'I need to be quite sure that if there is evidence to be found on the bloodstained vest it has to be in a form we can pass on to the police. Whatever we find, we can't either keep it to ourselves or destroy it.'

'This is the girl who was going to chuck the whole shebang into a skip,' he said, getting to his feet. 'See I knew you was the responsible type really—when some sadistic bastard wasn't frightening the life out of you. I knew you'd do the right thing in the end. Now let's go find the nearest cash-point.'

13

Packy Peedo

//

Nita sat in front of the TV watching the news. It was hard to believe that it wasn't yet six-thirty. On the screen men ran though hot, dusty streets firing guns and throwing rocks. A jeep exploded into an orange ball of flames. She hardly noticed.

Her current account was almost empty. Even more extraordinary to her, after she had given Zach seven hundred and fifty pounds, he kissed her. Not on the mouth she was consoled to remember. No, he took her hand and turned it palm up, then bent and kissed the bare spot between glove and coat sleeve. It was an ambiguous, intimate moment, almost more intimate than a kiss on the mouth.

She looked at her wrist. There was no mark on it to prove that anything had happened at all. What do your expect, she asked herself, some sort of carnal stigmata when you don't even know if the kiss was carnal or casual. Silly brown cow.

Zach bleached his hair. His spoken English was sloppy. Men with tattoos were immature and unreliable. It was a stupid, inappropriate thing for a man to do to his client. Nita wondered what his lips would feel like on hers.

A knock sounded on her door and Toby called, 'Neets, open up. Leo'll be back any minute and I need the prezzies. You haven't forgotten his birthday, have you?' He hurried in still wearing his woolly scarf and matching bobble hat, smelling of exhaust fumes.

Nita had forgotten and she quickly signed a silly birthday card while Toby rummaged in the bottom of her wardrobe for the hidden parcels. She couldn't help noticing the difference between the bright wrapping paper Toby used for Leo's presents and the brown paper bag and duct tape Harris Searle had used for hers.

Toby said, 'We're having a few friends over for drinkies, Nita sweetie, so do come. Have you got something sparkly to wear? A sari? One of those chemisey suits? And let your hair down, darling, you know Leo loves your hair. Oh and how long does it take to make those samosas? That'd be the best present ever—something you cooked yourself. Leo says you're the bestest cook, and so do I. About eight-thirty?' And out he breezed barely able to see over the armful of bundles and boxes.

He looked pink and polished, utterly untouched by life. And yet, Nita remembered, he was a medical student, faced with disease and death every day of his working life. Both he and Leo seemed to skim over dark water like two sleek dragonflies, barely touching the surface, untainted by what went on beneath. Was life really so easy for them? Or did they have a talent for making it appear so?

Something sparkly, she thought, looking with despair at her reflection in the wardrobe mirror. Unlike the guys, she was so tainted by the last three days that her skin looked yellowish—the way it did when she was sick.

At the back of the cupboard in a polythene drycleaner's bag was the aqua and rose concoction she'd worn for Mina's wedding. It should be sparkly enough even for Leo and Toby. The only problem was that it was a couple of sizes too big. Nita had assuaged the catastrophe of her sister's wedding, as she did all unhappiness, by many visits to the fridge. She turned away and went to the kitchen to make samosas.

While she was kneading the pastry dough she thought about Leo and Toby's place in the world, about how they approached every circumstance with the confidence that they would be welcomed joyfully. She thought about Toby rapping on her door, assuming she would be pleased to see him and that she'd want to be involved in Leo's party. By contrast, even though she was invited, she would be uneasy about joining the party unless she could hide behind a gift of perfectly cooked samosas. She had to earn her place—buy her way in. The world did not welcome her. At best it was indifferent; at worst it was hostile.

She didn't have the right ingredients for filling classical samosas so she improvised with onion, potato and the mushrooms she'd made on Sunday, as well as the usual red chilli, ginger, coriander, cumin and turmeric. Soon the whole kitchen smelled like her mother's hands.

She filled little triangles of pastry with the mixture and deep fried them in her karhai until they were crisp and golden brown. After nearly two hours there were about eighty delicious mouthfuls of spicy filled pastry draining on paper and resting in a warm oven.

Nita knew her samosas would be acceptable. It was a pity she couldn't say the same for herself and her appearance. She showered and washed her hair. A little makeup disguised the dark circles under her eyes. Then she dressed in aqua and rose coloured silk and tied a cerise scarf round her waist to offset the bagginess. In the mirror she looked like a kid dressed in a patchwork quilt. All the same the colours were beautiful. It was just hard to see the drab little creature who was wearing them. She wound another scarf loosely round her throat. When in doubt, Nita always added rather than subtracted clothing.

She was so much more comfortable in the kitchen. There she arranged the samosas on two large serving dishes. She found a jar of her own tomato chutney and tipped it into two bowls. 'Done,' she said, satisfied at last. 'Looks good enough to eat.'

The phone rang. Nita had been hearing guests arriving downstairs for the last twenty minutes so she almost ignored it. It was only her nervousness at the thought of entering a roomful of strangers that made her answer.

Miss Whitby said, 'You'd left by the time I got round to writing out that address. Do you still need the details of a solicitor?'

'Oh how kind of you to ring me,' Nita said, wondering how Miss Whitby had got her phone number.

After she'd dictated the name, address and phone number of the firm she was recommending Miss Whitby said, 'Look, I don't want to pry, but obviously you're in some sort of trouble. The only thing Mr Hughes would tell us was that you hadn't been sacked or suspended. This implies that the action he's taken against you is unofficial and therefore questionable. Do you want me to contact our local union rep?'

'I hadn't thought of that,' Nita said, 'but I think I'm going to be able to sort the problem out tomorrow without bothering any one else.'

'It isn't any bother. Think about it. You're a good teacher. Don't let the system grind you down.'

'Oh,' Nita said, and was unable to go on because she was afraid she'd start crying, and then she'd have to tell Miss Whitby what people thought the 'good teacher' was capable of.

'Well,' Miss Whitby said after a short silence, 'here's my phone number in case you change your mind. Oh and call me Helen, okay?'

'Thanks so much for your help,' Nita managed to stammer out at last. She was horrified to hear how trembly her voice was and how stiff and formal the words were.

Toby came dancing in on a cloud of cologne and champagne breath to help her carry the food downstairs. Frankie Goes to Hollywood was pounding out of the speakers and the guys' small flat was submerged under a flood of extroverts.

'Nita!' Leo cried when he saw her, 'what have you brought me? Samosas! Listen everyone, this is my friend Nita, and she makes samosas to *die* for, so dig in. Nita, you are an *angel* and I love you.'

Loved by Leo, Nita circulated bearing gifts. The young guy in the designer suit who was talking about hedge funds didn't know she'd just given seven hundred and fifty pounds in cash to a virtual stranger. The trio dancing together were unaware she was suspected of killing her own baby. The four medical students tipping back champagne as though it were beer hadn't heard that she'd been sent home in shame from her job. 'Mmm, fabulous,' they said. 'Wait. Can I take another? Ooh, *delicious.*' None of the people who crammed themselves into Toby and Leo's party had witnessed her making a complete jackass of herself about Harvard Slut. She was Leo's friend and she made samosas to die for.

People danced and shouted and drank. They spilled out of the guys' flat into the hall and up the stairs.

The heat and noise were so overwhelming that at first no one noticed when somebody yelled, '*Fire!*'

Then several people took up the cry, and grey, stinking smoke began to waft into the party. There was a stampede towards the front door until those in the lead saw that the front door was where the fire was hottest. But the people at the back surged on and pushed the ones at the front into the fire. They had no option but to open the door and run through the fire out onto Guscott Road.

Fresh air fed the flames and shoved the tail-enders back into the flat. Except for Toby who did no good at all by trying to extinguish the fire by pouring champagne onto it. Leo grabbed him by the arm and hauled him into the flat, slamming the door behind them.

One of the details Nita was to remember later was the way everyone drew their mobile phones as if they were weapons. The Fire Brigade must have received at least twenty calls simultaneously. It was a wonder the dispatch centre didn't collapse. Another thing she noticed was that all the samosas had been eaten, and she thought hazily that if she were to die now she would die popular.

But it was a Monday night, not the usual night for out of control parties, so the Fire Brigade arrived quickly and no one died. More by luck than good management the fire was contained in the hall and stair-well. It had spread upwards to Nita's door but no further and the firemen quickly doused it. The guys' flat suffered some smoke damage. They clung to each other saying, 'Omigod, omigod,' until a fireman firmly shepherded them out to the street.

'So hunky,' Leo breathed. 'Did you check him out? Was this your idea for a surprise present, Tobes? My party invaded by men in uniform? Cos if it was, it's the best damn idea you ever had.'

He wasn't the only one enthralled by the appearance of a truckload of fire-fighters at a gay birthday party. Several of his guests, while fleeing for their lives, had grabbed champagne bottles and were now offering drinks to the officers. And the sound system, unharmed and still playing Dexy's Midnight Runners' 'Come on Eileen' at full volume, added to the hysterically festive atmosphere.

Toby, though, had fallen silent. His attention had been diverted from the spectacle of men in uniform and he was staring grimly at the front of the house. One by one the party guests followed his gaze and saw, written in ragged black paint the message: FUCK OFF PACKY PEEDO.

Nita stared at it, taking several seconds to understand that a packy peedo was, in fact, her.

Just then, the most senior fire officer approached Toby and Leo and said, 'I'll send an arson investigator out tomorrow to confirm, but it looks to me like someone poured petrol through your letterbox and ignited it with burning rags.' He looked at the writing on the wall and went on, 'It's disgusting, but don't clean it off just yet. The police will want to see it.'

As if summoned, the last arrival at the scene was a police car. It stopped outside Women's Aid because the rest of Guscott Road was blocked by the fire engine. Two police officers, one man, one woman, got out and began to force their way through the crowd.

It seemed as if the whole street was outside in the freezing cold watching the fire and the party. Nita saw Daphne in her dressing gown flanked by her two stout sons on the edge of the throng. Jen and Dave were pointing out the subtleties of the graffiti to some of their neighbours. She couldn't see Diane and Stu or Rose Peters, but she was sure they were there somewhere. For a moment she thought she'd caught a glimpse of Harris Searle's laughing face, but he worked the night-shift so she must have been mistaken.

But what she was certain of was the fact that everyone could see the painted message, and that hers was the only face in the crowd it could possibly refer to. She was the only one in an ethnic costume. She couldn't have been more conspicuous if she'd ridden into the street on a pink elephant.

'Can we go back inside?' she asked one of the firemen who was sweeping sooty water off the pavement and into the gutter.

'Give it a couple more minutes for the fumes to clear,' he said, allowing her no escape from prying eyes.

For Nita, the worst pair of eyes belonged to Leo. Toby had not yet woken up to the full implication of the combination of graffiti and petrol poured through the letterbox. But Leo stared at Nita as if he were seeing her for the first time, and coldly weighing up what it meant to be her neighbour.

It came almost as a relief, then, when the two police officers succeeded in pushing through to the front of the house. They swept the revellers with keen eyes and settled on Nita. The woman took her wallet out and flipped it open to her warrant card. She said, 'Nita Tehri? I'm Sergeant Eavers, and I'm going to have to ask you to accompany us to Wallace Street Police Station.'

She spoke loudly enough to be heard by everyone, and the last humiliation Nita experienced before being led away to the police car was the party guest in the designer suit saying to Leo, 'I say, old man, isn't that your caterer being arrested?'

14

The Immigrant's Fear
of the Blonde

///

I n the car, Nita said, 'If this is about my letter to Sergeant
Cutler, I may have expressed myself badly, but I promise I've
no intention of suing anyone.' She was looking out of the
window, trying to see Zach's Toyota. Zach would know what
to do. Then she wondered how the fire would affect property
prices in Guscott Road. Maybe Zach's other client, Bret West,
would have grounds to sue *her*.

She said, 'I don't see why you had to come out to collect
me. I told Sergeant Cutler I'd come in voluntarily.' She'd never
noticed before how many people tried to stare inside a police car.

She said, 'I know I said I didn't agree with it, but in the end
it seemed as if giving a sample was the only way to solve this
thing.'

And she said, 'Why aren't you talking to me?'

⸺⸺

In the interview room Sergeant Eavers said, 'I wish you'd just
shut up about Sergeant Cutler. He worked the weekend and
now he's got days off. Nobody's seen your bloody letter.'

She said, 'You can have a cup of tea and a phone call.'

And she said, 'The machine's on the blink—you can have milky coffee or nothing.'

There was no one to phone but Toby and Leo. The solicitor's number, and Miss Whitby's, were at home on the pad next to the phone. She badly wanted to change out of the aqua and pink silk which made her look as if she'd raided the dressing-up box. How could she face Sergeant Eavers' sensible black trouser suit looking like a reject from a Bollywood movie?

Nita remembered with anxiety the expression on Leo's face, but she had no choice. She took a deep breath and dialled. The phone rang twenty times but there was no answer—even from the answer machine.

Sergeant Eavers said, 'Your family lives in Leicester. Is that correct?'

'Why?'

'You claim you withdrew your objection to DNA sampling in writing. Correct?'

'Yes.'

'And yet no one can lay their hands on the withdrawal. Funny, that.'

Nita looked at the sensible suit and the sensible buttoned up face and decided to say as little as possible. She said, 'I want to talk to Sergeant Cutler.'

Eavers said, 'You only talk to men, right? When I asked for a sample you told me in no uncertain terms where to go, but you want to give it up for a man. Typical.'

Nita stared at her in astonishment.

Eavers cleared her throat and said, 'I've been doing some research on you, Ms Tehri. Would it surprise you to learn that I've even been all the bloody way to bloody Leicester in pursuit of my enquiry?'

'You went to...? Why?'

'I'm asking the questions. You're good at withdrawals, aren't you, Ms Tehri?'

Nita looked at her hands which lay passive and plain on her gaudy silk lap.

Eavers' hands were stubby and red tipped. She said, 'Last time it was a charge of rape that you withdrew, wasn't it?'

Nita stared at the grey congealing coffee and imagined meadow flowers and a slow walk down to a clean, clear stream.

'Technically, I suppose you'll say it wasn't you who made the complaint in the first place—it was one of your college tutors on your behalf—but you do seem to make a habit of wasting police time. Am I right?'

Nita sat on a bank, warmed by the sun, and watched the shallow water flow clean and fast below her.

'You got everyone all excited and then you backed down.' When Nita didn't respond Sergeant Eavers went on, 'You make me sick. Know that? It's women like you who make it so much harder for proper victims to be taken seriously.'

A small blue butterfly flew a tattered path over the water. Among the stones in the stream Nita could see some turquoises. She breathed slowly and deeply.

Sergeant Eavers said, 'You were taking your final exams, weren't you? You even sat the last exam before you complained, didn't you? Passed it too, I shouldn't wonder. They said you were a bright girl.'

If Nita breathed slowly and deeply enough the hard chair, cheap table and strip lighting would simply disappear.

'So you claimed you were raped and all the good little feminists at your college supported you. And all the women police officers too, I expect. Only by then there was no physical evidence and in any case you refused a medical examination. Don't like giving physical evidence, do you? I'm sensing a pattern here.'

Water danced across smooth stones, but the sound of it wasn't loud enough to drown out Sergeant Eavers' voice.

'Do you want to know why I'm so angry? Go on, guess.'

Nita didn't want to guess. She tried to grasp the sight and sound of a clean clear summer morning and hold it in her mind as a barrier between herself and the angry Sergeant.

The third person in the room, a lanky young guy in uniform whose name she couldn't remember, stirred uneasily. Eavers glanced at him and said, 'Well, never mind why I'm so angry—have I said anything so far you want to respond to?'

Nita said, 'Why is any of this relevant?'

'Hallelujah, it speaks! I thought I was going to have to do all the bleeding work. I'll tell you why this is relevant, shall I? We have the body of a baby girl, new born, suffocated at birth. According to the ME's prelim report it, *she*, was stored frozen for as much as nine months. Nine months in the womb, nine months in the freezer—there's something poetic about that. Or is poetic the word I'm looking for? No, it probably isn't.

'And then we have you. When you moved into Guscott Road nine months ago—nine months, you see where I'm going with this?—your neighbours say you could've been pregnant. Let me quote.' Sergeant Eavers flipped through a file of papers and said, 'Yes, here's one: "She was a round little thing, broad as she was long, and we all thought she was expecting. Then she lost a lot of weight suddenly but there wasn't any baby. So we must've been wrong." Were they wrong, Ms Tehri?'

Nita looked at the thickness of the file. She couldn't count the sheets of paper in it. Suppose each sheet represented someone who knew her? Someone who was prepared to talk about her to a stranger.

She said, 'I went on a diet.' The clean shallow stream was being pushed out of her mind, swamped by a load of sewage surging downstream.

'You went on a diet,' Eavers said flatly. 'You must tell me all about it—a fucking diet that *works*. Well I never!

'But back to what's relevant: nine mouths ago you move here and the neighbours think you're pregnant. Nine months before that, there's a police report which says you claim you were raped. So I'm thinking, here's a coincidence—here's something that deserves a little more investigation. So I drag my sorry undieted carcass all the way up to Leicester to talk to my colleagues. But not only them—I want to talk to your friends and family.' She tapped the file of papers and waited.

Nita said, 'You talked to my family?'

'Oh yes.'

'But did they talk to you?'

'Well now,' Eavers said, 'that's got you apprehensive, hasn't it?'

'Sceptical.'

Eavers smiled a thin, knowing smile. 'You think they're secretive as all hell about family members, don't you? Yeah, they probably are. But you aren't a family member, are you? Not any more. Not since you accused your fiancé of rape.'

A door slammed shut in Nita's mind. On one side was the past; on the other was the present and future. It was very important to keep the door shut, to stop the past bleeding through and contaminating everything on the other side.

Eavers said, 'Want to tell me about it?'

Nita closed her eyes and tried to evoke the clean clear stream again. Relaxation techniques always employed images of nature: the other one she sometimes used was a walk down weathered wooden steps to a beach. Maybe that was why the techniques didn't work when a *city* girl was under pressure. And why did so many of them involve water? Why was that supposed to be relaxing when she couldn't swim and saw any water deeper than her morning shower as an invitation to a drowning? According to a first aid book she'd once read you could drown in two inches of water.

She looked up into Sergeant Eavers' implacable face and said, 'Sergeant Cutler told me the baby was of *mixed* race.'

'Did he now?' Eavers looked disgusted. 'Well, someone did suggest that as a possibility to begin with. But to tell you the truth it can be a tricky determination to make on a newborn who's been kept in a fridge for nine months.'

Nita said, 'And Sergeant Cutler told me the baby was wrapped in... ' She broke off. She couldn't use the red-stained vest wrapped in the local paper as a defence. Eavers would want to know where it was and why it hadn't been handed to the police. Wouldn't Zach get into trouble if it was known he'd taken it to a private lab? There was something prescient about Zach. How had he known the time would come so soon when she'd need an independent analysis more than ever?

She said, 'I mean, Sergeant Cutler told me he was going to have the doll tested. What's happened to that?'

'What doll?' Eavers looked confused. 'No one said anything about a doll.'

'And what about the fire and the racist graffiti on the wall?' Nita was determined, if she possibly could, to keep Eavers off balance. 'Don't you think all those things are connected to the attack Harris Searle made on me up in the Holyfield area?'

Eavers was flushed with annoyance. 'Don't keep changing the subject. You think you've so clever, don't you?'

Someone tapped on the door and a young woman in uniform put her head into the room and beckoned.

Eavers said, 'Don't go anywhere,' and went out.

Nita looked at the lanky guy who seemed embarrassed to be left alone with her. She said, 'I've forgotten your name.'

'Smith,' he said.

'Please may I use the phone again? My neighbour may be home now. I need him to ring my solicitor for me. I left the number on my phone pad.'

But the name on her phone pad was of Helen Whitby's solicitor. Not Nita's. She hadn't had time yet to introduce herself. Would a stranger respond to a call for help in the middle of the night?

Smith was about to speak when Sergeant Eavers came back into the room followed by a weary looking oldish woman in an ill fitting brown suit.

Eavers said, 'The duty solicitor's just arrived. Now I can arrest you for the murder of an unnamed infant.'

—∞∞—

Certain events stood out in Nita's mind: how nervous Smith seemed; how muddled the duty solicitor, Mrs Ormerod, was; how she kept calling Nita 'Mrs Terry' and then apologising; how impervious to reason Sergeant Eavers was.

'I'm volunteering my DNA,' Nita said. 'You don't have to arrest me.'

'So you say. And you want your own solicitor, whose name you can't remember, present when the sample's taken; giving you plenty of time to change your mind and make a fool of me like you did with my colleagues up North.'

There were long periods of waiting by herself in a white painted room containing a bunk bed and a toilet. Nita didn't want to admit it was a cell because she didn't want to admit that she had no personal power or freedom of choice any more.

Every twenty minutes or so someone she couldn't see stared at her through a hole in the door. She walked slowly up and down—six small steps in one direction, six steps back. She was exhausted but the room smelled of piss and she didn't want to sit or lie on the bunk.

They took away her scarves making her clothes sag and bag—imitating depression in spite of their inappropriately festive colours. Then she was glad Miss Whitby's solicitor wasn't there to see her. She could imagine a suave blond man laughing with blonde Miss Whitby over a cocktail, saying, 'Remember that teacher you gave my number to? The one who murdered her baby? She looked like a chorus girl from Ali Baba and the Forty Thieves. Pantomime stuff—I couldn't keep a straight face.'

'The immigrant's fear of the blonde,' Nita said, under her breath, accepting at last what Cutler, Eavers, Searle, *et al* had known all along: that although she wasn't technically an immigrant, she was, irredeemably, an outsider.

Even the precautions the cop took while handling the buccal smear looked like he didn't want to breathe the same air she breathed. He held the swab between thumb and forefinger as if it were poisonous and cut the tip off so that it fell into a tube. It wasn't to avoid contaminating the sample, her warped, exhausted, brain told her—it was because she and her DNA were untouchable.

And then, suddenly, it was exactly the way the homeless man with the red beard told her it would be: she was bailed to appear again at Wallace Street Police Station in a week, and turned out into the icy morning street to find her own way home.

She walked, freezing in the sparkly silk she'd put on to please Toby and Leo, and there was nowhere to go except back to her scorched, vandalised home on Guscott Road.

15

Pinning Her Hopes on a Man

//

Sometime during the night, while Nita was at the police station, the yellow skip goddess farrowed six bulging black bags. One had already been torn open to display in its guts the dirty, uncared for clothes of an old woman, too shabby for a charity shop. Torn skirts and sweaters hung forlorn with greying sweat-stained underwear on the disembowelled armchair, rejected, it seemed, even by scavengers.

Partly obscured by the clothes, Nita recognised the little hall table she, Toby and Leo used for post or messages for each other. It was charred and missing one leg. She was shocked to see something she'd used and cared for in the belly of the beast. Shocking too in daylight was the graffiti savagely spoiling the honey stone façade of her house. It made the street look like a war zone.

The paint on the front door was blistered from the heat of the fire but the door itself was sound. Nita let herself into a blackened scene of burned carpet and curtains. Soot and watermarks covered the walls and ceiling. The charred air carried the reek of violence and hatred.

The postman, with a fine sense of irony, had delivered gas bills. With no hall table to put Toby and Leo's on, Nita leaned it against their door. She tapped on the door but the silence was so profound she needn't have bothered. Upstairs, pinned to her own blistered door was a note. It read, 'Oh Nita, what a drag! I do hope you're alright. Leo and I are staying with Mike and Pete until we can sort out decorators. That ghastly dyke cop took your spare keys. She had a warrant. I'm so sorry. Love, Toby.'

Nita opened her door with caution. Obviously the firemen had come in with their hoses to make sure nothing was hot enough to catch fire behind the closed door. There was damage to the carpet close to it. The walls and ceiling of her little entrance lobby were smoke and water-stained. Her coat and a couple of jackets hanging from hooks next to the door were pickled with smoke and water. She would never be able to wear them again.

Her book bag, the real leather reward she'd bought herself after she'd passed her teachers' training course, was ruined; the papers and booklets inside were pulpy and stuck together.

She moved further into her flat, thanking the developers for insisting on a fire door close to her front door. Neither smoke nor heat had penetrated past it.

But Sergeant Eavers had. Here, in her living-room, study and bedroom was the evidence of a different kind of violence: the exercise of power by one person over another. The UK, the State, the government, the Home Office, had given Sergeant Eavers permission to invade and search Nita's little flat. British society sanctioned the intrusion. England required that she submit to the handling of all her possessions. It was for the safety of the nation and the neighbours that someone had been in her kitchen to make sure she'd hidden nothing in her rice, flour, and spices; that her pots, pans, oven, fridge, freezer, washing machine and dishwasher were free from crime.

Nita hurried from room to room opening windows, pouring icy air over everything the intruders had touched. She put on rubber gloves and scrubbed her bathroom from top to bottom. Then she took off the unlucky aqua and pink silk and scrubbed herself from top to toe.

Dressed in jeans and a sweatshirt she attacked the kitchen, scrubbing, wiping, bleaching; throwing out what might be contaminated by the touch of a stranger; cauterising the power of the state, the infection of suspicion, rumour and racism.

There is nothing like a spotless kitchen for defeating the evils of an unjust society.

Aware of acting irrationally but unable to stop, Nita extended her field of operation to include the other three rooms. She worked like a dervish in the freezing cold. The washing machine and dishwasher were her only assistants, but by mid afternoon she could make a cup of tea without poisoning herself. She could sit on her own chair without feeling the fingers of the unknown men and women who'd searched behind the cushions. And she could lie down on pristine sheets without her skin puckering in revulsion.

But first she picked up the phone, cleansed of strangers' breath with antibacterial wipes, and called a locksmith. Sergeant Eavers had her spare keys and although she might give them back Nita couldn't trust her not to make copies.

Even as the locksmith worked, tutting about the fire damage, sympathising about the vandalism, drinking tea out of a mug almost scrubbed free of its glaze, Nita realised that she would never again feel safe in her home: it would never be quite clean enough or quite secure enough.

After he'd gone, she closed and locked the door, closed and locked all the windows and drew the curtains against the darkening sky. She took another shower and dressed in layers of clothes till the flat began to warm up again. The jeans and sweatshirt she'd worn for her cleaning marathon joined the aqua and pink silk in a bin bag. So did the rubber gloves, the cleaning cloths, sponges and scourers, along with anything she'd felt could not survive handling by an intruder.

Her final problem was deciding what to do with the bin bag. She couldn't throw it in the skip to be picked over by scavengers and exposed to Guscott Road. In the end she put it outside her door on the chargrilled landing, neither upstairs nor down, neither in nor out. She was too tired to make a decision.

It was time to sleep, but first Nita turned off all the lights and raised one blind so that she could look out at the evening on Guscott Road.

First she saw Tigs and Joe with their mother and another little boy she recognised from Midford Junior walking home carrying the shopping. The children ran ahead chattering in high voices, their stripy scarves flying like banners on the freezing air. They didn't look up as they passed Nita's house but their mother glanced sideways and hurried on. Nita remembered her as a sweet-tempered competent woman who worked part-time at a toyshop. The father did something in transport. Tigs and Joe were bright, friendly and keen. They read books and finished their homework. If any of that family were to write graffiti it would probably be correctly spelled.

Directly opposite was number 15 which of course was empty. The house to its left was occupied by a retired couple. They'd left for Spain in November and wouldn't be home, except for flying visits, until April. On the other side, Nita noticed lights showing between the cracks in the curtains. The two girls who lived there were weekly boarders at an out of town fee-paying school. Nita had never spoken to them. According to Daphne the man of the house was something big in retail. The woman was mad about horses. It didn't seem to be the sort of family who'd stuff burning rags through a letter box or write on walls.

Nita was tired enough to sleep standing up, but she couldn't leave the window. She watched the people who'd only parked in Guscott Road unlock their cars, put shopping in the boot or back seat and drive away. Some of them looked at the graffiti, wondering perhaps what a packy peedo was and why it should fuck off. Others noticed nothing.

Harris Searle's car wasn't visible, and Nita couldn't see any lights on in his flat. He should be at work. Obviously he'd mended the puncture. She wondered if he'd seen any connection between the nail he'd hammered into the mouth of the little brown doll and the nail she'd hammered into his rear tyre. Or did he just think he'd been unlucky?

Nita saw the two white-haired women from Women's Aid turn out the lights, lock up and start off towards the bus stop. The madman on the floor above had his window open which usually meant he'd thrown something out. Sure enough, on the pavement outside, were the torn scraps of paper that signalled his outrage at something official. Would he have called her a peedo? Wasn't he more obsessed with bombers and terrorists?

Why was *anyone* calling her a peedo? Was it worse to be a paedophile than a murderer? It was more inflammatory, that was for sure, especially for a school-teacher. But which was worse for a victim, to have a damaged life, or no life at all? Some children's lives were so damaged that they killed themselves or were lost to depression. Others grew up and perpetuated the cycle of damage on more children. Still others turned it all around and stubbornly made the most of themselves, promising to get through life never doing harm to a child, and succeeding.

The old saw was true, Nita thought wearily. While there was life, there was indeed some hope—no life, no hope. Ergo, murder was worse than paedophilia. But try telling *that* to someone who couldn't spell paedophilia.

Unless, of course, the graffiti writer was perfectly well able to spell but pretending otherwise. Nita leaned her tangled head against the cold glass. She felt feverish.

Down below in the street Rose Peters emerged from her house. She was wearing layers of bright wool and carrying what looked like a newspaper. She turned to look at Nita's house, then saw Diane. The two met outside number 15. Rose showed the paper to Diane who looked without expression at Nita's windows. They exchanged a few words. Diane walked on towards her own house and Rose crossed the road.

Nita couldn't see her any more. She waited. Miraculously, the doorbell was still working. She rested her burning forehead against the glass. The bell sounded again. After a few minutes

Rose appeared once more, crossing the road towards her own house. She was no longer carrying any paper and she seemed to float along the pavement on yards of coloured fabric.

Nita left the window and went to the kitchen to make tea. She hadn't eaten since tasting Leo's party samosas last night and she was quite proud of herself. The danger was always sorrow. It was sorrow that took her by the scruff of the neck and forced her to open the fridge door; sorrow that led her by the hand to where the chocolate biscuits lay on supermarket shelves; sorrow that reminded her of the tastes and smells of her childhood and persuaded her to replicate them in her own kitchen.

She could remember playing upstairs with Ash and Mina until the smells of cooking, like invisible cords, drew them closer and closer to the kitchen. They would end up under the kitchen table, which was as close as they could get without annoying their mother so much that she'd slap them and send them outside.

Drinking her tea now, Nita could still see her mother's plump feet in perpetual motion between cooker, fridge and sink, and hear the rustle of her skirt. She could hear too the snorts of suppressed laughter as she, Mina and Ash tried to keep quiet and failed. Those were the days when she'd thought their mother was all-powerful. Her hands dealt out nourishment and punishment. Their lives were governed by her will and whim.

Then, one dreadful day when Nita was about six, without meaning to, perhaps by asking for help with some schoolwork, she discovered that she could read English better than her mother.

Even now she wasn't sure why, but from that day on her attitude to her mother changed. She no longer saw her as capable of advising or protecting her—especially from the world outside. Later she realised that her mother was incapable, even unwilling to protect her at home. And that, in the end had far more lasting consequences.

But on that first day, when, aged six, she felt she was smarter than her mother her reaction had been fear and sorrow. It was as if she were standing at the edge of a cliff with no guard-rail between her and the abyss. Her mother, noticing nothing, gave her a drink of cold shurbut and a mouthful of sweet halva and sent her away. Maybe it was the first time Nita accepted food as a substitute for what she really needed. Whatever that was.

The phone rang. She let it ring and went back to the window, standing in the dark watching Guscott Road. She was waiting for Zach's Toyota. She wanted to ask him what he'd seen last night although the answer had to be nothing. Because if he'd seen people scrawling on the front of her house or shoving petrol-soaked rags through her letterbox surely he would have stopped them. Most likely he was at the private lab giving a red-stained vest to his friend Woody for testing.

A car turned into the road and parked down at the end by the river. It looked as if Tigs and Joe's dad had come home early.

Nita's legs started to shake. Too tired to stand she turned on the TV and sat in the dark watching the children's programs. She didn't want to ask Zach what he'd seen last night; she wanted to show him. She wanted to say: Look what they've done to me. Help me.

But last time she did that, there'd been no help. Instead there'd been blame and banishment. She knew that the instinct to go for help to a big man was something she should have conquered by now. But she was too tired. It was as if she spent her whole life at war with herself, trying to defeat the self-destructive urges that seemed so natural: eating, and looking for love and comfort in all the wrong places.

Even now she automatically thought of Sergeant Cutler as the man to complain to about Eavers. And Harris Searle—the memory of herself sitting passive and compliant in his car hit her like a brick. There was an appalling truth to what Eavers had said about her: when it came to 'giving it up' men *were* at the top of her list.

It appalled her because she'd come from a family where men controlled everything: money, education, children, business.

She'd been forced to reject it because it had rejected her. Once she'd recognised the damage and contempt she couldn't take her place in the system that damaged and despised her. So she'd found another way of life, a lonely one to be sure, but one where men, women and children were supposed to respect her. In return, she had taught herself to accept that if her family was so completely wrong, she must learn to offer other women the esteem she wanted to receive. And yet her first crucial memory was of scorn for a woman, her mother.

And now, in trouble, she was pinning all her hopes on a man.

16

No More Nasty Surprises

///

The doorbell woke her up. Automatically she stumbled out of her chair and over to the entry phone. Zach said, 'What the fuck's been going on here? Let me in.'

Fuddled, and forgetting everything she'd been thinking about before falling asleep, Nita pressed the button that let him into the hall and then went to open the door to her flat. She could hear him fumbling his way upstairs and realised that the minor miracle which had saved the entry system had not been extended to the hall lights.

He appeared at her door looking furious, his hands black from feeling his way up in the sooty dark. Nita led him to the kitchen sink and found him a clean towel. Her watch told her she'd been asleep for three hours. Her neck hurt.

He said again, 'What the fuck's been going on here?' He scrubbed at his hands but still left sooty marks on the towel. He brought the smell of the fire in with him. Nita started to tell him about what happened last night as she filled the kettle and began to make tea. She got to the bit about Eavers showing up when her knees buckled and she had to sit down. Without a word Zach finished making the tea and put two slices of bread into the toaster. He said, 'Your trouble is you don't eat enough. Every time I see you, you pass out. It ain't clever.'

In spite of everything, Nita was thrilled that he thought she didn't eat. It almost caused her to forget the discomfort of having a man serve her in her own kitchen. But he seemed to know his way around. He even complimented her on the logic of her layout.

She ate toast and honey and drank tea, finishing her story for him.

He said, 'Know what? Cops is insane. That flamin' Eavers, she's out of her mind.'

'She certainly seemed to have an axe to grind.' She was remembering Eavers' weird anger, especially her rant about Nita only 'giving it up for men', which she did not tell Zach. Nor did she tell him the bits she wanted to forget—the bits she'd slammed the door on.

'You gonna take it to the Complaints Commission?' he asked.

'I haven't thought about it.'

'Well think about it. Compensation. Could help with the bills.'

'Oh,' Nita said, anxious, 'Do I owe you more money already?'

Zach grinned his crinkly grin at her and said, 'Not yet, but wouldn't it be nice if, in the end, the cops paid for everything? Huh? Like when your test results come through and you sue the arse off of them.'

'Doesn't it take forever, complaining to the police about the police? And wouldn't it make them so angry they'd find some other way to get back at me?'

'The trouble with you is you got too much respect for authority and authority don't deserve it. Cops is out for themselves just like everyone else. It's your duty as a citizen to keep 'em in line and give 'em a slap when they fuck up.'

Nita licked honey off her fingers and watched him drinking tea, comfortable wherever he found himself: comfortable in his own tattooed skin—so comfortable that he felt immune to the wrath of the establishment and he used her kitchen as if it were his own.

Maybe, she thought tiredly, if I were a guy, blond—even dyed blond—over thirty, over six feet tall, then, just maybe, I could think about giving the authorities 'a slap'. She wondered if Zach felt wonderful about not being scared. And then she decided he probably never knew the difference. He'd probably been born cheerful, cheeky and charming, and nothing in his life had forced him to change.

Now he was looking in her freezer for something to heat up for supper. She said, 'Did you see your friend Woody last night?'

'Yeah.' He had pulled out a tub with 'Chicken & Tomato' written on the lid.

Nita got up and took it out of his hands. He sat down in her place at the kitchen table and said, 'Woody's a good bloke plus he owes me a favour. First he'll find out what that red substance on the vest is. Then he'll find out where the vest came from—like, is it new or has it been worn, and if so, who by? But it's only when he knows what the red stuff is that he'll know what to do next. Doing one thing at a time saves us money, but it takes longer. Just let me know if you want to speed up.' He watched while she measured rice and shook a few green cardamom pods into the palm of her hand.

She said, 'I was going to ask for the vest back. I thought if Eavers knew what'd been going on...'

'She does know.' Zach snorted. 'She saw the fire and the graffiti. What did she do about *that*, eh? I'll tell you what she did. The fucking lame-brain arrested the victim. That's what she sodding well did. Don't you give her *nothing*, girl.'

Nita had been hesitating about whether to flavour the rice with turmeric or the vastly more expensive saffron. Instantly she decided on saffron.

As usual, cooking calmed and revived her. Eating did too, but that was a different story—as was Zach's approval. He said, 'Know what? I'm fussy about my food but that was as good as you get in any frigging five-star.'

She smiled and stacked the dishes in the dishwasher. They took tea on a tray through to the living room. Before sitting down, he switched off the lights and stood looking down on the road from her window. 'Wish I'd known you a week ago. I could of done my surveillance a heap more comfortable from here. Tomorrow's my last day, you know. I'll write my report and then goodbye Guscott Road.' He let the blind drop.

'But you'll be working full time for me, won't you?' Nita turned on the light again and hoped dismay didn't show in her expression.

'Wish I could, darlin',' he said, taking the steaming mug of tea she was offering. 'But we both know I need another client. I can't afford to work on half pay. That's the way it's goes—you ride piggy-back on a richer client. I've got another prospect, but I won't be in the same street no more.'

'It's just...' Nita began, and then stopped. She couldn't begin to express the way her heart and lungs seemed to contract, squeezed too small for pulse and breath.

'I'm really sorry,' Zach said, his eyes creased with concern. 'I thought you understood. I got overheads, see, an office, a bookkeeper, people who gotta eat. But I never knew anyone who needed help more than you. Maybe I could ask around, see if I can find someone cheaper who can do it fulltime.'

'I need...' This time Nita was interrupted by the doorbell. She jumped to her feet and went to the entry-phone.

A voice distorted by static seemed to say, 'Bee key fours misery.'

'Sorry?'

'Sorry. Bobby Kees for Ms Tehri.'

'I don't know who you are, Mr Kees.'

'I write...' the static came back full force, '...tea chronic.'

'I can't hear,' Nita said. 'You write?'

'For the City Chronicle. Can we talk?'

Zach appeared at her shoulder saying, 'Hang up, Nita. Quick.'

Nita said, 'Sorry,' and hung up.

'Was that a reporter?' Zach asked. 'I thought it wouldn't be long. That's another thing you gotta be careful about—who you talk to. If you don't watch out you'll be national news.'

Nita sat down abruptly. 'Mr Hughes said...'

'Who?'

'My Headmaster. He was talking yesterday about headlines—"Junior School Teacher" side-by-side with "Baby Killer". But they can't say that. I haven't done anything.'

'They can say, "Junior School Teacher Accused Of" or "Arrested For". Anyone who knows anything knows you're innocent but the media don't know you and they'll say anything. And once it's out there... well, you can't blow smoke back in the cigar, can you?'

'Oh God.' Nita slumped. 'Zach, I've got one last credit card I haven't beaten to death. If I pay the full retainer, please, would you postpone your other client and work for me?'

'Like a shot.'

The doorbell rang again, making Nita jump.

'Ignore it. Screen your calls. Pity there ain't a back way out of these terraces.'

'How do they know where I live? Who gave them my phone number?'

'Don't panic. Look, we'll wait a few minutes and then I'll go. If there's anyone out there I'll say I was giving you a quote for redecoration. Speaking of which, I got a mate working with one of those stone cleaning companies—y'know, with pressure hoses. I can get him to come and clean that crap off of the front of your house if you like. Just say the word.'

'Yes please.'

'You can afford it?'

'I think vandalism's covered by the house insurance.'

'Cool,' Zach said. 'I might of known you was the type of girl with paid up policies. Look, I gotta go. I'm still working for my other client till tomorrow. But I'll try to make sure you don't get no more nasty surprises tonight.'

'What about the rest of your money?'

'Tomorrow,' Zach said. 'I trust you.'

She fetched a torch from the kitchen and they went downstairs together, Nita lighting the way. At the front door she looked at the scorched doormat to see what Rose Peters had pushed through her letterbox, but there was nothing.

She said, 'You didn't pick up some papers on your way in, did you?'

'It was so dark I couldn't see me own feet.' He paused with his hand on the latch. 'Don't let anyone in and don't talk to strangers. Okay?' He leaned forward and cupped her cheek running his thumb softly over her chin just once. 'Get a good night's sleep. Your worries is my worries now.' With that, he opened the door and slipped out into the night. Nita dropped the torch.

Before going to bed she checked her emails and found one from Mina. 'Dearest Nita,' her sister wrote, 'I wish we could have talked more. Is something bad happening? My husband has been talking to Dad. He doesn't say much but I gathered it was something to do with the police. Ma won't say anything as usual, but Ash rang and told me to warn you. Of what? Why won't anyone tell me anything?'

Nita wrote, 'Don't worry, sis. There was a little misunderstanding but... ' She looked at what she'd written and hit the delete key.

She started again. 'I've been accused of killing a baby. But I've met a man... ' Delete, delete, delete. The phone rang. She checked the screen but didn't recognise the number so she ignored it.

She wrote, 'Last Thursday someone found a dead baby in a skip. The police think it's mine... ' Delete.

She could see Mina a long, long way away. She was wearing her wedding finery. Rolam, the familiar stranger, was at her side and she would never be alone again. She was Rolam's wife now, the mother of his children. She could no longer make the leap into Nita's life. Nor could Nita understand hers.

Nita shut down her laptop with tears in her eyes. She unplugged the phone and then went to bed.

———

She woke up trembling with fright two hours later smelling smoke, hearing the rustle of flame. There was nothing. It was so quiet her breath sounded like a haunting.

She got up and looked out onto the street. Zach's Toyota was parked close to the skip where another dead Christmas tree now leaned drunkenly against the ripped armchair. The sky had cleared enough to show a faint glow of moon behind watery clouds.

She woke again an hour later from a dream of drowning. When she looked for Zach all she saw was a space next to the skip. She thought, if Rose Peters had posted something through her letterbox, where was it? She thought, who gave my name to Bobby Kees? She thought, were the doll and the vest sent by the same person who set fire to the hall and called me a packy peedo? The last two don't sound like Harris Searle. But if it wasn't him, how many people hate me enough to burn my house?

She got up and dressed in her warmest clothes. She filled a bucket with hot soapy water and went downstairs to attack the graffiti with a scrubbing brush. Half an hour later her arms were shaking with fatigue but the writing was as clear as ever. She should have known: she had never been able to erase her shame with soap and water.

The sound of two cars on the main road reminded her that although the hour was neither late nor early she was not alone in the world. Someone would be getting up, maybe only for a drink of water, and looking out of a window to see Nita Tehri fail with a scrubbing brush. She tipped the water into the gutter and took the bucket back upstairs. Then she picked up the bag of discarded clothes from the landing and went out again. There was a recycling bin outside the all-night supermarket.

17

Being a Bad Girl?

///

A part from rubbish caught by the whirly-gig wind the car park was empty. Nita carried her black bin bag over to the brown metal recycling container. As she opened the bag a gust of wind blew a sheet of newspaper against her legs and she saw the headline: Teacher Accused. She grabbed the paper before it could dance away again.

It was an inside page of the City Chronicle and under a dim yellow light she read the first two paragraphs. They began without much embellishment by telling the story of the newborn baby found in the skip. The second paragraph told of a young teacher working in 'one of our City's many primary schools.' The teacher had been sent home as soon as her link with the dead baby had been established. This prompt action assured readers that there was absolutely no danger to any child in the system. The story continued on the next page which Nita did not have so she couldn't tell if either she or the school was named.

She began to tear the paper to shreds until a sudden thought made her turn and look down the rows of empty parking spaces. There were two CCTV cameras that she could see. One of them seemed to be pointing directly at her. Automatically she stuffed the pieces of paper into the hole in the recycling bin even though that particular bin was for clothing. The single eye seemed to be fixed on her and she realised that under its gaze she could not throw away the bag of clothes and cleaning rags she'd brought. The phrase, 'Disposing of the evidence' came into her mind. It wasn't what she was doing, but it was what it would look like to the spy on the pole. If Bobby Kees bought the footage, what would he see? A bundled up little figure furtively stuffing things into a recycling bin in a deserted car park at four in the morning.

What would the police see? The destruction of evidence? If she were to thrust her spangled pink and aqua concoction through the hole marked Clothing, would the car park fill instantly with police cars and howling sirens? Would she be arrested again under the gaze of a CCTV camera and the flashing bulbs of a City Chronicle photographer?

Anything a person did in an empty car park at four in the morning would look bad or mad when seen on TV.

Nita shouldered her black bin bag and trudged round to the front of the supermarket. She was thinking about the dozens of people who'd managed to transport and fly-tip objects as big as dead Christmas trees and armchairs into the skip on Guscott Road without being seen, while she couldn't even recycle clothes in a receptacle marked 'Recycled Clothing'.

She wheeled her refuse round the shelves on a trolley, sadly aware that now she looked like a bag-woman to the two bored guys manning the single open checkout and the many interior CCTV cameras.

It was her own fault—she shouldn't be in the shop at all. Zach told her not to go out but she had to be able to cook and eat.

She began to plan siege menus: everything from simple kheema to chicken chitani, and as usual, when thinking about cooking, her breathing steadied and her pulse returned to normal. The siege faded from her mind as she began to visualise the steps she'd take to make chicken moghlai. She ran through the list of spices: ginger, cinnamon sticks, whole cloves, cumin seeds, coriander, cayenne, bay leaves, saffron, garlic. She knew she already had them in her kitchen, and a notion struck her—that whatever hand life dealt could be endured if you had a cupboard full of good spices.

She wondered if she would do all her shopping at four in the morning from now on. It wouldn't be so bad, she thought, daydreaming in the aisles where usually you had to negotiate for a place like a car in a jam.

Her fantasy of life as a recluse came to an end with the shouts of three boys in hooded jackets running past, barging each other, passing a watermelon from hand to hand as if it were a ball. She watched them go, amazed. Did nobody miss them at home? She thought about Ash—her parents knew where he was twenty-four hours a day. When did care become control or freedom become neglect?

She had submitted to control for most of her life—she was trained for it. Freedom had not been on offer. But wasn't obedience simply a lack of courage and imagination? She tried to see herself racing through a shop, throwing a melon to her friends. She couldn't, and she had to admit that freedom, when it came, had been forced on her rather than snatched by her. Like everything else, she thought angrily. She was so damaged that she experienced freedom as abandonment, and she still fenced her life with rules and limitations, literally going to school on time every morning. Now she had been forced to stop going to school and she didn't know what to do.

A man said quietly, 'We can't keep meeting like this.' And she found herself pushed and trapped against the shelves with her nose pressed against a row of canned lentils.

Harris Searle stepped out of her nightmares and said, 'Been having some trouble lately, haven't you?' His arm snaked around her body and under her sweater.

'Not going out much any more, huh?' he whispered. 'Staying home for surfer-boy? Being a bad girl for him now—is that what you're doing? But I can find you wherever you hide. And that's what you want, isn't it? To be found.'

His hand discovered her breast and squeezed. He said, 'You're like a little kid, aren't you? You don't want to get away with it.

You want to be caught and punished when you've been bad. Otherwise it might mean Daddy doesn't love you any more.'

He began to twist her nipple. 'It might mean Daddy isn't strong enough to make you do right. And you want a strong Daddy, don't you? Surfer-boy just doesn't cut it, does he?'

His words hurt more than his hands.

Nita tore herself out of the hypnotic state his voice put her into. She kicked backwards to give herself space. In the same instant she grabbed two cans of lentils and whirled around. She hit him, whack-whack, in the face. He staggered back, tripped against her trolley and fell down.

Someone, off to the left, a long way away, started to clap.

Harris raised his hand and touched the blood crawling out of his nose. He looked at his hand.

When he spoke his voice had lost its dreaminess. 'What did you do that for?' he asked, seeming to be truly puzzled. It was as if he thought she had broken a contract with him.

'You hit me,' he said, astonished. 'I could sue you. I've got witnesses.'

Nita dragged her horrified eyes away from the worm of blood on his upper lip and saw that the three guys in hooded jackets were standing a few paces away. The melon lay smashed at their feet.

The one in front said, 'What him sayin' man? Witness what, man? He muggin' her for her phone, isn't it?'

The one who was clapping said, 'Could be's her old man, innit? He a wife beater?'

'Could be, could be,' the first one said, nodding judiciously.

Nita turned and fled down the aisle, past the check-out and into the freezing darkness.

Even after a hot bath and a drink of warm milk and honey Nita's hands were shaking so violently that she could hardly turn on the computer. I hit him, she thought repeatedly, I made him bleed. Tremulously she found City Chronicle Online.

I made him bleed, she thought, and the sky did not fall. Yet.

The front page headline said simply, 'Police Quiz Suspect.' That's me, she thought, her heart staggering. I'm a front page headline.

But she wasn't. This suspect was a man called Ahmed Karavez from Tajikistan, and he was not suspected of killing a baby. He was being questioned about the death of a Philippine woman who used to work at a 'so-called massage parlour' in the Holyfield Industrial Park. The woman, who the reporter kept referring to as Maria, was apparently an illegal immigrant who seemed to have no friends, family or, most importantly, documents. It was hinted at but never stated that Ahmed was a member of a people-trafficking gang. He didn't appear to have correct documentation either. A police spokesman expressed horror at the notion that 'these people' were bringing their lawlessness to 'our beautiful, historic city.'

Maria, Nita thought. Mary, Miriam—almost generic names for a woman. Was it really her name? Or was it simply a name given to a woman with no papers, no rights, and not enough English to contradict?

Maria, without question, was not Harvard Slut, the long-legged, scarcely-skirted blonde in pink. And Harris Searle, greying, reliable-looking, English, was not the suspect.

Nita felt extremely stupid. She had looked at one of the many women who might have become a victim of violence that night and put her together with a man demonstrably capable of violence. She'd just picked the wrong woman and the wrong man. Apart from that, she thought, it was a good guess. But she wished she hadn't made it out loud so many times.

She scrolled on till she came to the smaller headline: Teacher Accused. The paragraphs she had not yet read were devoted to a statement by a local Labour Councillor who insisted that all the teachers in her constituency had undergone rigorous background checks by the authorities. Unsuitable candidates were weeded out at an early stage. She supposed that very occasionally a bad apple might go undetected for a very short time, but she could assure the voting public that the system was working well: their children's education was in safe hands.

Nita closed the page with contempt. She knew the councillor lied. Midford Juniors had employed her for months and there'd been no background check. People didn't do their jobs. People lied. All they had were untrue words to disguise a collapsing system. No one was looking after the children.

It was still dark outside but already there was the sound of more traffic from the main road: people were beginning to get up and go to work. Soon it would be light and Nita would feel safer in bed. While it was light her ill-wishers would find it more difficult to attack.

She knew there were those who watched her door. Harris Searle was one. He knew about Zach. Surfer-boy. That was good: it meant Harris hadn't identified Zach as a P.I.

But Harris was watching her. He'd followed her to the supermarket. And now he had the bag of clothes and cleaning cloths she'd left behind when she ran away. An ancient fear made her catch her breath—what if Harris used her possessions against her? Suppose he made an effigy of her and clothed it in her silk? Suppose he burned the effigy? Would she not die next time someone poured petrol through her letterbox and set it alight?

She could almost hear Mina say, 'You'll have to get that bag back, Nita darling. Or move across the water to break the curse. The man who controls your possessions has power over you.'

And you should know, Mina dear, Nita thought. She put on her thick sweater and then stood in the hall feeling foolish. Why didn't education and reason save her from ancient fears? Sternly she removed her sweater and went to bed.

18

Lovely Neighbours

///

A blonde woman in a sensible sheepskin coat stood outside Nita's front door doing a short piece to camera. Zach was watching from an open window. The flat was freezing. Nita sat in the kitchen, her head in her hands. The doorbell rang continuously.

Zach called from the living room, 'There's a woman out here saying you shouldn't be allowed to breathe the same air as decent folk. I don't think the silly bitch even *lives* in Guscott Road. Come and look.'

Nita didn't answer.

He went on, 'Nobody'll see you—I've rigged up a mirror. Come on, how often do you get to be on TV?'

'With any luck, never,' Nita said, emerging reluctantly from the kitchen.

'The reporter's from City News,' he said, playing with the angle of the mirror. 'I seen her loads. There, how's that? Sit on the floor so you can't be seen.'

Nita sat and looked into the cleverly placed mirror. At first all she could see were the camera and sound men and some of Guscott Road's residents. But with a bit more fiddling Zach was able to show her the blonde reporter and an excitable woman who seemed very familiar.

'Ryan's mum,' Nita said, her heart sinking. 'I was responsible for her son being excluded from school.'

'Ooh, bad move,' Zach said. 'There's nothing worse than a mum for holding a grudge. Unless it's a gran. What'd he do?'

'Threatened another kid with a knife.' It seemed like months ago.

'Who's the old bird?'

Through the mirror Nita saw Daphne push her way to the front of the little crowd. She could hear clearly when Daphne shouted, 'What you listening to her for? She doesn't live here. Nita's a lovely girl. Why don't you all push off and leave the poor kid alone?'

Nita burst into tears and rushed back to the kitchen. After a few minutes Zach followed her. He said, 'Well the old bird killed *that* interview stone dead. They're packing up now so you won't have to hide for much longer.'

Nita blew her nose on a piece of kitchen paper and dabbed her swollen eyes with cold water. Zach watched with interest.

'I don't understand you at all. All this crap happening to you and you just grit your teeth. But one little old lady says something nice and you collapse in a soggy heap.'

Nita could feel tears welling up again. She turned away.

'Oh fuck,' Zach said. 'You need a cuddle. Come here.'

'I can't,' Nita said, pulling back although she'd never wanted anything more in her life.

'Suit yourself,' he said, sitting down at the kitchen table. 'I got to admit it ain't very professional.'

'It isn't that.' She couldn't explain. Harris would have grabbed; Ahmed would too, giving Nita no choice or responsibility. But then it would be an assault and not a cuddle. That's not what I want, she thought, truly it isn't.

What overwhelmed her was that, once pushed away, Zach did not persist. Nor did he punish her for turning him down. His light remark about professionalism was an excuse they could share equally. It made him unique among the men she'd had any physical contact with. It made him utterly trustworthy.

She said almost stammering, 'We've got to talk. Nothing is clear. I owe you money and we have to decide what to do first.'

'True, but you can't go out. You also need to go shopping but you keep running into your evil stalker at the supermarket. Looks like you gonna have to be the princess in the tower for a while.'

'The Lady of Shalott,' she said remembering the mirror. 'The trouble is things keep happening so fast we've never talked properly about what I'm hiring you to do.'

'I do whatever you need—taking shit to the lab, bodyguarding, surveillance—just name it.'

And that was unique too: a tall blond man putting himself at her service, under her leadership. Giving her control.

'I think I've been passive for too long,' she said, astonished.

'Not your fault—like you said, shit happens fast round here. You can't help reacting to the last thing.'

'But who's doing those things? Isn't it time I found out more about my neighbours? I think what I want is for you to do a background check on some of them.'

'Can do,' Zach said. 'Which ones?'

'Harris Searle,' Nita said promptly.

'Now you're talking.' Zach grinned.

'Also Diane and Stu. They went strange on me very quickly. We used to talk, but mainly about property prices. I wonder if they think I'm bad for their investment.' She broke off. 'Don't you want to write this down?'

'If you think I'll forget two names... ' He started to fumble in his pocket.

'Er, three, actually. But there's more—there's Jen and Dave. Not so much Jen—the dead baby couldn't be hers because Craig is about a year old and he's definitely hers. But it might be Dave's. And then there's the Nazi above Women's Aid.'

'Hang on.' Zach stopped in the middle of an undecipherable scribble. 'What do you want to know exactly? What do you suspect these people of? Being the baby's parent? Trying to intimidate you? Arson? They're different questions.'

'Maybe,' Nita said, 'maybe not. We don't know that. We don't actually know anything for sure. I just thought if you investigated their backgrounds you might turn up a pattern. Like a history of violence or racist attacks. I don't know.'

'Okay.' He bent his fair head and started to scribble again. Nita watched his square competent hands struggling with a pencil and smiled. He looked up and said, 'One of them's a flaming Nazi. I'd of thought racist attacks was his thing.'

'He's probably only mentally ill. But maybe he does more than just rant and throw his gas bill out of the window.'

He stopped writing and looked at the notebook. 'Lovely neighbours you got here.'

'I used to think so,' Nita said sadly. 'But you should know: you've been watching us for nearly a week.'

'I been checking out the area for a guy who bought a property at auction, sight unseen. He didn't know nothing about the *area*, see. I didn't do no background checks on *people*.'

'And it's a nice area, isn't it?'

'Not bad. Nothing fancy—just some nice old houses, most of 'em really well kept—like this one. It's quiet because it ends at the river—no through traffic, see. Growing middle-class component. The only problem is the pub on the main road—it's a bit noisy Friday and Saturday nights. But that's true of anywhere in a city centre.'

'Are you quoting from your report?'

'Yeah.' He stirred self-consciously. 'How does it sound? You're a teacher. I was always crap at the written work.'

'Very professional. What did you say about all the fuss with police and stuff?'

'I ain't supposed to divulge a confidential report. But I called it atypical.'

'Good word.'

'Think so? My secretary suggested it. She's better at writing than me. What was that boy's mum doing in your road if she don't live here?'

'Oh my goodness,' Nita said. 'I should've thought of that. She isn't supposed to know where I live.'

'She's one for your list then, eh?'

'I'll ring the school and find out where *she* lives.'

'It'd be flaming hilarious if you had *two* stalkers, wouldn't it?'

'I didn't know you had a secretary. Is she someone I can ring if I can't reach you?'

'I sort of share her with an antiques dealer. She's more of a typist really. I'll give you my mobile number. What're we gonna do about money?'

'Can I go out now?' Nita asked. 'Has everyone gone?'

'I'll look.' He got up and went to the living room.

While he was gone she checked his list. She wrote in the numbers of the houses people lived in and bit her lip, resisting the temptation to correct his spelling.

He came back and caught her looking. 'I was always better at the verbals,' he said, snapping the book shut and hiding it away in his pocket.

'I was just...'

'No sweat. But don't go out. There's people rubber-necking out there, and a couple of 'em look like journalists.' He stood looking awkward and impatient to be gone, jangling the keys which hung from a chain on his belt. 'You got any cash?'

'Not much. Why?'

'Well I thought I'd go to the office and call Woody, see how he's getting on, make a start on this list of yours. Then maybe come back here with some shopping—since you can't get out no more.'

'That's so thoughtful,' Nita said. 'Thank you. Look, take this credit card.' She rooted in her bag for the last of her cards. 'If you go to the cash point and take out three hundred pounds, that'll be the two fifty I owe you and then some for the shopping. I'll make a list.'

'Are you sure about this?' he asked, watching as she bustled round the kitchen rewriting the list she'd lost last night. 'Giving me your card? What if I abscond to Barbados? S'pose I'm run over by a bus?'

'I'll go hungry then, won't I?' She looked up into his transparent tobacco eyes and smiled. 'And you'll either get a great tan or you'll be on the tarmac, flat as a pancake.'

'Oh, that's alright then,' he said, smiling back. 'You'd better not forget the PIN number or I won't make it as far as the airport, will I?'

She added the number to the bottom of the list and handed it to him along with the card.

'I'll be back around six,' he said. 'Think you can hold out till then? Tell you one thing you can do for me, eh—when the phone rings and you don't recognise the number, write it down and I'll check it out later.'

When he'd gone all she could think of was the tone of his voice when he'd said, 'You need a cuddle. Come here.'

She rejected warmth, sympathy and understanding. 'A cuddle,' she said out loud, exasperated with herself. 'What's so bad about that?'

Deciding that as she didn't have a sister to talk to anymore she should employ a therapist, Nita went to her phone pad to call the solicitor.

The page on which she'd written his number and Helen Whitby's was gone.

Nita was shocked. Could Eavers, when searching her flat, have been so vindictive as to destroy the only contact number she had for her solicitor? In the long run, what had she gained by forcing Nita into the temporary care of an overtired duty solicitor?

She phoned the school office to ask for Helen Whitby's phone number and Ryan's mum's address. The office manager told her that the children really missed her but seemed to be coping well with her replacement. Her tone was bright, chirpy and completely false. The woman did not want to chat with a teacher under suspicion.

'Give the kids my love,' Nita said sadly, knowing full well that she wouldn't.

19

Atypical

///

A t six o'clock Nita was brushing her hair. It shone like black satin and she thought that it was the healthiest looking part of her. Instead of dragging it back into a severe knot she twisted it loosely and fixed it with an antique silver clasp. Staring critically at her tired, pinched face she dabbed a little concealer on the circles under her eyes.

I'm only twenty-three, she thought, but I look forty-three and I feel a hundred and three.

The doorbell rang and she went to the entry phone. Zach's voice crackled and said, 'Hi.' She pressed the button that opened the front door, grabbed a torch and went down to meet him.

The man standing in the dark hall was not Zach. He had a torch of his own and was examining the damage.

Nita stopped halfway down the stairs and said, 'I thought you were someone else. I shouldn't have let you in.'

The man turned and smiled, saying, 'I'm Bret West. I own the property across the road from you.'

'What can I do for you, Mr West?' Nita said coldly.

'It looks more like I could do a little something for you.' He directed the beam of his torch up to the ceiling, squinting along it at the light fitting. 'Like maybe send over one of the guys working for me. See if he can fix your electrics. Otherwise, the structure don't look too bad. You were lucky.'

He was short and square-looking, dressed, as far as Nita could see by torchlight, in an expensive coat which might have suited a taller man better.

She said, 'Thank you for the offer, Mr West. I rang the insurance people and they told me not to touch anything till they'd sent someone out to inspect the damage.'

'What b... rubbish,' he said cheerfully. 'If you don't mind me saying, they're giving you the run-around. You'll be sending them the fire-officer's report, I take it? So there's no need for them to inspect. You should just get the work done and send them the bill. Pronto. They can't expect you to go up and down stairs in the dark till they decide to get off of their fat fannies and send someone. I'm sorry, but it ain't safe.'

'That's really good advice, Mr West, and thank you for your offer.'

'Just being neighbourly.'

It was as if a little bubble burst in Nita's chest and she started to laugh. 'I'm sorry,' she said, catching her breath, trying to contain herself, 'but "neighbourly" isn't a recommendation just at the moment.'

He stared at her for a couple of seconds before his face cleared. 'Oh, you mean the good wishes on the front of your house? That was the neighbours?'

'It might have been. It might not.'

'Look, Ms Tehri,' he said, 'I'll come clean about this visit. Of course my offer of help stands—I'll send a guy over, just say the word—but that wasn't my only reason for calling. I'm a property developer, as you could've already heard, and I like this little road. It's got potential. So I'm wondering, if you're having trouble here, or maybe you're unhappy with the neighbours and such, and you're thinking of moving on, well, I'd like to make an offer on your flat.'

'How do you know I'm not renting?'

'Well obviously I asked around.'

And obviously Zach would have mentioned in his report about how many owner-occupiers there were because that sort of thing affected property prices in an area.

She said, 'So you've seen what's happened here and you still like the road?'

'Well, that was really tough. But I'd say it was atypical.'

'I think what you mean to say, Mr West, is that it's a nice little road, but *I* am atypical.' Nita found herself shaking with rage. Atypical was Zach's typist's word. In Zach's mouth it'd seemed harmless, even cute, but in the mouth of a man who wanted to buy her flat and profit from her distress it sounded like a weapon of war. She said, 'Again, thank you for your offer, but I'm not interested. Now please would you go?' Why did she *always* say please? Even to the people who meant her harm?

'I've offended you,' Bret West said. He seemed genuinely puzzled. And the sincerity of his confusion only angered her more. How could he fail to see what was so offensive? How could she stand on the stairs and talk to a guy who failed to understand what was so offensive about burning her house and calling the graffiti on her wall 'atypical'?

'Think nothing of it,' Nita said, knowing that was what he'd do anyway.

She was kicking herself for saying anything at all. Silence would've been much more dignified. She started down the stairs so that she could usher him out and close the door on him. But he anticipated her, turning away and opening the door himself.

He said, 'Well, I'm sorry. But here's my card in case you change your mind.'

When he saw that she wouldn't take it he put it down on the burnt doormat and left, shutting the door quietly behind him.

The phone rang. Nita checked the screen and saw that her caller was not Zach but Helen Whitby.

Helen said, 'The old bag in the office told me you'd called. She also told me that she wouldn't give you my number.'

'Strictly speaking she probably did the correct thing.'

'Strictly speaking she's an interfering cow who wouldn't know the correct thing if it flew up her nose.'

'As I suppose you took pleasure telling her,' Nita said. 'I rang because someone removed the solicitor's number you gave me.'

'Have you had a break in?' Helen asked. 'The old bag said you wanted Ryan's mum's address too. Has she been giving you any trouble?'

'She was here. Have you watched City News this evening?'

'I have, actually.'

'Was she on it?'

'Ryan's mum? No, why?'

'She was talking to that blonde reporter on camera. So she's either hanging around me or she's hanging around the reporter. Did they show the front of my house on TV?'

'I'm afraid they did,' Helen said.

'I know you'll say I'm being paranoid, but given what the graffiti says, what am I going to do if Ryan's mum starts accusing me of... you know?'

'Maybe she already has. Mightn't that crap on your wall be her work?'

'It's one of the possibilities I'm having investigated right now. I meant she might start making accusations to the school board.'

'Nita dear, the accusation was on the front of your house, and also on local TV. The school board knows.'

'I need your solicitor's number more than ever,' Nita said, fighting panic.

'I think you do,' Helen said, and gave it to her. 'What did you mean when you said you were having possibilities investigated?'

Nita told Helen about Zach as briefly as possible. Even so, there was a lot to say, and when she'd said it Helen was silent

141

for a few seconds. Then she said, 'Nita, you've been arrested, accused of infanticide, forced to give a DNA sample, and yet you'd rather employ a PI than a lawyer? What're you thinking of?'

'He was just *there*,' Nita protested, feeling foolish. 'He nearly ran me over. I thought he was a policeman. I told him about the doll. And later, when someone sent me the blood-soaked vest, he... '

'Doll?' Helen sounded shocked. 'Blood-soaked? Nita, I'm coming over and I'm bringing a lawyer. I'll drag one out of bed if I have to. I had no idea you were in this much trouble. Why on earth didn't you tell me before?'

'Things only happened bit by bit.' Nita felt suddenly crushed by the weight and number of the bits. 'And besides we don't know each other all that well.'

'I don't care if you're a total stranger; I'm on my way.' Helen Whitby hung up.

Half an hour later the buzzer on her entry-phone sounded. It wasn't Zach, nor was it Helen Whitby.

Rose Peters said, 'I've brought you a plate of brownies. Daphne insisted on coming too.'

Nita let them in and rushed downstairs with the torch.

Daphne said, 'Oh my good gawd what an 'orrible stink. You're never gonner get shot of that.'

'It'll be fine once she's decorated,' Rose said impatiently.

'You can never really get rid of the stink,' the old woman said, starting to climb the stairs slowly, puffing. 'My sister had a fire once—her old man went to sleep on the sofa with a beer and a fag and the football on the telly and never woke up again. 'Course they redecorated but she always complained of the smell. They had to re-house her. She said it was like pork chops burning.'

'Charming,' Rose said, bringing up the rear.

'Ooh, this is nice,' Daphne said when they finally reached the sitting room. 'You done a lovely job here.'

'I can't offer you much,' Nita said, 'I'm waiting for a friend to bring back some shopping. But would you like tea?'

'We didn't come for tea,' Rose said, and gave Nita the plateful of homemade brownies.

'That's so kind,' Nita said, 'thank you.'

'I take mine with milk and sugar,' Daphne said, giving Rose an evil look. She followed Nita into the kitchen and watched while she filled the kettle, her opal eyes turning from time to time to check the equipment and the cleanliness. 'Nice,' she said. 'I expect you make all them curries like you get in restaurants. My two boys love them. Too spicy for me, though—they repeat all night. Do you like cooking?'

'I love it,' Nita said.

'Thought so. It's that sort of kitchen.' She wandered away to join Rose in the other room.

When Nita came in with the tea Rose said, 'We're here to show solidarity and to say we aren't associated with what's being said in the street.'

'Solidarity, my arse.' Daphne added milk and sugar to her cup and stirred it noisily. 'It just ain't fair, people turning on you. You never did no harm to no one. I don't know why the cops picked on you and I ain't asking, but that don't give nobody the right to say bad things on your front wall. And as for the fire, I thought at first those fairy boys you got living downstairs was the cause of that. I thought her neighbour, what's his name?'

'Harris Searle,' Rose said crossly.

'Harris Searle,' Daphne went on, oblivious. 'He don't like fairy boys. He told me so. But they always been more than civil to me, as I told him back. So I thought when they had that party and all the loud music...'

'Harris wouldn't do that,' Rose said, 'he isn't violent.'

'Yes he is,' Nita said. 'I've been trying to warn you.'

'I live in the same house and he's never lifted a finger to me.'

'He attacked me in the supermarket last night.'

'Why on earth would he do that?'

'I don't know. I think he's watching me.'

'Why would he do that? Look I told you it wasn't wise to go out with him.'

'You never bleeding went out with him?' Daphne said. 'I thought you had the sense you was born with.'

'I met him in the supermarket and he suggested a drink. It wasn't a date.'

'It would of been when I was a girl,' Daphne said. 'Anyway he's too old for you.'

'He didn't seem to think so.'

'They never do,' Rose said. 'That's our job.' She pushed a tendril of greying hair behind one ear and smiled knowingly at Daphne.

'All the same,' Nita said, 'he *is* violent. He was on Saturday and then again last night.'

'Are you sure you aren't just giving off the wrong signals?' Rose said.

'I thought you was a bleeding feminist.' Daphne cackled gleefully. 'Leastways, you was a feminist when you was telling me my boys is too old to live with their mother no more.'

'They're in their fifties, for God's sake, Daph. You're still cooking for them, cleaning, doing their laundry.'

Daphne cackled again. 'She was seeing my eldest,' she told Nita. 'She wanted him to move in with her. She can't forgive me for making him more comfortable than what she could.'

Nita stared at them in amazement. It was a feud that went back years, and yet here they were, side by side on her sofa to offer their support. They weren't doing a very good job but she was grateful. She wasn't friendless. The doorbell rang.

It was Helen Whitby without a solicitor. 'I really tried,' she said, climbing the stairs by torchlight. 'A younger partner will call on you tomorrow morning. But... '

'I'm ever so grateful,' Nita said. 'It's so kind of you to come.'

She showed Helen into the sitting room and introduced her to Daphne and Rose. They all stared at each other with a subtle form of wariness which Nita didn't understand. She disappeared back to the kitchen hoping they'd have made peace with each other when she came back with fresh tea and Rose's brownies.

Before she'd even had time to put the tray down Daphne said, 'Miss Whitby tells us you're involved with that geezer in the big bleeding monster-motor who's been hanging round at night.'

'He's a private detective,' Nita said.

'He's a twat with tattoos,' Daphne said, staring belligerently at the others, daring them to contradict her. 'I hope you didn't give him no money. You never want to give no money to twats with tattoos.'

'Tattoos are folk art,' Rose said unwisely

'Folk art, bloke fart,' Daphne said triumphantly. She seemed to be enjoying herself.

Helen Whitby was looking bewildered.

Nita felt, for one astonished moment, that she might have too many friends. She put down the tray and poured the tea. Helen Whitby accepted a cup. Out of school she wore designer clothes and very expensive looking shoes. Nita didn't understand why she was a teacher or what she was doing sitting in Nita's armchair.

Daphne, still on the subject of tattoos, was like a dog with a bone. 'Those greasy fairground blokes who gave the young girls trouble on the dodgems—they had tattoos. And earrings. You can't trust 'em further than you can post 'em in an envelope. I hope you got a reference.'

'Sort of,' Nita said. She knew Zach was genuine: it was the word 'atypical' turning up in Bret West's mouth which proved that he had been doing surveillance and had written a report exactly as he said. But she wished he'd come home with her shopping; or ring to say why he was delayed; or somehow let her know he'd forgiven her for turning down a cuddle.

Late that night, waking with a shudder from dreams of drowning, she went to the window. Sleet had frozen on the skip and dignified with improbable sparkle a new addition to the rubbish family. Sometime in the last couple of hours someone had managed to off-load a broken-backed piano and drive away without being noticed. It looked as if the keys and fascia board had been smashed with a hammer. The once fine inlaid wood was splintered; the keyboard looked like an old man's mouth.

Nita opened the window and peered up and down the street. There was no sign of a Toyota four-by-four.

20

Incredulous

///

At eight o'clock the next morning Nita rang Zach's mobile. It was switched off. It was still switched off at nine and ten.

At ten-fifteen a young and breathless voice told her that in spite of what Helen Whitby promised, he would not be able to come to her house as arranged. He'd ring again later and maybe they could 'conference' by phone.

Zach's phone was switched off at eleven, half past eleven and twelve.

At twelve twenty-five her doorbell rang. Sergeant Cutler said, 'You want to let me in?'

'Do you have a warrant?'

'I just want a chat. You might want to hear what I've got to say.'

'Well, I don't,' Nita said. 'Please go away.' She hung up the entry phone and went back to the window, sitting on the floor watching the road through an angled mirror the way Zach had taught her.

The bell rang again. She ignored it. Why had she said 'please' to Sergeant Cutler? Out loud to Zach she said, 'Please ring, please ring, please ring.'

The phone rang. She didn't recognise the number so she let the machine take the call. An Irish voice said, 'Would you ring

147

Credit Direct about the atypical activity we've been alerted to on your credit card number... '

Nita leaped to the phone and said, 'I'm here. What's happened?'

'I'm Orla. First let me take you through some security details.'

It took only a couple of minutes to establish her identity and stop the card. Orla was sympathetic but incredulous. 'You gave him your PIN,' she kept saying. 'Usually the company would reimburse you if someone steals or abuses your card. But I think we have an altogether different policy if you actually *gave* him both card and PIN.'

'He only went to buy groceries,' Nita said helplessly. 'Because I couldn't go out. He was kind. He was helping me.'

'He was helping himself,' Orla said.

'Maybe it's something he can explain,' Nita said without hope.

'I doubt it. One of his purchases was an air ticket, business class, to LA. He bought the phone, camera, suit, shoes and booze at Heathrow Airport.'

'Can you stop him?'

'Your card is flagged now. It'll automatically trigger certain measures if the vendor has the nous to avail himself of them. I suppose if you contact the police they could alert airport security.'

'Oh dear,' Nita said.

While she was blowing her nose and rinsing her face with cold water the doorbell sounded again.

A woman said, 'I'm Alicia Tamblin. You don't know me but you might've seen me on City News? On TV?'

Without thinking, Nita said, 'What do you want?'

'Can I come up and talk to you?'

'Regarding?'

'Well, regarding the accusations made against you.'

'Oh,' Nita said, still hoping it was all a huge, horrible mistake and she was actually talking to Zach. 'I thought you were someone else.'

'I can give you the chance to put your side of the story before the public.'

'I haven't got a side,' Nita said, her heart aching. 'I haven't got a story.'

Another voice, Daphne's, interrupted and said, 'I told you yesterday—leave the poor kid alone.'

A third voice, Cutler's, said, 'A little less noise if you don't mind, ladies. Or I might have to do you for disturbing the peace.' With his mouth closer to the speaker he said, 'I'll send the media away. I got to go now but I'll be back soon, crime and accidents permitting.'

In the grip of a sudden spasm of optimism Nita hung up. She was thinking, if Zach had been in an accident, or if he'd been mugged, he could be lying in an anonymous hospital bed right now, in a coma, while a thief with her credit card was flying, business class, to LA. She ran to find the phone directory.

After a wait of nearly fifteen minutes a woman at St Martin's hospital returned to tell her that no one called Zach Eastwood had been admitted in the last twenty-four hours; nor was there a man without identification in a coma. It took nearly as long for someone at City General to tell her the same thing. Both women advised her that if this was a missing person inquiry she should go to the police.

Instead, she went back to the phone book. There was no entry for Zach, Zachary, Zachariah or Z. Eastwood. She tried the Yellow Pages. Between Desk Top Publishing and Detectors (Metal) she found a list of thirty-four Detective Agencies. Zach's name did not appear but that didn't worry her: a lot of the agencies had names like Key, Peace of Mind or Tracer.

She began at the beginning with ABC Investigations. It was simple. She asked, 'May I speak to Zach Eastwood, please?' And the respondent at the other end of the line said, 'Who? No Zach Eastwood here.' Or she left a message on a machine asking

Zach to ring her. When there was no answer she made a query mark on the page and went on to the next. Her only worry was that Zach's business might be so confidential it wasn't listed in the Yellow Pages.

After about an hour the doorbell rang. Nita paused with her finger marking her place on the page. The bell kept ringing.

Sergeant Cutler said, 'I'm back. I could go and get a warrant, or I could put my shoulder to this poor excuse for a front door. But that's too much like hard work, so why don't you give a poor old copper a break and let me in? I've come to say I'm sorry.'

Nita said, 'Are you going to clean my wall, mend the fire damage and restore my reputation? Are you going to take DNA samples from all the men and the rest of the women in Guscott Road? Are you going to delete my sample from your permanent database? No? Then go away.' She put the receiver down gently, thinking, I didn't say please. Hallelujah!

The doorbell rang and kept on ringing. Nita went to the window, trying to ignore it. She thought of throwing water down on him. She remembered Zach calling her a princess in a tower, and her own poetic notion about the Lady of Shalott. 'Four grey walls and four grey towers,' she thought.

Years ago when she was a schoolgirl and her class read the poem in English, someone had come up with the idea that the nameless curse, which kept the Lady indoors and prevented her from seeing the world except through mirrors, was a description of agoraphobia. The Muslim girls didn't see what all the fuss was about: the curse needed no explanation—sexual longing was sometimes punished by death, even now. The white girls meanwhile succumbed to fits of the giggles at the line, 'The curse has come upon me!'

From her window, without the intervention of a mirror, Nita watched a midnight blue Mercedes park outside number 10 and a man, get out. It was Bret West in his oversized coat. She ran for the door, dashed downstairs and pushed Sergeant Cutler aside.

'Mr West,' she called.

He turned and crossed the road towards her. She said, 'Can I talk to you for a minute?'

'Okay,' he said. 'Have you had a chance to think about my offer?'

Sergeant Cutler said, 'What's he got that I haven't? Oh, let me guess, a Mercedes.'

'Please,' Nita said, 'can you tell me where Mr Eastwood lives?'

'Who?' said Sergeant Cutler.

'I'm sorry,' Bret West said, 'I don't know a Mr Eastwood.'

'He worked for you,' Nita said. 'He wrote a report for you.' Then because Bret was staring at her blankly, she added. 'The private investigator.'

'Oh, *that* investigator.' Cutler snorted. 'The one you accused me of putting outside your house?'

'What did you say his name was?'

'Zach Eastwood,' Nita said. 'I know it was supposed to be confidential, but this is urgent.'

'Fucking Ada's tight trousers!' Bret West looked angry enough to spit bullets. 'Zach fucking Eastwood!'

'I know he shouldn't have told me about it,' Nita said, alarmed by his anger.

'I wish we *had* put someone outside your door,' Cutler said. 'We could at least have avoided the bleeding fire.'

'Who the hell's this joker?' Bret asked.

'Sergeant Cutler,' Cutler said, 'police. Not private.'

'Well, this here's supposed to be a *private* conversation.'

'You sounded very upset,' Cutler said to Nita. 'Has a crime been committed?'

'Well, yes,' Nita admitted. 'But not by Mr Eastwood, I'm sure.' She was shaking with cold. She turned again to Bret West. 'But I really do need to know where to find Zach.'

'What crime hasn't he committed?' Bret asked. 'You haven't given him any fucking money, have you? Please say you haven't.'

'She fucking has,' Cutler said, examining the expression on Nita's face with interest.

'Shit, double shit,' Bret said. 'How could you be so flaming stupid?'

'Don't cry,' Cutler said attempting to put a comforting arm round Nita's shoulder before she edged away from him. 'I'm sure it's nothing we can't put right.' He turned to Bret. 'So who is this Zach Eastwood and where do we find him?'

Bret looked as if he would explode with fury. 'There isn't any frigging Zach Eastwood. There's a Zach *West* though. West. East. Clint Eastwood? Don't you get it?'

'Related to you, is he?' Cutler asked.

'I hate to sodding say it, but the arsehole's my brother. Every now and then my old mum gets on to me and I have to give him some sort of job. And he always finds some fresh new way to embarrass the shite out of me.'

'So where does this black sheep live?'

'As far away from me as possible,' Bret said. 'He's staying in one of my properties, sort of flat-sitting till I get a chance to put a crew in there.'

'But where?' Nita cried. 'I have to go there. It's all a mistake. It *must* be.'

'How much did you give him?' Bret asked.

'I don't *care* about the money,' said Nita who had been panicking about the money. 'It's the baby's vest. He took it to his friend Woody at the lab. It's important.'

'What you on about? Baby's vest?' Cutler said.

While Bret said, 'Woody? He got wood on the brain when he met you, didn't he? Woody, East*wood*. He doesn't like to overwork his imagination on names, my bastard baby bruv.'

'Hang about,' Cutler said, suddenly sounding authoritative, 'I need to know about this vest.'

'Maybe we should go somewhere a bit warmer,' Bret said. 'Miss Tehri looks like she's going to keel over.'

'Her flat,' Cutler decided.

'No,' Nita said. 'I want to go to Zach's place.'

'Okay, I'll take you there,' Bret said. 'But fetch a coat first.'

'I haven't got one anymore.'

'You never gave him the coat off of your back too?' Cutler said.

'Smoke damage,' Nita said. It was true: she was feeling so cold, so sick, so stupid, so utterly betrayed, she wished she could fall down unconscious or dead and leave real life far behind.

Bret took her arm and led her to his Mercedes, saying, 'We'll get in the car. It's got a decent heater—you'll soon warm up.'

Sergeant Cutler said, 'I'm coming too.'

Bret paused with his hand on the passenger door handle and asked, 'Do you want him along, Miss Tehri? We don't have to bleedin' take him just cos he wants to come.'

'You don't want me to make this official, do you?' Cutler said.

21

Dirt-bag

//

Zach was tall; Bret was short. Zach was blond; Bret was dark. Zach's face was symmetrical; Bret's looked as if he'd once been an unsuccessful fighter. Zach's clothes were casual surfer chic; Bret's were straight. Zach had square strong hands; Bret's were squarer and stronger.

They are not alike, Nita repeated to herself like a mantra. This isn't true; they are not brothers. But the thought was blown apart by the bombshell of Bret's voice. If she closed her eyes and heard him say, 'You'll soon warm up,' it was Zach's voice she could hear, his accent, his tone and his rhythm. It was a tone and rhythm that must have come from the same house, the same family and the same parents. It was why she'd opened the door to Bret yesterday. She'd thought last night that she'd wished Zach's voice into Bret's mouth, but it'd been there all along.

It wasn't something she'd ever wondered about before but tone of voice was a cultural transmission as distinctive as anything genetic. It ran through a family like brown eyes or a turned-up nose.

She sat beside Bret in his midnight-blue Mercedes, wrapped in his tartan car rug, as he drove, grim and silent across the city to the flat Zach was supposed to have been looking after. Now and then she sneaked a look at his profile and couldn't help making comparisons. He's ugly, she thought. He can't be Zach's brother—he's too ugly. And then she thought: he isn't ugly; he just isn't Zach.

He drove smoothly through the city streets past the mass of ordinary people going about their ordinary afternoon business: shopping, pushing prams, collecting kids from school, talking, holding hands. To Nita the ordinary looked bizarre—like a view of an alien species seen through smoked glass. And yet, she kept reminding herself, it was she who was wrapped in a rug like a cartoon Bedouin, not them. It was she who had been under arrest, not them. They had not handed thousands of pounds to a complete stranger. They were the sane, ordinary citizens of the UK. The one who stood out in the crowd, who would fail any test of commonsense, was Nita Tehri.

Bret broke his silence to ask, 'That cop—what's his game?' He checked his rear view mirror to see if Cutler, in his dented old Audi, was still following.

'I first met him a couple of days ago,' Nita said, 'when they were going from house to house asking about the baby in the skip.'

'A week ago,' Bret corrected her. And she realised with shock that he was right. 'Yeah, Zach told me all about that,' he went on.

'In his report?'

'Report? Ms Tehri, I don't know what my flaming brother told you, but a detective he bleedin' well is not. It's true I asked him to suss out the neighbours and check if there was any outstanding planning applications, but that's the lot. He ain't Shylock Holmes, except in his warped little imagination.' He scowled ferociously at a van driver who was trying to cut him up.

'Charm and potential,' he added, sneering to himself. 'That's our sainted mum's brilliant opinion. Just how much potential can a thirty-five-year-old man still have, eh? When he's done nothing in his whole life except hang out in betting shops and go to jail for ripping off... There, now I've told you—you ain't even the first.

'Do we really need the flaming cops? Can't we settle this between ourselves?'

'Settle what?' While he was talking Nita had sunk down into the blanket, ashamed and hoping no one would look into the car and see her brimming eyes. 'Do you always pay his debts?'

'Not if I can help it.' He looked towards her as he braked at traffic lights. 'But it nearly killed my mum when he got sent away. When he came out she believed he was, whatchamacallit, rehabilitated. So to please her I let him do a little caretaker stuff at one of my properties. That way he could live rent free. But I wasn't going to give him much cash or he'd just blow it all in the frigging casino. It's a disease, my mum says. Some fucking disease! Proper diseases kill the patient. This fucker kills everyone *except* the patient. Including you this time.'

The lights changed and he drove on. After a few minutes silence he flicked his eyes in her direction and said, 'Tell me to mind me own bleedin' business, but what was it about him made you give him money? I mean, it's just sodding unbelievable—I could sit here and ask you for dosh till the cows come home and you'd laugh in my face. Why him?'

'I don't *know*,' Nita said. It came out like a sob. 'I've tried to think and all I can come up with is that he was there at the right time and he said the right things.' She struggled to find something Bret would understand. 'Imagine that it's raining cats and dogs and there's a huge damp patch appearing on your kitchen wall and someone turns up and says, "Don't worry, your gutters need cleaning and I just happen to have my ladder here. It won't take a moment but I'll need a small payment."

'You say, "Oh thank you." He comes down from his ladder and says, "Problem solved." And you feel so much better because he's made it simple, and you're not coping all on your own any more.

'Then he says, "While I was up there I couldn't help noticing you've got a couple of loose tiles." So you say, "You're already here with your ladder would you mind having another look?"

'He goes up again and calls down, "It's a bit tricky and I'll need some money for materials but I'm pretty sure I can fix it."'

'You see, you're just so grateful you've met this nice helpful guy with the right skills exactly when you need him.'

'Meanwhile he's stolen all the tiles and sold them to the builder down the road,' Bret said sourly, 'and he's sitting in your fucking attic making free with your stuff.'

Nita, huddled in the blanket, said nothing, and after a minute Bret went on, 'I'm sorry. No one's ever explained it in a way that makes any sense before. Your English... '

'What?'

'Nothing. I was about to make a complete tit of myself, wasn't I? You ain't really from Pakistan?'

'Leicester,' Nita said, warming to him slightly. 'Don't believe everything you read on walls.'

'I'm going to clean that off for you.'

'Oh don't do it for *me*,' Nita said. 'I'm getting used to it. Besides it isn't me it diminishes.' She was lying: it made her feel marked out for the utmost contempt.

Bret took this in silence. Then he said, 'Zach might understand what you just said, but I fucking don't.'

'Zach would say nothing,' she explained bitterly. 'But I would interpret his silence as total understanding. While in fact it was total indifference. Zach is my own sorry invention.'

My understanding of people is limited and banal, she thought. I populate my imaginary world with people just like me, whereas the real world is far more strange and dangerous.

Bret said, 'Don't blame yourself for *his* sodding failings.'

'I'm not. I've got failings too. You said it yourself. How could I be so stupid? Well the answer is—easily.'

He didn't reply to this. They were now in a newly developed part of town. Small blocks of twenty or so flats in converted warehouses overlooked the river. Bret parked outside one of them, and Nita realised she'd passed close by without seeing them on her way to the Cut, the day the Head sent her home from school. How many days ago? She couldn't remember.

They got out of the car—Nita still wearing the blanket like a cloak. Sergeant Cutler pulled in behind the Mercedes. The freezing wind blew off the river and forced them around the side of the building to the entrance.

Inside, Bret West turned to Cutler and said, 'If Ms Tehri wants to make an official complaint against my brother, that's her business. She's entitled—in spades. But she ain't done it yet. Okay? So you're here as a private citizen. Right? If you ain't a private citizen you ain't coming in. Got it?'

'Invitation only,' Cutler said, looking disgusted.

They ignored the lift which Bret said was a death-trap and climbed the wide staircase.

'It's a lousy fucking conversion,' Bret said on the way up to the second floor. 'If I owned the whole building I'd turn it into a top end property—covered entrance, doormen, separate service access, the bleeding lot. Riverside, see? People pay silly money for a river view.'

There were four doors off a corridor on the second floor. Bret stopped at one of them and selected a key from a huge ring. Nita stood behind him. She wanted to knock. There was still a chance. In a parallel universe, she would knock at this door and a tall, blond guy with Maori tattoos on his arm would open it and smile his crinkly warm smile.

Not bothering with parallel universes, Bret opened the door. It was dark. The air smelled faintly of cigarettes, mouldy bread and unwashed hair. Somewhere, to the left, a refrigerator hummed and a boiler clicked into life: sounds you only notice when there's nothing else to listen to.

Bret switched on a light and then went around opening curtains. Nita followed.

The flat was unfurnished except for a sofa and two canvas chairs in the living room and a mattress on the floor in one of the bedrooms. The bedding was dirty.

'Typical,' Bret said, 'he's nicked the bleeding telly and DVD player.'

Cutler wandered bad-temperedly with his hands in his pockets pretending to look like a private citizen.

Nita found the kitchen. It was grubby and old-fashioned. There was nothing in the fridge but some milk, a cracked lump of cheese and half a sliced white loaf. The freezer contained three frozen pizzas and too much ice. She started opening cupboards and drawers.

'What're you looking for?' Cutler said, standing in the doorway.

Nita found some wrappers of the juicy fruit gum he chewed. She said, 'Papers. The lab—maybe there's an invoice or an address.'

'There ain't any lab or any Woody. His brother told you. Weren't you listening?'

She smoothed a gum wrapper, running her thumb over it to iron out the creases. 'Maybe something was true.'

'In your dreams,' Cutler said. 'The guy was a dirt-bag.' He walked over to the sink and opened the cupboard underneath it. 'No imagination,' he said, pulling out a bulging plastic rubbish sack. 'It's always under the sink.' He tore it open and dumped the contents into the sink.

Nita turned away from the mess. She folded the gum wrapper into a perfect square. Before putting it into her pocket she surreptitiously held it to her nose and sniffed.

'Is this what you're looking for?' There was an unmistakable tone of triumph in Cutler's voice. With a pen, he lifted a tiny stained vest from the chaos of used teabags, cigarette ends, banana skins and beer cans.

Nita sighed.

'Tell me again how you found it,' he said. 'Describe the packaging.'

'I think it was Monday. It was in a taped-up brown paper bag with "How Now Brown Cow" where an address should be. Inside was the vest wrapped in the local paper and duct tape just like... '

'Okay,' he interrupted, separating some soggy brown paper and newspaper from the rest of the rubbish. 'We're going to need your Mr West in here. I'm about to break the terms of our contract.'

Bret West said, 'He didn't send it. That's not his style.'

'But he suppressed evidence,' Cutler snarled. The two men had built up a working animosity.

'I did too,' Nita said. 'I wanted lab tests.' They ignored her.

Bret said, 'If *she* wants him charged with fraud or thieving, I'd back her all the way. It could be her only chance to make her bank or card insurance agree to frigging pay her back—if there's a police report. But the sodding vest's your own fault. If you'd done anything but sit on your fat thumb about the doll, or been more fucking sensitive about the DNA it wouldn't of happened, now would it? By your own admission you're only here cos your twatting bosses want you to mend fences.'

'That's none of your flaming business,' Cutler grumbled. 'That's stuff I told *her*, not you. Your brother's in deep shit whether she makes an official complaint or not.'

'What you got here,' Bret said, enjoying himself, 'is a law-abiding kid, a teacher, for fuck's sake, who won't give the police the time of day no more. All because of your thick-headed, dumb nonsense. And you expect me to serve my little brother up to you on a sodding plate.'

'I told you once—I'm not talking to you about her. That's an ongoing investigation. But I do want to talk to that brother of yours.'

'But he's gone to LA,' Nita said. 'How can Mr West help you get him back?' They both turned to her, surprised she was still in the room.

A knock sounded at the door, making them all jump. Bret got up to open it and a plump man dressed in a mustard coloured sweater, which clashed horribly with his pink flushed face, lurched into the room. He carried a fistful of newspaper in one hand and a golf club in the other. He was brandishing both and sobbing uncontrollably at the same time.

Bret, knocked back against the wall by the force of his entry, tripped and landed on the floor.

'Where is he?' the man cried, his head turning from side to side, snot and tears flying.

'Uh-oh,' Cutler said, sounding almost bored, 'looks like there's another customer for the missing scum-bag.'

Bret scrambled to his feet saying, 'Oy, mate, you can't just gallop in here. It's private property.'

The man hit out wildly with the fist that held the newspaper and sent Bret tumbling again. He was screaming, 'He promised. He fucking swore. How could he do this to me?'

Bret said, 'Hey, Cutler, you're a policeman—fucking arrest him!'

'Private citizen,' Cutler said, 'or are *you* changing the rules now you're on your arse?' But he heaved himself slowly to his feet.

The man placed the end of the golf club in the middle of Cutler's chest and shoved. Cutler sat down so fast he almost somersaulted over the back of the sofa.

Shocked by such naked, undignified emotion in an adult, Nita got up. She said, 'Shush now, come here. What on earth's the matter? Have you got a handkerchief or a tissue? It's alright, really, it's alright. We'll make it alright.' While talking, she walked over to the man holding her hand out the way she would to a hysterical child. Gently she took the club away from him. She patted the hand, saying, 'What's it all about, then?'

He turned to her, hunching over, and put both arms around her, weeping into her neck and shoulder. He was so heavy he nearly pushed her down, but she struggled to stay upright and awkwardly stroked the mustard coloured wool. He smelled of citrus and diesel.

He said, 'I never knew I'd feel like this. I didn't care at the beginning—it was just another problem to solve.' His words were muffled by her shoulder and choked with tears. 'But it just wouldn't go away. *She* wouldn't go away. I just couldn't take it any longer.' He hiccupped twice and then seemed to pull himself together for a moment. Still speaking into Nita's neck, he said, 'Oh flick, did I just hit a policeman?'

'Don't worry about it,' Nita said. 'He's a good guy.'

'Don't flaming listen to her, sunshine,' Sergeant Cutler said, untangling himself from the sagging sofa.

'Oh crap,' the man said, letting go of Nita and straightening. 'Sorry—really, really sorry.' He turned and ran out of the room. Nita followed.

The man turned right, stopped, felt in his pocket for car keys, turned left and sprinted for the stairs.

Cutler and Bret arrived in time to hear his footsteps pounding down to the ground floor. They ran after him.

Nita turned right and walked to the next door down. It was wide open. A suitcase and a computer bag sat in the lobby with a thick black cashmere coat partially draped over them. Three copies of the Daily Telegraph and a What Car? Magazine lay on the floor. She didn't touch anything but went slowly back to Zach's flat.

The crumpled newspaper mustard man had dropped on the floor was Tuesday's copy of the City Chronicle. On the front page was the large article about the dead 'masseuse' in the Holyfield district, and a small one about a dead baby found in a skip on Guscott Road. Nita smoothed out the paper, folding it so that the two headlines could be seen, before placing it on the sofa next to where Cutler had been sitting.

She went to the window hoping to see what the men were doing. 'If you don't run, they won't chase you,' she murmured to herself. But the view from the window was of the river, grey and black with ice forming at the edges, sliding sullenly by. Nita shuddered and turned away. She couldn't understand anyone paying silly money to see it.

She wrapped herself in Bret's tartan rug once more and waited for the men to return.

22

Debts

///

They walked through the door pink with cold and exertion, out of breath—two middle-aged men, fresh from the hunt. Their prey escaped, but Nita could see the gleam in their eyes. Bret said, 'He had too much of a start,' while Cutler was on his mobile phone giving mustard man's vehicle registration number to a colleague.

Nita waited politely till he'd finished and put his phone back in his pocket. Then she said, 'He lives next door. He's just come back from a trip... ' She would have gone on but both men left the room at a brisk trot. Their sense of purpose made them alike.

When they came back Cutler was saying, 'It isn't a search, see. The guy left his door wide open. I just went in to make sure the premises are secure.'

'And you just happen to trip over his flight bag which fucking falls over and out spills his passport.'

'Accidents do happen,' Cutler said, sitting down almost on top of the newspaper Nita had folded for him.

'And you wonder why nobody effing trusts you.' Bret turned to Nita and went on, 'He's Ian Atwell. It doesn't look like he's lived next door long.' He paused, frowning. 'And what the fuck was you thinking about, just walking up to him like that?'

'That was stupid,' Cutler chimed in, seeming more than ever like Bret's twin. 'You could've been walloped. Golf clubs can make a nasty mess of your face, you know.'

'Oh please don't thank me,' Nita said, too miserable to be polite. 'He wasn't the violent type. He wanted someone to stop him.'

'And you're such a good judge of character,' Cutler said. 'Let me see now, do the names Zach West and Harris Searle ring any bells?'

'That's just nasty,' Nita said. 'If I wasn't forced to try and clear my own name I'd leave you to stew in your own juice and not point to the copy of the Chronic Mr Atwell had in his hand.'

'Where?'

'You're sitting on it,' Nita said, 'which is typical.' She bit her lip.

Cutler ignored her and raised his hammy thigh to pull the Chronicle from under it.

'Who the fuck's Harris Searle?' Bret asked.

'Harris Searle lives in Guscott Road,' Cutler explained. 'First off, she goes out with him. Then she accuses him of killing this woman.' He showed Bret the headline which said Local Youth Finds Dead Body. 'And after that, she thinks he sent her stuff like a doll with a nail through its mouth, and that baby's vest I just found in your brother's garbage.'

'Well, *someone* fucking sent them,' Bret said. 'And someone set fire to her house. I don't notice anyone falling over himself to investigate that. I'd say threats, intimidation and arson was worse than a piddling case of credit card fraud, wouldn't you?'

'The difference is I'm 125% sure your bleeding brother's guilty, and I like the stuff I'm sure of. I know what to do, see. And it isn't pissing about with someone who suppresses evidence. Have you looked at that vest? What use is it now? Talk about tainted! Forensics will just laugh.'

Nita said, 'It's Tuesday's Chronicle. He read something on the front page that really upset him.'

'What?' Cutler came back from his invigorating, manly argument with Bret reluctantly. 'Who?'

'Ian Atwell,' Nita said. 'There are two articles: one's about the dead baby. The other's about poor Maria.'

'Who's Poor Maria?' Cutler stared at her, mystified.

'The woman who was killed on the Holyfield Estate. You investigated it?'

'Oh, right. Her boyfriend practically coughed to that one.'

'Ahmed Karavez?'

'Oh, is that how you say it?'

'How would I know?' Nita asked in despair. 'He's from Tajikistan. I've never been there and I don't know how they pronounce names there.'

'See, I didn't even know how to pronounce Tajiki-whatsit. It's her superior education.' He looked towards Bret for support.

Bret ignored him, and said, 'He came in here waving the paper and asking for Zach. He said... what did he say? I was giving that fucking five iron my full attention.'

'You were flat on your arse, mate.'

Nita, on the point of giving up, said, 'He said Zach promised him something. He said, "How could he do this to me?"'

'A superior education *and* a photographic memory,' Cutler said. 'Isn't she something else?'

'Give me a break!' Nita shouted. 'What's your problem?'

'What's yours?' Cutler suddenly looked disconcerted. 'Relax. Where's your sense of humour?' He turned to Bret. 'They just don't get our sense of humour, mate.'

'Who's "they"?' Nita asked furiously.

'Oh crap,' Cutler said, 'women? Women don't understand my jokes.'

'You're fucking busted, mate,' Bret said, grinning from ear to ear. 'Racism or sodding sexism—which'll it be?' To Nita he added, 'Ignore him. He's just playing games. Be grateful he ain't on the fucking victim support team.'

'I'm just an old copper,' Cutler said, as if that excused everything.

Bret said, 'Then fucking listen, will you? She's saying Zach promised to do something for Ian Atwell and, big freaking shock, Zach didn't do it, or fucked it up. She's saying it has something to do with the dead baby or dead Maria. So she's saying if and when you catch up with Ian don't just steam in and charge him with knocking both of us flat on our flaming arses. How'm I doing so far?'

'Fine, thanks,' Nita said, 'but I'm afraid, if that's so, it follows that Zach's also involved. Sorry.'

'You don't have to tell me how to do my job,' Cutler said. 'Just cos I don't use fancy words doesn't mean I ain't a good copper.'

'I'm 125% sure Zach never killed a fucking soul. He's a lot of bad things but he ain't capable of killing. I know that 125%.'

'I knew that about myself too,' Nita said wearily. 'But look what's happened to me.'

'Cops won't fuck with my family. Wanna know why? It's because they knows people involved in property development got fucking lawyers popping out their fucking ears. That's why.'

'Are you threatening me?'

'Wouldn't fucking dream of it... mate. I'm suggesting if you want to search this flat you'll need a warrant. And I'm saying we're all leaving now. I'm locking up and then I'm taking this kid home. She looks done in.'

'Do you really want me to go to all the trouble of getting a warrant? It might piss me off.'

'Be pissed off with my blessing. You need one for next door anyway. Just do the job properly for a change.'

He showed exactly the same lack of respect for authority that Zach did, Nita thought. She didn't know if it was frightening or impressive.

She waited while he left the room, afraid that in his absence Cutler would turn on her. Instead he said, 'There are two things I'm authorised to tell you about Sergeant Eavers which might help you understand her behaviour. Wouldn't you like to drive home with me? Then maybe we can talk properly without always jumping down each others throats.'

Bret came back into the room cutting off her answer. He was carrying Zach's padded gilet. 'I suppose he didn't fucking think he'd need this in LA,' he said. 'It'll be way too big, but it might keep some of the cold out till you buy another coat.'

'Now who's being flaming insensitive?' Cutler sounded delighted. 'Why would she want to wear the jacket of the guy who's just ripped her off in the cruellest possible way?'

'To keep warm?'

'Feeling guilty? It's because of your dog-breath brother cleaning out her bank account she can't *afford* a flaming coat.'

He seemed to need an enemy, someone to clash with. Nita wondered how popular he was with his colleagues. She held out her hand for Zach's jacket. If Cutler hadn't spoken up she thought she would have refused it. It hung down halfway between her knees and hips, inadequate but better than nothing.

'That looks terrible,' Cutler said.

'Let me guess,' Bret said. 'You ain't married. Am I right?'

Cutler ignored him and turned to Nita. 'Are you coming with me?'

She said, 'Thanks for the offer, but I need to discuss property with Mr West.'

'Okay,' he said. 'Try not to get fleeced by both brothers in one bleeding day, eh? And when it all goes turd-shaped, don't say I didn't warn you.'

In the Mercedes, driving back across town, Bret said, 'It had to happen one day: the silly bugger had to be right once. But I withdraw my offer for your flat. It really don't seem fucking honourable.'

Nita fought off another attack of panic by deciding that if Bret thought Guscott Road was a desirable part of town then so would others. In any case it wasn't wise to consider the speedy sale of her flat before finding out just how much she owed to the bank and credit card companies. It was very odd but whenever she tried to decide which was worst—physical danger or debt and destitution—the two seemed equal. She could imagine herself filthy, homeless and in rags with the same horror as her painful death in a burning flat or suffocation in freezing water.

Not that Guscott Road seemed a particularly desirable part of town when they pulled up outside her house a few minutes later. It was not yet completely dark, but the street lights were already lit giving the road a grey and orange limbo-like look and turning all the rubbish strewn on her doorstep into weird sculptural shapes. Her front door was wide open showing the burnt interior of the hall like the blackened cavern of a corpse's mouth.

'Wait here,' Bret said getting out of the car.

Nita found a huge torch in his glove compartment and forced herself to get out too. It was her property after all, not his.

They stepped over the rubbish and shone the torchlight into the hall—just as Toby, Leo and an elegant stranger came out of the ground floor flat.

'Who's that?' Toby said, squinting into the light. 'Nita, is that you? This is so spooky. We didn't think about bringing a torch. This is Armando; he's going to give us a quote for redecoration.'

'And while we're at it,' Leo said, 'we thought we might do the whole flat. Armando thinks Bauhaus but we're worried about the Georgian proportions. Aren't we Tobes?'

'I'm so sorry about the rubbish,' Nita said in a rush.

'Not your rubbish,' Bret said loudly.

'Not your fault,' Toby said.

'But it wouldn't be happening if I wasn't living here.'

'Do not on any account give in to the small-minded insects of this sad world,' Armando said. 'I think we have an opportunity. We could cover front of house with graffiti art. I know many graffiti artists—is not a problem. Bring brutalist beauty to this little, little street.'

'I still worry about the Georgian proportions,' Leo said.

'But it's an absolutely *super* idea,' Toby said, 'and we'll give it lots and lots of thought, won't we Leo?'

'Oh lots.'

Bret said, 'I was telling Nita, I can fix your hall lighting very quickly.'

'Would spoil brutalist theme. With imagination we could make this tame little hall like Palestine. Create world statement in one little, little terrace house. Make cover of Design Interiors.'

'I don't know,' Nita said. 'I might not want to live in a statement.'

'How quick is very quickly?' Leo asked Bret.

'I have an electrician working across the road. He could be over here in five minutes. I can get one of the lads to clear up the rubbish and make a start on your wall right now.'

'How much?'

'For the cost of materials.' Bret said. 'If you want more than just the basics to make it safe we can talk. But I owe Nita a favour.'

'You can't pay Zach's debts...'

'Nothing to do with Zach. It's for saving me from Ian Atwell and his fucking five iron.'

Leo glanced meaningfully at Toby who said, 'We'd be very grateful if someone could come over now.'

'Cowards. Armando cannot work except for clients prepared to take risk.'

Seeing Toby and Leo's stricken expressions Nita said, 'I'm sorry, Armando, I'm the coward. I'm scared of falling downstairs in the dark. I really need a light. Toby and Leo are very serious risk-takers. Honest.'

'Yes, honest,' Toby said. 'And we're *very* interested in Bauhaus. But Nita's sensitive to graffiti, aren't you Neets?'

'I am.' She watched Bret turn and cross the road to number 15 unsure of how she felt about allowing him to help. He said

he owed her, but she doubted the truth of this. She was glad
it had been Leo and Toby who'd given him the go-ahead. She
didn't want to have too much to do with him. Maybe he was
reliable and a man of his word, but in this case words were the
problem—he simply sounded too much like Zach. And Nita
promised herself that she was going to forget all about Zach
as soon as she possibly could. It wouldn't be easy because of
the debts, but she knew she could find a way to dissociate his
memory from those. She'd done it before. But she couldn't do
it if she kept hearing his voice.

Toby said, 'Nita? You're off in fairy land. Leo was just asking
if we could have a cup of tea in yours. We're out of fresh milk
and nobody's cleaned up since the party and our place pongs a
bit. So would you be a darling...?'

Leo said, 'Have I got this right? Bret West is the developer
who's doing up number 15? So presumably he knows what he's
up to where electricians et cetera are concerned.'

They left Armando gazing critically at the front door and
went upstairs. Leo was muttering, 'Statement, my arse! This is *foul*.
The more I think about it, Tobes, the more I think Armando's
full of BS.'

'But he's hot.'

'Yes but haven't you noticed, Tobes, hot guys are often full
of BS?'

'I usually don't notice that until too late,' Toby said sadly.
And Nita found his sadness comforting.

Even more comforting was the look in Leo's eyes when
he accepted a mug of tea. It was the way he normally looked.
After the fire she'd caught an expression which made her think
he was blaming her. Now they wanted to sit, relax and coo
with sympathy about the way the police had treated her. It was
friendship, she thought. It didn't go very deep but it was there
and she was grateful.

23

Destroying Daughters

///

Bret West tapped on the door and came in. 'You've got light. Your friend walked off in a tantrum. I don't know why. And my guy, Baz, found something interesting in the garbage he cleared off of your doorstep.' He showed them an envelope, soggy and stained by kitchen waste.

Toby said, 'Means nothing to me. Do you think Armando heard us talking about hot guys?'

'Oh dear,' Nita said, recognising the name on the envelope.

'What I thought I'd do,' Bret said, 'is photocopy it and then give it to sodding Cutler. See if he can move his lazy arse if someone's already done most of the work.'

'He'll say it isn't evidence because we didn't leave it on the doorstep for the police to deal with.'

'Like we left everything else,' Leo said. 'I mean, the Fire Brigade said it was as clear a case of arson as they ever saw. They sent a report to the cops. But have the cops been here to look? Have they? No they have not. And why? Because we're just a couple of fags and a brown girl. I said to my solicitor, "This wouldn't have anything to do with sexuality and ethnicity, would it?" And he said, "I'm afraid you might be right." But I don't want to be right. I mean we're medical students—about to become pillars of the community. And she's a teacher. But the cops don't care. We're queer and foreign. End of.'

'There are worse things to be,' Toby said, taking Leo's hand. 'Aren't there, Neets?'

'Yes,' Leo said, 'racist, sexist, cruel. Like the pond-life who threw rubbish on our doorstep.'

'Actually, she's just a working mother who thinks I've been unfair to her son,' Nita said, looking at the soggy envelope and the red lettering on it which meant it was a final demand. 'She's a terrible mother. And she's ignorant. And she thinks everyone else is responsible for her troubles. But when you think about it she's just a representative of yet another minority having a hard time.'

'So what do you want to do?' Bret was looking uncomfortable. 'Set up a sodding support group or stop the bitch harassing you?'

The phone rang and without thinking Nita answered it.

Mina said, as she always did, 'Nita, is that you?'

'Mina, how wonderful—but this isn't Sunday... '

'I haven't got long.' Mina sounded very shaky and as if she was speaking from under a blanket. 'Ash just rang. He says I must warn you. Shsh, don't interrupt—he says someone in the British police has told Father where you live. He says Father has consulted Uncle Jag. Ash is afraid they will bring all the cousins to find you, and he's afraid they will make him go too.'

The room darkened and seemed to lurch ever so slightly. Moisture suddenly glued her hand to the telephone. She said, 'Is this true?' But she knew it was true and that this was the call she'd been expecting for over a year.

Mina said, 'Nita darling, this may be the last time we will talk to each other directly. I think perhaps you ought to leave your home—Ash sounded very scared. But I don't know. We might be worrying unnecessarily because, well, my husband says you are wrong—if this family is as bad as you think you would be dead a long time ago. He says many girls have paid a far greater price for what you did.'

'For what was done to *me*,' Nita began, outraged, and then became aware suddenly that Toby, Leo and Bret were staring at her. She was on her feet looking down at the street as if she were on watch for an invading army, but she couldn't remember getting up from her chair. She turned to look at Toby, willing him to take some initiative and lead the others out of her flat. But he smiled at her, not understanding.

Mina started to speak, but Nita cut her off saying, 'Thank you so much for warning me. I know how difficult it is for you.'

She was about to ask the men to leave when Mina began to cry. 'Nita darling, sisters should stick together, but... but... '

'Please don't cry, Mina. I'll be alright.'

'It's always a question of loyalty to the family. But I am not allowed to decide who is my family.'

'Oh Mina.' Nita was fighting tears. 'Your *children* will always be your family. I don't understand how anyone can turn you against them but... '

'*Our* mother turned against *you*.' Mina was sobbing. 'Why is it alright to murder a daughter? Why could I not keep my last daughter? Why must I pray each night that the child I'm carrying is a son?'

'Come home,' Nita cried. 'Bring the babies. We'll find somewhere to live. Somewhere no one can find us. We'll raise the kids together and they will be safe.'

Mina was crying so hard she could scarcely speak. She said, 'Ash told me you are accused of killing the daughter of your betrothed. I told him it can't be true, but he said this man shamed you.'

'The shame part is true. The rest is a lie.' Nita could feel the eyes of three strange men boring into her back. 'That man brought me nothing but shame and it has followed me into my new life.' The back of her head prickled and she felt queasy. She should not be talking like this in front of men.

Mina said, 'Why didn't you tell me? All you said was that you refused him.'

'It was when Ammy was being born. What could you have done? I thought they must've told you everything later.'

'They may have told my father—I mean my *husband*. But he didn't bother to tell me. What happened?'

'I can't talk about it now.' Nita was caught between Mina and her alien audience like a bug is caught between wind and windscreen. It could be the last time she'd hear her sister's voice. She gestured forcefully to the men that they should leave and turned again to the view of the cold road. She said, 'You know I didn't want to leave college. I didn't want to live abroad with strangers. I didn't like him. You know all this. So I refused, which I thought was my right.'

'It *is* your right. In theory.' There was bitterness in Mina's voice that Nita had never heard before.

She saw, in reflection, the men leaving the room so she said hurriedly, 'He followed me to college and to the halls of residence. And he... he refused my refusal. He thought... he had been told... after... after what he did to me... that I could no longer refuse because... because otherwise I would be outcast or worse. You know all this.' Mina must have known this, she thought. The family could not have spoken about anything else. Even in Mumbai.

'Where did you find the courage, Nita? How did you grow to be so brave?'

Yes, Nita thought. Of course she knew. She'd simply been unable to face it so she'd turned away. Which is the only thing left for the totally powerless to do.

'I wasn't brave,' Nita said gently. 'I thought I had the right. I thought my family would support me. And then, when he did what he did, I thought they would punish *him*. And when they didn't, I thought the law of this country would protect me. Mina, I wasn't brave; I was stupid.'

'I hate them all,' Mina cried. 'Even the women. Nita, they agree to everything. They support the system and bully their sisters. They can't help it because they didn't go to school. But, oh Nita, I'm turning into one of them. I'm even forgetting my language. I sound like them now, and I'm beginning to hate myself. If I can't find my own courage to refuse, I might even accept destroying another daughter.'

'Come home. Say that the heat is making you too sick this time—that you have to see your parents.'

'Yes, yes,' Mina muttered, 'that's what I'll say. It's true: I am sick and weak all the time now.'

'You've never been home. Mina, I haven't seen you for six years.'

'And Ash. But Nita, you must leave your home. Now. Right now. It's been two hours since Ash rang. I couldn't use the phone—I'm never alone.'

'I'll be alright. Don't worry. Just come. And remember, if we can't talk, there's email, snail-mail and Ash. I can protect you and the babies.'

'But Nita...' Suddenly there was a click and silence followed by the despairing growl of dial tone.

'Don't go,' Nita wailed. She hugged the plastic receiver. Outside, the road went in and out of focus and she found herself staring, brainless, down into the skip where a mess of nearly twenty empty paint cans lay tumbled on top of another dead Christmas tree.

There was a tap on the door. The men, it seemed, had removed themselves only as far as the kitchen. They'd made a fresh pot of tea and Leo was carrying the tray. He said, 'Are you all right? You look terrible. That was more bad news, wasn't it?'

Terrified of what they might have heard, what she might be forced to explain, Nita turned back to the window and said, 'It's the middle of February.' She addressed Bret's dim reflection in the glass. 'Where do all the Christmas trees come from?'

'It's one of life's little mysteries,' he said easily. 'It doesn't matter what fucking time of year it is—even June or July—you stick a skip out in the road—you score Christmas trees. Fact of life.'

'It's like they're offerings to the skip goddess,' Nita said, 'or is it the other way round—like she's generating them? An appropriate offering to modern society—dead symbols of what used to be fertility which now have come to signify unconfined greed.'

'Sit down before you fall down,' Toby said. 'Now is not the time to wax whimsical.'

'You're right. I need to be practical.' She had a stark choice to make: she could ask a stranger for help or she could live on the street. Last time she'd gone to a strange man she had thought it was a professional relationship, one governed by the exchange of money for expertise. Now she had no money left, and consequently, no control.

She turned to face Bret directly this time. 'I need to ask another favour. I have to move out of here. It's only temporary, but can I stay for a short while at the flat Zach was looking after? I'll pay rent and I'll clean it up.'

Before he could answer, the phone rang again making Nita flinch. She answered cautiously. A young, pompous voice said, 'Ms Terry? I'm so sorry I haven't been able to contact you until now—today has been brutal.' It was the solicitor from the firm Miss Whitby had recommended.

She said, 'Can I call you back in a couple of hours?'

'I was rather hoping to get home in time to help bath the baby,' the plummy voice wheedled. 'Unless, of course this really can't keep till tomorrow?'

Would there be a tomorrow? Nita wondered. She couldn't even remember what it was she needed a solicitor for. It was too late for him to prevent the police from sampling her DNA or to stop Mr Hughes from suspending her. Which of the current crop of catastrophes was he qualified to assist with? Could he ask a judge to put a restraining order on her father, her uncle and her cousins? How long would that take? There was no time.

In the end, because there was too much to tell, she told him nothing and rang off after agreeing to call in the morning. Bret was staring at her so she said, 'Really, ignore me. I shouldn't have put you in such an awkward position.'

Toby said, 'It sounds to us like you're the one in an awkward position. What the hell's going on, Neets?'

Bret said, 'You're crap at asking for help, aren't you? Or is it just me? Because of my miserable kak-covered brother?'

'So many things have happened,' Nita began, 'graffiti, fire through the letterbox, rubbish on the doorstep. Now someone from the police has told my father where I am. So he and my uncle have rounded up a posse of cousins and I can't let them find me here. I can't possibly tell you the reason because it's one of those stories that create prejudice against families like mine. I sort of feel embarrassed—it's as if I've stopped being me and become an immigrant cliché.'

'Bit of a mess, isn't it?' Leo said. He took her hand and made her sit next to him on the sofa. Toby put a mug of tea in her other hand saying, 'Being a cliché is *such* fun.'

Leo as usual saw the serious implications. 'Is the house going to come under attack again? We ought to think about protecting our property as well as our persons. It's a pity recent events have dented our faith in the boys in blue.'

'I know,' Toby began enthusiastically. 'We should hire the penthouse suite at the best hotel in town and live on room-service till the threat has passed.'

Bret took a deep breath and said, 'Okay, okay—you can all stay at River House if you want to—I don't bleeding care. Just don't paint the fucking walls pink.'

'See what I mean about clichés?' Toby sighed dramatically. 'You're very sweet, big butch Bret, but Leo and I are staying with Pete and Mike who would be thrilled if we had time to paint the walls pink instead of saving the world with our burgeoning medical skills.'

'Well excuse the fuck out of me,' Bret said. 'I'm just trying to save your scrawny necks.'

'Well excuse the fuck out of *me*.' Toby loved a good scrap. 'Nita's neck is *so* not scrawny. She's small but perfectly formed.'

'I didn't mean...'

'Oh do shut up,' Leo said. 'The speed with which you can turn tragedy into farce constantly amazes me. How are we going to protect the house?'

'Daphne!' Toby said, with the air of a man who's discovered gravity. 'Nita, you go and pack. Big butch Bret, you get someone to change the locks. Leo, where's that list of things we want? You could get started on that. I'll go and talk to Daphne.'

'Who the fuck's Daphne?' Bret said, looking bemused.

'And we do have to tell the police,' Leo said, 'at very least for insurance purposes. Sorry Nita, I know it's your family, but we can't afford another fire. I'll do that, and I'll give them the envelope Bret found—for all the good it'll do.'

'I don't think my family would vandalise the house,' Nita said. 'They have great respect for property. Ryan's mum is a different matter. I'm sorry for her but she endangered lives when she started the fire. If it was her.'

'Have you any bleedin' doubt?' Bret asked.

'Always,' Nita said. 'And Leo, whatever you do, don't tell the police about River House. It was a cop who told my father where to find me.'

24

River House

//

The flat in River House smelled of Zach's hair—the sharp foxy scent of male sebum that was stored in old pillows and leaked slowly into stale air like blood into water.

For the second time in two days Nita put on rubber gloves and attacked dirt and the subtle odour of a thief. She scoured away at the greasy print of alien hands on the surface of what was to be her home. She tried to clean from her mind the memory of his fair head and tobacco coloured eyes, the sight of his strong square hands and the way he smiled when she cooked for him. It seemed in keeping with what she now knew that though his hair had always appeared clean, his pillow was filthy. She was glad she'd brought her own.

While she worked she also tried to blot out her last sight of Guscott Road. As she'd loaded her things into the back of the Mercedes she saw an elderly woman, who had no gloves to protect her swollen purple hands, peer hopefully into the skip. Hope died when she saw the mean harvest there, and she shuffled away mumbling to herself. The city wasn't kind to homeless women.

A couple of minutes earlier Diane and Stu had walked by. Diane saw her and instead of a greeting she ostentatiously held her nose as if Nita smelled foul. Bret watched and said nothing.

Nita was grateful for his silence but wished he had not been a witness.

As she scrubbed she felt the bitterness collect beneath her skin like an abscess—an abscess so inflamed and swollen she was afraid it would burst and flood the whole flat with corruption and anger.

Or maybe, she thought as she scoured the bathroom, her rage would break out of her like fire and cauterise everything in its path, cleansing all the insults and betrayals, burning to cinders everyone who had insulted or betrayed her.

Then she thought, no, I'm not that lucky: my rage is not fire, it's pus. When it breaks it won't cleanse, it will soil. And who will be left to wipe up the mess? Me. Just as I am doing now.

—⁂—

Even though she'd brought her own bedding she lay down to sleep on the sofa. Sleep didn't come willingly. She could hear the screams of urban foxes from the riverbank and occasionally the cry of a city seagull sounding like a baby in a tantrum.

She thought about her father chasing her out of her bed, her house, and forcing her to this flat where all the cleaning in the world made no difference to its shabbiness and need of decoration. She thought about her own fresh white paint and vibrant fabrics. She thought about the faint warm scent of cooking that clung to her kitchen curtain. Whatever happened, until her father's death, she would never be able to live there again.

Her father's rage had centuries of tradition behind it and was supported by his whole community. Her father's anger was righteous: it was the anger of a man—one who was accustomed to being obeyed without discussion. His rage had certainly been fire and all she could do was run away.

Maybe it had cooled now, become a frozen, solid thing like a glacier—slower moving but just as capable of destroying everything in its path; an anger justified by custom; a huge and terrible force rolling down a hillside towards her.

Nita, who had been bred for obedience, even when she had reason and simple humanity on her side, could not quite accept that her own anger was justified too. Her own anger, she felt, could only destroy herself and she didn't need any more destruction.

After an hour she got up and went to the kitchen. There was a bottle of Southern Comfort in one of the cupboards. She'd put it there along with a handful of juicy fruit gum packets she'd been unable to throw away. First she unwrapped a stick of gum and popped it into her mouth. Maybe it was time to pick up a habit that involved chewing but would not make her fat: comfort without punishment. There was a small explosion of metallic sweetness in her mouth and the back of her nose that almost made her gag. She thought, What kind of fruit is this? And almost spat it out. What had been an endearing smell on Zach's breath was a foreign taste in her mouth. She reached for a glass and poured herself a shot of Southern Comfort. She didn't know if she was supposed to add water so she hesitated for a moment before tipping some into her mouth. Juicy fruit and Southern Comfort collided on her tongue and this time she really did gag, spitting it all into the sink.

There were centuries of tradition behind her gag reflex, she thought, annoyed with herself. Bugger centuries of tradition; tradition is no friend of mine.

Southern Comfort tasted a bit better without the chewing gum. It was sweet and sticky, but it hit the back of her throat like pepper. She finished the shot as if it were medicine. She poured some more and went back to her lumpy, sagging sofa.

In her mind was the picture, taken from books, TV and film, of someone, usually a man, passed out on a sofa, oblivious to noise and emotional storms. Oblivion was what she needed now, or failing that, Dutch courage. She was entering a new alcoholic world where courage was Dutch and comfort was Southern, she thought, doggedly swallowing more booze. If it could make her forget her family, the police, the credit card company or Zach, then, unlike tradition, it could become her new best friend.

Look at me now, she thought with a kind of awe, it's three in the morning and I'm drinking alcohol.

She was just beginning to relax when someone knocked softly. She leaped to her feet and stared at the door as if it had produced a voice of its own and spoken to her. Wrapping her duvet around her like a cloak she tiptoed across the room. The tapping repeated and a human voice said, 'I know you're there—I can see the light under the door.'

It could not be a member of her family because the voice was too English, so her first horrified thought was that Harris Searle had followed her to River House.

'Let me in,' the voice pleaded. 'Surely you don't want the police to find me here.'

It couldn't possibly be Harris Searle: he would never plead. Her reasoning was as slow as a country bus. She thought, If it isn't Harris it can't be dangerous, and opened the door without even putting on the security chain.

The man in the mustard sweater looked as startled to see her as she was to see him. She stepped back, tripped on the trailing duvet and fell. Ian Atwell came in hurriedly and closed the door behind him.

'Where's Zach?' he asked. He looked terrible: his eyes were bloodshot, his skin was mottled with cold and his nose was red and raw. He turned away from her and took a quick tour of the flat, looking in cupboards and behind doors.

Nita scrambled to her feet trying to reassemble both her cloak and her dignity. The last time she'd seen Ian Atwell he'd wept on her shoulder. He didn't seem at all threatening.

He returned to the living room saying, 'What were the police doing here? Where's Zach? Who are you?' He stood in front of her swaying unsteadily. 'Have you got anything to drink?'

'You're drunk,' Nita said, realising with astonishment that she was too. It had happened too quickly for her to have noticed.

Previously she'd assumed that you achieved inebriation only after several hours work. She went to the kitchen and brought back the bottle and another glass.

He wrinkled his nose in distaste. 'Is there any ice?'

'No, but there's frozen pizza.'

'Who the hell are you?' He stared at her in confusion.

'My name's Nita Teh... Teh... Tehri and Zach ripped me off for thoushands and thoushands... thousands of pounds. He told me he was a private investigator and I believed him. How shtupid am I?' She poured him a hefty splash of Southern Comfort and added a little more to her own glass. Being drunk, she decided, was really quite pleasant. It made her feel reckless and feckless, entirely foreign to herself. No wonder alcohol was forbidden.

'What were the police doing here?'

'Only one of them was a poleeshman, Shergeant Cutler, and he's a jerk. The other one was Zach's brother. He only shounds like Zach. Otherwise he's quite nice. But he isn't going to pay Zach's debts. And I don't blame him.'

He sat down in the chair opposite the sofa. 'Were they looking for me?'

'No, but they are now.' She sat down and balanced the bottle on the arm of the sofa with exaggerated care. 'You should never, never run. It's like a ball to a dog—if you run they chase. Shimple as that.'

'What do they know about me?'

'Not as much as I do. But even the jerk will work it out if you give him enough time. You should just confesh all and blame Zach. He's gone to LA. I didn't mean to, but I bought him the ticket. I gave him my last remaining credit card and away he flew. How shtupid is that?'

'About as stupid as me thinking he'd give her a decent burial. I gave him five thousand pounds and he gave me his solemn promise. He's just a conman, isn't he?'

'He's a guy with tobacco coloured eyes,' Nita said sadly. 'He looks at you and you think he's lishtening so you tell him shtuff. He isn't lishtening; he's waiting for an opportunity.'

'You know, I think you may be right.' Ian took a deep draught of his drink and closed his eyes. 'I got drunk with him and told him things—the worst, biggest secrets—things I should never have told anyone. He said, "Just leave it with me; I'll take care of everything." He said, "I have a friend. He can find us space in consecrated ground. It'll be expensive but respect and peace of mind don't come cheap." That's what he told me.'

'What was his friend's name?' Nita had tears in her eyes.

'Josh. Why?'

'It doesn't matter. Well, it does to me. At least the imaginary friend he told me about had a different name. At least shome of what he told me was original.'

'You're in love with him, aren't you?'

'No way!' Nita was utterly dismayed. 'I didn't fall for him; I fell for his line. I trushted him, and sho did you.'

Ian said, 'Gimme another slug of SC,' and Nita passed him the bottle.

She said, 'Why is it called a slug? I don't see shlugs when I think of alcohol.'

'Slug as in hit, dummy,' he said, 'not as in garden pest. Where were you brought up?'

'Leicester.' Nita was so unused to being called a dummy that she started to giggle. 'It wasn't a drinking culture. I wonder why the language of booze shares some of its vocabulary with the language of violence. Like, shlug, shot, hit, ooh and bombed.'

'Slaughtered.'

'Dead drunk.'

'Dead,' Ian said and burst into tears. 'Where is she now? Where are they keeping her? What're they doing to her? They're cutting her up, aren't they? To find out her secrets. They're chopping bits off her to keep in bottles. Men with microscopes and no pity.'

Nita felt sympathetic tears well up in her own eyes. She was vaguely aware that he was saying things she needed to hear, important information. But the sight of his distress was so overwhelming that she just wanted to comfort him. She wanted to go to him as if he were one of her kids and let him cry on her shoulder the way he had before. But she was paralysed by the knowledge that under the cloak of her duvet she was only wearing her Snoopy pyjamas. In her eyes that made her almost naked. She absolutely must not, never, no way, comfort a man in her pyjamas.

It was a difficult, delicate matter to which she gave slow rococo thought. Then she said, 'Have you eaten at all today?'

'Eaten?'

'You've been drinking but...?'

'What're you talking about?' But he was a plump man and Nita watched the idea of food take hold of him. 'I had breakfast in Strasbourg,' he said, 'and then I came home and saw the headline.'

'Nothing since?'

'Well, crisps and beer nuts.'

'Thatsh not enough, is it?' Nita said, trying for her best junior school teacher voice. 'The only food here is frozen pizza. That'll have to do.'

'I like pizza,' he said following her to the kitchen. He blew his nose on kitchen paper and rinsed his face under the tap.

Nita drank two glasses of water. She didn't think she should be drunk in charge of an unfamiliar microwave. But she liked being drunk. She loved feeling that things didn't matter very much. They weren't tragic, they were only temporary. It was wonderful to be able to talk without inspecting her words in case she was saying too much or telling things that should be kept secret. Restraint and reticence weren't worth the effort.

It was hard to cook pizza with a duvet round her shoulders so she went away to the bathroom to put on more clothes. It didn't matter how relaxed she felt—pyjamas were not suitable attire for pizza with a strange man.

25

Confession

///

I an said, 'I met her in Berlin at a trade fair. She was there with her father. She was already very good at languages. She said it was because she'd lived in so many places.' He tore at his pizza slice with big healthy teeth. He didn't look like a man built for misery; it had been thrust upon him.

'I was doing business with her father. His English was pretty good but my Arabic is frightful so he brought her along to help translate—oil the wheels. She was only sixteen then but very confident and well-educated. He was looking for an English boarding school for her last two years. He was hoping she'd go to an English university. I don't know where he got the idea that the English provide a superior education.'

Nita cut another slice and passed it to him.

'My company was courting his company at the time, so I sort of agreed to help find a suitable establishment for Alia. Which I did. And then I kept in touch, and me and my girlfriend would take her out for a meal sometimes or the theatre. I swear, at the beginning, I was just doing a favour for a rich client. I don't know how it happened. I just got more and more fond of her. And she'd come to me about anything at all, like if she was having trouble at school, or she'd overspent that month. My God, could that girl spend money! But, see, she was daddy's little princess and he just extended her credit every time.

'I don't know, maybe the money made her seem more sophisticated than she was. I promise you, up till then all my girlfriends had been roughly my own age. I'm not a guy who drools about schoolgirls, honestly I'm not.' He stared at Nita with damp blue eyes. 'You've got to believe me—I've never done anything like it before and I'll never do anything like it again.'

'Okay,' Nita said warily.

'I knew it,' he said in despair. 'You don't believe me. No one's ever going to believe me. I didn't rape her, and she didn't come on to me. It just happened. And I felt like the luckiest man in the world. I was that stupid. I'm hardly a stud, but maybe it was because I look so very English, so belonging to the host nation. I don't know. Even now, I can't understand what else she could've seen in me. I was just an employee in a firm her father was doing business with. I'm nothing special.'

He did look typically English, Nita agreed silently. Not that she thought it was much of a recommendation.

'*Do* you believe me?' He asked as if her answer really mattered to him.

'I think so.' But Nita wondered if he had any idea of the power the older man, the father-figure, wielded over some young girls. It seemed inconceivable that anyone as wishy-washy as Ian wielded any power at all, and maybe Alia had never seen him with tears and snot pouring down his face. But that surely was the point; there was genuine grief behind his drunken show of emotion.

He was still staring at her, wanting something, so she said, 'Sometimes mistakes are made between people of different cultures.'

'Yes,' he said, relieved. 'She wasn't sophisticated at all. She didn't even know she was pregnant till it was way too late for an abortion. And then of course it was panic stations. She was a big girl who could take extra weight without showing too much so we had a bit of time. She told her father that she was being sent on a course to Scotland. She told the school her father was taking her to Switzerland for the skiing. I backed her up. Then I broke up with my girlfriend and Alia moved into my flat.

'We were going to do everything properly, I swear, and put the baby up for adoption. Don't look at me like that.'

'Like what?'

'You don't understand: I *wanted* to marry her. I couldn't think of anything I wanted more. But she wouldn't. Apparently her future was all mapped out in her father's mind and it didn't include an ordinary, not very wealthy, Englishman. Or an unwanted baby. She told me that promises had been made since before she was born and you can't change those kinds of plans.'

'Some families in some cultures are very inflexible.' Nita was feeling a lot less drunk now. She wasn't sure she wanted to hear the rest of the story. With a sick lurch she realised it could only end one way—in a skip outside her house.

Ian went on: 'It didn't matter how westernized her father was, she simply could not be pregnant by me. I never really understood—what could he have done to her that was so awful?'

Nita shuddered and said, 'I don't know where she comes from or who her family is but her father can probably do quite lot. Including having her killed.'

'All girls say, "My dad'll kill me".'

'Some girls mean it.'

'But then, you see, it seemed to have more to do with losing face than with morality. She met a woman from her own country in London and she came back much more cheerful and told me what this woman had said. Apparently there's a doctor in Harley Street who does a thriving business in reconstructing virgins so that the men they're supposed to marry won't suspect a thing. Did you know that? I didn't, and I was really shocked. Can you imagine, you're so ignorant you don't know you're pregnant but you do know a doctor who'll restore your virginity? How bizarre is that?'

'I think it should tell you something about the importance of virginity in some cultures.'

'It tells me more about hypocrisy.'

'Maybe,' Nita said, 'but you're not entitled to make that judgement unless you have to live with the consequences of breaking a certain culture's rules.'

'But I do have to,' Ian cried. 'I've lived with the consequence in my freezer for nearly a year. I've kept Alia's secret, and changed my job so that I'd never have to meet her father again. But she just walked away and became a virgin again as if nothing happened.'

He reached for the bottle and poured himself another shot.

Nita was beginning to think that she wasn't tipsy enough to talk to a man about virginity. She helped herself to a little more Southern Comfort too. There wasn't very much left.

She tried to focus on what was important. 'What went wrong? Why did you end up with your daughter in your freezer?'

'Oh God,' he mumbled, 'this is so ridiculous. When I told Zach he just sat there with his mouth open. He could not believe it.'

Of course this wasn't the first time Ian had got drunk and told this story. He'd done it once before—with disastrous consequences for both of them.

He took a sip from his glass and went on, 'Like I said, we were supposed to be doing it properly, with scans and hospital visits. She said she kept all the appointments. She said... But I came home one evening—I'd spent two days abroad—and I found her on the bedroom floor. She was in labour. Of course I was going to take her to hospital. Of *course* I was. But she became hysterical. She said she'd never registered. She wasn't in the system. She'd been too afraid to go the hospital in case anyone ever found her medical records.

'It was an emergency—I didn't think to ask the obvious question: if she wasn't registered as pregnant, how could she legally put the baby up for adoption? Was she planning to leave it outside a hospital somewhere?

'I wasn't thinking about logical questions, I was running around like a blue-arsed fly with towels and water. Things were moving so fast I could hardly keep up. I mean, one minute I'd been parking the car and the next I was up to my elbows in blood and shit. I never knew having a baby was so gory. I think I was in shock.

'But somehow or other the baby was born and I think she was fine. She had all her fingers and toes. She was covered in blood but it was all stuff that would wash off. I wrapped her in a towel and gave her to Alia. The bedroom looked like a car crash. Alia was on the floor and I got her into bed. I think I'd used every towel I had in the place. There was blood everywhere. When I try to remember, that's all I see. I even thought, looking at the blood, this could just as well be a murder as a birth.

'Alia was very tired. I was still trying to persuade her to let me call an ambulance, but she said, "Bring me a drink. I'm parched. I need sweet tea." So I went and made the tea. I was nearly finished when she called me back into the bedroom. She said, "There's something wrong with the baby."

'I looked and the baby was still as bloody as if it'd been in a car crash. But she said, "It isn't breathing."

'You know what the really, really stupid thing is? I don't know for sure it was breathing when I gave it to Alia to hold. I hadn't held it upside-down and smacked it till it cried like they do in the movies because I was afraid of hurting it. I didn't know what I was doing, see. I'd just wanted to wrap it up warm and give it to Alia.

'But you know what? She said, "It's dead," and she handed it back to me. Then she rolled over to face the wall and, I swear to God, she went straight to sleep.'

'But why didn't you call an ambulance then? They might've been able to help.'

'Because, oh God, because when I looked at Alia sleeping I noticed blood on the pillow next to her and—I don't know what I was thinking—maybe I was hallucinating—but the bloody image on the pillow was like the Turin shroud—I could've sworn I could see the little baby's face there. I thought Alia must've taken that pillow and put it over the baby's face and smothered it. And I realised that if I called an ambulance or a doctor there'd be a post-mortem and then they'd know. I couldn't do that to Alia, I just couldn't.'

'What did she say?'

'She was asleep. So I sat on the edge of the bed and I didn't know what to do. It was already wrapped in a towel so I put it in a clean pillow case so that I could cover its face. Then I drank the tea I'd made for Alia and waited for her to wake up.

'She slept for ten hours straight, and I'm ashamed to say I did too. When she woke up it was morning. I took her tea and toast, and then I said, "Alia, what're we going to do?"'

'And she said, "About what?"'

'I said, "About the baby."'

'And she said, "What baby?"'

'I said, "Your baby."'

'She said, "I haven't got a baby." And she just stared at me as if I was stark staring mad. It was as if we were total strangers: we'd never met, never fallen in love. And she'd never been pregnant.

'That's when I thought she was acting, and I was absolutely convinced she'd killed the baby. Then the next minute she said, "I'm going to be late for school, will you give me a lift?" And then I was equally convinced she'd gone bonkers and blocked everything out. Her eyes were completely blank, like some time in the night she'd built a wall in her head. She was on one side and I was on the other.

'She got up and went to the bathroom and I heard water running. When she came back she was staggering slightly and she said, "I've got a really heavy period; will you phone the school?" She was obsessed with her school.

'I reminded her that the school thought she was in Switzerland with her father, and she seemed to accept that. But when she looked at me I caught this expression of such fear and, I don't know, it wasn't exactly hatred—I don't know what it was but I was afraid to go anywhere near her.

'Then I thought maybe it was me. Maybe when I was helping deliver the baby I'd accidentally done something terrible. I'd killed it, and she was blaming me.'

'Didn't she need a doctor?' Nita asked hesitantly. She was horrified by the story, and confused, not knowing which of the participants she identified with most. She wanted him to go on, and yet she didn't want him to finish the story. Because when he finished the story she would have to come face to face with the truth. This was the story Ian had told Zach. Ian said, 'Of course she needed a goddamn doctor. But as time went by we were sort of stuck in this web of secrecy and silence. I rang my boss and told him I'd caught a virus on the plane. So I was with her, looking after her for a few days. But we didn't speak. I wanted to, and now and then I'd try, but there was that mad panicky expression again and I couldn't. I put the baby in the freezer so that she wouldn't have to see it. I didn't want to see it either.

'Then of course I couldn't put off going back to work. To tell the truth, I wanted to go. I couldn't wait to get out of there. Work was normality. When I was at work I could cope. Everyone there thought I'd been really ill—I'd lost so much weight, see. But when I went home I was as mad as she was. Or bad. I didn't know which. It was an unreal place—full of nightmares.

'On the third day I came home from work and she was gone. By then it was over a week since the birth. I was out of my mind with worry. She was still bleeding heavily, and I thought she was completely insane. I waited for her to come home. I even cooked a meal before I realised she'd taken all her things. The flat was a mess, you see. She never cleaned up. She never tidied and she was way too much of a princess to use the Hoover. God forbid she should break a nail or something.

'Don't look at me like that. I know what I sound like. And it's true—by that time maybe I did hate her a little. I was terrified for her, but at the same time I was so relieved. I had a big drink and put on some loud music, R.E.M, I think—I remember *Bang Blame* and thinking: how appropriate.

'But of course I had to find her. So finally I plucked up enough courage to ring her school. I asked to speak to her but they said she was ill in bed. Apparently she'd caught a virus on the plane back from Switzerland! Can you believe that? She even stole the lie I told my boss.

'The people at the school obviously knew I was sort of her father's factotum so they said they'd keep me informed and let me know if she needed anything. But they never got back to me. Before all this she always used to ring me once or twice a week—if nothing else because she needed me to arrange more money. But after that she never rang again. She cut me out altogether. It was as if I didn't exist any more. She simply walked away and left me with a dead baby.

'And to begin with that was okay—it was just a problem I was going to have to solve one day. So I resigned from my job because I didn't want anything more to do with her or her father. Then I got the job I'm at now.

'But as the days, the weeks went by it seemed more and more as if she hadn't just left me with a little dead creature. She'd left me with all the horror and pain and *pity* of it too. And it grew. Like the baby should have grown, I suppose.

'She, meanwhile, blanked it out completely and then presumably became a reconstructed virgin. What kind of woman could do that? I still don't understand.'

Someone twisted into the shape of a corkscrew by the expectations of her family, her community, her culture, Nita thought. Someone terrified of punishment. Someone too young and inexperienced to cope. She said, 'She was out of her mind. Women can become very strange after the birth of a child. She was very young herself, remember.'

'But to kill her own baby...'

'It could've been a stillbirth,' Nita reminded him. She didn't want to go on speculating about Alia because it made her think about Mina's aborted daughter. A nasty, infested corner of her mind wondered if Alia's baby had been a boy, would she have found some way to keep it alive? She shut the thought down and said, 'What changed? Why did you have to do something about it now?'

Ian tipped the last of the Southern Comfort into his glass and drank deeply. 'My boss wants to relocate me to New York. It's a promotion. I want the job. But I'd be away for at least two years. Either I have to sell my flat or I have to rent it out. Or I turn down the job and live the rest of my life with a baby in the freezer. I didn't know what to do. I want to get on with my life. I want to forget. I mean I wanted all that. I really, really wanted to move on but I didn't know what to do with Alia.'

'I beg your pardon?' Nita was almost too shocked to speak.

'The baby was all there was left, so one night I got steaming and christened her Alia.'

'Christened?'

'Okay, I mean named. I had a private ceremony in the kitchen with a bottle of champagne and I called her Alia. I was remembering her as Daddy's little princess when I'd thought I was the luckiest guy in the world because she was so young and pretty and rich. She was such fun then. The world was her playground and for some reason I'll never understand she wanted me to be part of it. So I gave her daughter her name and my name: Alia Atwell. Nice, isn't it? Because I thought I'd never have another child, because I'd never have another girlfriend. You can't have normal relationships when you're hiding a terrible secret in your freezer.

'In the end I was getting drunk a lot and talking to Alia in the kitchen. I don't know which one. And then my boss calls me in and offers me New York. So I had to do something or sit here and rot for ever.

'And then just a couple of days later along came Zach West, the man with the plan, drinking buddy, Mr Fixit. Mr Wonderful. Mr Practical. Is there anything else to drink in this dump?'

'It's all gone,' Nita said, examining the bottle.

'Right,' Ian said decisively. 'Go to my place next door and bring us back a bottle of scotch. I can't go because I hit a policeman and they're just waiting for me to go home and then they'll arrest me.'

'It's four in the morning,' Nita protested. 'Everyone's asleep except us. Why did you tell Zach?'

'I've thought a lot about that, especially today, and I can't find an answer. He just seemed to turn up when I was at the end of my tether and had to tell someone. He was one hundred percent non-judgemental and on my side. And he knew a man...'

'Yes,' Nita said with feeling, 'that sounds like him.'

'All that bullshit about an ethical humanist ceremony, consecrated ground and a coffin...'

'Which turned out to be the skip outside my house. Which he chose because it was also outside the house his brother was re-modelling, and his brother had employed him to check out the neighbourhood. Just my luck.'

Ian stared at her. 'I didn't know you were involved. What's going on?'

'When the police found your baby, Ian, they decided, for reasons all their own, that it was mine. So they arrested me and took my DNA.'

'I thought you were Zach's girlfriend. You're living here...'

'I'm staying here because Zach dumped your poor little daughter in the skip outside my house and let me take the blame on account of mine being the only brown face in Guscott Road. It just became impossible to live there any more. Don't ask.'

'Oh, right, I was forgetting—you said at the beginning that Zach ripped you off and went to LA. But you listen really well, like he did. I guess I joined up all the dots the wrong way. Sorry.'

'What're you going to do?'

'Do?' Ian said. 'There's nothing more to do. I've told the wrong person the wrong story again. My life is over. And so is Alia's. I mean I won't tell the police her name, but you will. And even if you don't the connection can be easily made by anyone investigating my past.'

'Well yes,' Nita said, 'I suppose I could clear my name a few days before the DNA test results come in. I could save the police some work, couldn't I? Cos I'm a good girl who's never had a drink before in her life and I always do the right thing, don't I?'

26

Save a Sister

///

In the morning Nita discovered why it is that the first time
you get drunk you always promise yourself it will be the
last. She threw up the remains of her share of the frozen
pizza and nearly spewed her empty stomach into the kitchen
sink when she caught the whiff of stale Southern Comfort from
the glasses she was washing.

She stood under the shower for ten minutes with her eyes
shut because she couldn't stand the glare of morning light on
the bathroom tiles. She tied her wet hair back because the sound
of the hairdryer nearly made her teeth fall out. An iron hand
grabbed at her temples and squeezed. Nevertheless she resisted
the urge to go back to bed and die. Instead she staggered bravely
out into the world.

During the night council trucks had carpeted the roads
with coarse salty grit to cover the ice. The freezing air hurt her
lungs as, dressed in layers of jumpers topped by Zach's gilet,
she wandered unfamiliar streets to find aspirin and a new coat.
Nobody knew her in the shops close to River House. No one
waved to her on the street. No one pointed a finger or turned
away without speaking. No one held her nose. It wasn't like
home.

She bought a thick quilted coat in olive green and a woolly
cap and scarf, paying for everything with the cash Bret had lent

197

her. Then she stuffed Zach's gilet into a rubbish bin and walked away without looking back.

She wished she could do the same to Zach—consign him to a dump, preferably a skip, and never look back; never wake at four in the morning sweating and re-examining all his betrayals—revisiting every step by which she'd walked so eagerly into his traps. Which was worse, she wondered, her idiocy or his cruelty? Could it even be called cruelty? He was too indifferent to anything but his own advantage to be called cruel. Cruelty implied a personal connection with the victim. Zach had no more personal connection with Nita than a milking machine has with a cow.

There was more personal connection between herself and Harris Searle... Nita stopped dead in the middle of the pavement, hugging her new coat close to her chest, feeling again the pain in her nipple when he'd twisted it in the deserted supermarket on Tuesday night. That's preferable to Zach? She asked herself. What're you thinking, girl? Are you mad?

What is the matter with me? she asked herself, disgusted. She couldn't stand the thought that she was so habituated to dominance that she almost *expected* a man she hated and feared to hurt her. It was as if he had the right, and so she had to dredge up a forgotten anger, an extra ounce of courage, to thump him. An English girl would've thumped without hesitation; certainly without feeling guilty afterwards.

At an internet café she ordered black coffee and thought very carefully about what to write to Mina. She had to presume that whatever she wrote would be read by Rolam and whatever he read would be told to their father. As the aspirin and black coffee began to work their magic she began: 'Dearest Mina, I've gone away to Scotland to stay with friends for a while. I need a holiday. I wish you could come too with the children. The snow is so fresh and clean—the kids'd love it—yet the thick walls and log fires keep everyone safe and warm.'

It would tell Mina that she was alright and that she wasn't in Scotland. She was hoping Mina would remember a children's story they'd read years and years ago about a camel who'd wanted to see the snow and persuaded his friend Tommy Truck to take him up north to see it. The two friends went further and further north but didn't find any snow until they got to the top of a mountain at the top of Scotland where the camel almost died because it was too cold for him. When they got to the end of the story Mina said, 'I never want to go to Scotland,' and Nita said, 'Me neither.'

Every time they reread the story the sisters ritually said the same thing until Scotland slowly became the mythical last place either of them would ever go to. But the cottage with the log fire was the place Tommy Truck took the camel to recover from his ordeal. The very last line of the story was Tommy's when he said, 'You'll always be safe with me.'

Nita hoped that Scotland would alert Mina to the notion that from now on Nita would use the language of their shared childhood and she was going to help Mina escape and come home. She wanted her to know that though the journey would be difficult and dangerous they would succeed and recover—provided Mina could summon up the necessary willpower and courage to start.

That, of course, was the biggest question: could Mina extricate herself from her own fear and her inclination towards submission? Or would the effort and the sacrifice be too great? She knew she was asking Mina to join her out in the cold with no love or support from the family. She was asking her to tear her children away from their father and look to strange Auntie Nita for protection—the same Auntie Nita who couldn't go back home because she was afraid that *her* father, their grandfather, would kill her in order to restore honour and balance to their family.

Nita ordered more coffee, this time adding milk and sugar. Mina wouldn't come because Nita wanted her to. If Mina came it would be for her own reasons and because she was prepared to take the risk.

Nita drank her coffee and tried to organise her mind for the next two meetings: her bank manager and the boy-solicitor. She reminded herself that she was still on salary from Midford Junior School and that other people lived for years on credit without their noses falling off or going insane. It wasn't the worst fate in the world.

Nevertheless, on her way to the bus stop, as she passed a small café called The Soup Kitchen, she noticed a sign in the window saying, Help Wanted. On impulse she went in and made an appointment to see the owner later in the afternoon after the café closed. Having two jobs wouldn't be the worst fate in the world either.

On the bus she checked her phone for text or audio messages. There were none and she almost sank under a wave of loneliness. She was broke and alone. There was no one she trusted to help her. Even her enemies were silent. It should've been a welcome release but it made her feel as if she didn't quite exist. Maybe it was the contempt of her neighbours that gave her life shape. She had no will or character of her own. Her personality was shaped by the will of others.

She was horrified by the notion. Oh yes, she thought, I'm the heroine who can save my sister and her kids. Come to me for strength and initiative.

What Nita really needed was an iron-willed bank manager to take her in hand and tell her exactly what she must do to climb out of debt while at the same time kindly extending her credit. She was only asking for the chance to accept and obey.

But what if her real, sick, and secret desire was to go back to Guscott Road and wait for her father? That would be the ultimate in acceptance and obedience. Her death would bring her back into the family. It would prove her loyalty. It would show that she belonged—she could accept her fate and her family at the same time, and give up on this bitter struggle with free will.

Sitting, jolted, at the back of a bus, Nita realised that she should be more afraid of herself than she was of her father. She was afraid of the self that was afraid of free will, afraid of making decisions, afraid of too much choice. She was ashamed of the Nita who still wanted to go to school every morning and live by school rules. This was the same abject creature who might easily have lived for the rest of her life with the man who raped her—just to win the approval of the man who sent him to her.

The other Nita, the one who fought back, fought for choice and free will, the one who would move heaven and earth to save her sister, cowered at the back of a bus exhausted.

27

The Flaming Enemy

fterwards, Nita was left with the impression that both
bank manager and solicitor were at their most engaged
when figuring out ways to pay themselves. That was
when their professional expertise went into overdrive and Nita
felt that if nothing else they had solved their own problems.
Hers had been explained as two related but different stories and
she was depleted.

She would have to use her insurance policies as collateral
and sell her flat to prove that she was a good credit risk. But at
least she had them to sell and she could start life again as a fiscal
entity poorer, sadder and not much wiser.

The solicitor was both out of his depth and gung-ho. He
was all for suing the police and slapping restraining orders on
her family. Nita felt she had talked a lot but hadn't been heard
which was not unusual when explaining things to professional
people.

By the time she was finished it was late afternoon so she
caught a bus back to The Soup Kitchen. She was so tired that
she dozed off and almost missed her stop.

The kitchen at the back of the café was tiny but well
equipped. There was room for only one cook and a very limited
menu, and that was all the owners, Sherry and Ollie Richards,
were interested in.

'We've just been granted a liquor licence,' Ollie said, 'so we're looking to open three evenings a week, Thursday, Friday and Saturday.'

'To begin with we want to do what we're already known for—our lunchtime menu,' Sherry said.

Nita looked at the menu board and saw that today's soups were Cornish Seafood with soda bread, Chilli Con Carne with Saltines and Winter Vegetable with granary.

'Obviously we change soups all the time,' Sherry went on. 'Tomorrow we're doing Granny's Chicken soup and for the vegetarian option, Pumpkin and Broccoli.'

'Are the vegetarian options properly vegetarian?' Nita asked. 'I mean, do you make a proper vegetable stock?'

'Well I never!' Sherry exclaimed 'She's the first candidate to ask us that, isn't she, Ollie?'

'I'm impressed,' he said. 'Tell me how you'd make vegetable stock.'

Nita described how she would make the stock and added, 'But of course I'd do it whichever way you want.' She was looking round. There were only six small tables downstairs. She hadn't been upstairs but there could not be many more. Obviously the three vats of soup would be prepared beforehand, so, unless she was expected to be the waitress too, there wouldn't be much to do but pour soup into bowls and cut bread.

Ollie said, 'What sort of soups do you make in your culture?'

'My, er, "culture" doesn't go in much for soups,' Nita said. 'But many things could be adapted.'

'What about Mulligatawny?'

'Isn't that Anglo-Indian?' Nita asked. 'That's what I mean—one could easily combine the ingredients of one culture with the spices of another.'

'But not for classics like lobster bisque or clam chowder?' Sherry said sounding alarmed.

'Well, no.' Nita sighed. 'You have your own recipes—I wouldn't interfere with them.'

'I'm just afraid you'd find it a bit *tame*, working for us,' Ollie said. 'We aren't very spicy.'

'Okay.' Nita reached for her bag. 'Thank you for seeing me anyway.'

'I didn't mean we wouldn't offer you the job,' Ollie said hurriedly.

'We think you'd be just perfect,' Sherry put in. 'We just wanted to be sure you wouldn't change the *tone* of the Soup Kitchen.'

'But we were wondering if you might like to do a deal about the advertised wages. I think we might be able to work out something to our mutual advantage.'

'Excuse me?'

'Well, you'd prefer cash wouldn't you? And we'd really like to help although it puts us in a slightly awkward position regarding employment laws. But maybe with a little negotiation we could all be happy.'

They think I'm illegal, Nita thought. They think I'm an illegal immigrant and I'll work for black-market wages. Weary but curious, she said, 'What did you have in mind?'

Moonlighting, she thought, walking back to River House in the dark, now that could be a second career opportunity. I could do home tutoring in the evenings. Or run a homework club for the children of working parents. I could advertise on the internet and nobody would be any the wiser. That'd make more money than cooking soup for below the minimum wage. I'd pay off my debt much more quickly. And I would be lost to the system and therefore hard to trace. There could be advantages in that.

But when she thought about teaching children again she realised that something inside had died. She had been accused of killing a child. Even if the charge was publicly withdrawn, the fact that she'd been accused would remain. It would stain her employment record and persist for ever just like her DNA in the police data base. The questions about why she'd been unofficially suspended from school would crop up any time she was considered for promotion or a job at a new school. They would follow her like a pack of hungry dogs wherever she went.

Nita stood stock still at the entrance to River House while the full impact of this realisation fell on her. She stared sightlessly at the black river knowing that she had lost. There was no going back.

A voice from the car park shouted, 'Oy, Ms Terry!' And there was Sergeant Cutler waving to her from under a sulphurous yellow lamp.

'I thought I'd find you here,' he said, 'although that bleedin' builder friend of yours was about as much help as a sponge hammer.'

Behind him a car door slammed, and with horror, Nita saw Sergeant Eavers standing next to his old Audi, her fair hair discoloured by the poisoned light.

'What the *hell* did you bring her for?' Nita shouted, fright freeing her from politeness.

'What do you mean?' Cutler was surprised by her ferocity. 'She's come to apologise and explain.'

'You *idiot!*' Nita cried. 'She's the one who told my father where to find me. Don't you know anything? Why do you think I'm hiding in this horrible flat?'

'She never!' Cutler said. He turned to Eavers. 'She's making that up, ain't she?'

'She's right,' Eavers said, 'you *are* an idiot. I thought that was one of the things I was supposed to be sorry for.'

'If I'm killed it'll all be down to her! Lock her up so she can't do any more damage.'

'Oh please tell me this ain't effing true, will you?'

'Let's go, Cutler. I told you this was a bad idea.'

'It wasn't mine—he who must be obeyed on the frigging third floor said "make it so". Don't look at me like that.'

'Well he's an idiot too. Don't you think it would've been fairer to wait for the result of the DNA test before he exonerates her and condemns me? People in her community got bloody strange ideas about women and babies.'

'And you've got bloody strange ideas about me and my "community".'

'Do you know?' Cutler said wonderingly, 'I never heard her fucking swear before.'

'Go away,' Nita said slowly and carefully, 'and take this... this malicious person with you. I'll be gone in ten minutes so don't bother to look for me here again.' She turned away and walked into River House.

'See, she's the type I busted my hump for up north,' Eavers shouted after her. 'But would they cooperate? You'd think *I* was the flaming enemy.'

'You *are* the flaming enemy,' Nita muttered, slamming the outer door behind her and running to the stairwell. She went up the stairs two at a time thinking, I'll have to find a shelter. How'm I going to do that at this time of the evening? She opened the door to Zach's flat and went in, locking and bolting it after her.

She knew there were no phone books in the flat so she took out her mobile phone to ring directory enquiries and saw that there were two missed calls and a text from Ash.

Ash's text said, 'On way. Run.'

Nita's eyes filled with tears—her little brother had found two ways to warn her. He could probably get away with talking to Mina about her father's plans, but texting Nita directly would be considered extreme disloyalty.

Pounding on her door made her drop the phone.

Cutler shouted, 'You're making a mistake. Eavers ain't the problem no more. She's on a caution. One more wrong move and she'll be out on a psych report. She knows that. You won't get no more fucking trouble from her. It's the Commissioner, see. He got more complaints since Monday than he can fill a cocking double garage with. And they're all about you.'

'Complaints?' Nita said, standing close to the door but still unwilling to open it.

'Yeah, a shitload—like someone's organised something. Only it ain't a whatchamacallit, minority led campaign. It's proper people, like doctors and teachers.'

'Proper people?' Nita stuttered with rage.

'It looks like you got friends out there,' he said.

'Proper friends? From Proper People Land?'

'Oh fuck,' he said, sounding tired. 'I ain't frigging said something again? What've I said now? Know what?—you're too sensitive by half.'

'Know what? You ain't half sensitive enough.'

'You made a joke,' he said astonished.

'No I *didn't!*' Nita ground her teeth in frustration. 'I'm just trying to make you understand me. Eavers told my family my home address.'

'She didn't know about this new one though.'

'She does now. You brought her here. She's on her own agenda and she's got police authority. How do you know she isn't phoning my father right now?'

'Do you think you're more important to her than her job? If your dad turns up here there's only one person could of told him where to come, right? That's logic. Then she's frigging fired.'

'And I'm dead. Do you see my problem Sergeant Cutler?'

'But he's your dad.'

'Unfortunately your colleague's right—my so called "people" are a bit strange about women.'

'The thing is, about Eavers, she was pregnant, see, when she was involved in a nasty car smash and she lost her baby. There were these internal injuries, see, which meant she could never have another one. The baby was a girl.'

'What're you saying?'

'I been told,' Cutler said, 'that she was working up north at the time and there was this rash of infanticide cases, well, two actually. Both involving girls, so she sort of wigged out.'

'What's that got to do with me?'

'Well, see, she thought the police was taking a way too soft line with the perps on account of bleeding "cultural differences." She thought there was some cultures literally getting away with murder.'

Nita could never admit out loud that she agreed with Eavers, but she did.

'You still there?' Cutler said, tapping on the door. He sounded as if he was leaning on it with his mouth against the crack.

'Where else would I be?'

'Dunno. You usually got more to say than this.'

'Not this time. I'm too tired and I've got to find somewhere else to stay.'

'You ain't been listening.'

'No Sergeant, *you* ain't been listening.'

'Yeah I have—your dad's on his way with a meat cleaver. I heard.'

Nita said, 'Talk to Eavers, Sergeant Cutler. I hate to say it but she's got a more realistic picture than you have.' She stepped away from the door. Her head was pulsing with pain and she needed tea and an aspirin.

The worst thing was that in spite of all her efforts last night the flat still smelled of Zach. There was detergent, yes, and bleach, but under it all was the earthy scent of the man who had hurt her so badly. This was the place where he heard Ian Atwell's story. Maybe he even kept Alia Atwell's body here till he could dispose of it under cover of the night.

This was where he slept while she thought he was working to help clear her name of a crime he, above all others, knew she hadn't committed. He was the only one who had always known she was innocent because he was the one who had dumped Alia Atwell in the skip. Yet he heard her distress and took her money without the slightest twinge of conscience.

She had stood at her window, watching for his car, and when she saw it she felt safe. When she saw his bleached blond hair she smiled. And when she heard his voice over her entry phone her heart danced.

She went to the kitchen and filled the kettle. Cutler pounded on the door again.

She swallowed two aspirin tablets and went back to the door.

Cutler said, 'Okay, okay, I'll go away in a minute. But while I'm here, have you heard anything from that bloke who bopped me? The one who lives next door?'

'I've been out all day,' Nita said.

'Okay, but if you do see him, be a good girl and give me a call?'

'I don't know how many times I can bear to say this, Sergeant Cutler, but I won't be here for much longer.'

'Yeah, but if you do...'

Nita went back to the kitchen to make the tea. She promised herself that whatever happened she would not be the one to give Ian Atwell up to Cutler. He'd been betrayed enough already, and caught up in emotions and events which he would never truly understand. Let him go to New York to start a new life if he could. She wouldn't stop him.

He was not a man who had no conscience: he would always be haunted by one little ghost who would never give him peace. Surely that was expiation enough.

As always there was good and evil in one act: she could only stand by Ian and his poor wounded princess if she broke the law which says that crime must be reported.

She sat in the kitchen and ignored Cutler until he went away. Then she picked up her phone and listened to the two remaining messages. The first was from Helen Whitby who said, 'I gather you've had to leave your home, and unless you're really comfortable where you are now I'd like to invite you to come and stay with me. It's a huge flat in a mansion block so it's pretty well protected. And I've been rattling around here on my own since Mummy died so you'd be doing me a favour. Do give me a ring when you get a minute.'

It was as graceful an invitation as Nita had ever received, and she met it with equal measures of gratitude, resentment and embarrassment.

The second voice on her phone was Rose Peters'. She said, 'Bret West told me where you're staying which is just as well because some members of your family turned up this evening for a visit. I'm sure you wouldn't want to miss them. Call me if you'd like me to bring any of your things over in my car. I don't blame you—the builders have been using power tools and pressure hoses on your house all day. It's a mess but it's got to be done. Bret West's a bit of a dish, isn't he? He seems to like you, you lucky thing.'

Even before the message finished Nita was on her feet rushing to find her bag. She packed quickly, throwing things in anyhow. Then she remembered City Cabs' phone number and called for a taxi to meet her as soon as possible.

She rang Helen Whitby back and said she'd come over to explain why it wouldn't be a good idea to accept her invitation.

'Don't be silly,' Helen said. 'We have a doorman here. You won't put me in any danger.'

'I might,' Nita said. 'But I do need somewhere for a short time where I can use the phone and figure out what to do next.' She was at the window waiting for the sight or sound of her cab.

'Come anyway. We'll discuss it over supper and a glass of wine.'

'My taxi's just come,' Nita said, seeing headlights blinking. 'I'll be there soon.'

28

Let the Water Take Her

///

Nita shouldered her bag and rushed downstairs to the
front door. The cold wind hit her face with an icy
blast making her eyes water. She ducked her head and
ran towards the waiting cab.

It was the sharp sound of the horn that stopped her.
She cleared the tears from her eyes and saw that the car was
already occupied and that a scuffle was going on between the
occupants.

A door opened and two men fell out onto the tarmac. One
of them scrambled to his knees and shouted, 'Run, Nita! *Run.*'

He was brought down again and an arm rose and fell.

'Ash!' Nita screamed starting towards him. 'Don't hurt him!'
Absurdly her first incoherent thought was about how much
he'd grown in the time she'd been away.

Another door opened and three more men emerged from
the body of the car. Three big men. Father. Uncle Jag... and
Nariman.

Nariman, who she'd last seen in police custody after she'd
identified him as the man... the man who...

She dropped her bag and started to run to the road. Towards
bright lights and passing traffic.

The three big men spread out and cut her off from the
exit, turning her back towards the river. Cousin Ardesar now

stood at the door to River House, cutting off retreat. Ash lay motionless on the ground.

There was only one way to run. Nita sprinted across the car park with the sound of their hard shoes close behind her. She scrambled over the low stone wall that separated the car park from the riverbank.

There was a frozen mud path that ran parallel with the wall. She started along that, stumbling in the dark.

Cousin Ardesar vaulted the wall into her path. She turned the other way and came face to face with her father.

He said, 'Shameless animal, you have no name and no right to walk the same ground as clean people.'

'Dad.' She spread her empty hands, trying to appeal to him.

'You have no father.'

'Dad, at least go to Ash. He's hurt.'

'You have no brother, no mother, no sister. You live with whores and faggots. You live in filth, with filth. You're a filthy creature with no family.' As he spoke, he took slow steps towards her. It was too dark to see his face or what he had in his hands.

She backed away from him until she felt Ardesar's hot breath on her hair. Then there was nowhere to go but down to the river, tripping over roots and bushes, falling to her knees at the frozen edge of the black water.

Her father came down behind her. He said, 'I could drive my knife between your dirty ribs and good people would feel nothing but joy.'

She struggled to her feet, but he came closer and closer. He forced her backwards into the water till she was up to her knees in it.

He said, 'You think I will kill you? I will not pollute my hands with your unclean blood. I will not soil my knife.'

But Nariman and Uncle Jag came down behind him, and Nariman walked into the water towards her.

Her father's voice seemed to come now from a long way off. 'No—let the water take her. Then she will no longer defile the air we breathe.'

But Nariman came on, wading towards her.

Nita backed into deeper water, shaking with cold and screaming with fear until her foot hit an obstacle. She tripped. The river covered her face. She came up gasping and screaming. The water dragged hard at her coat pulling her down. It hauled her away from the bank.

She beat the river with her hands, trying to grab it and pull herself up. But she sank again. Water filled her nose and mouth.

She kicked hard. Her feet tangled with her coat. The quilting weighed a ton. It grasped her legs, binding them, holding tight.

Again her face broke the surface. She screamed to the banks and black trees.

Down she went. Her foot struck a hard wire cage. It rocked. She slipped and hit it with her hand. Something to stand on. She grabbed and got her knees, then her feet, onto it. A supermarket trolley.

She thrust with legs too weak to fight the waterlogged quilting. Her head met the air. She took huge sobbing breaths.

Killed by a coat, she thought. Saved by river rubbish. She opened her mouth to scream again. For what? Her voice was puny. She could hardly hear it herself. Only her blood rasped in her ears.

Then she was dragged off her rocking perch. For the fourth time the river won, overwhelming her, turning her lungs to a sponge.

Accept, she thought; accept and obey. And the thought was met with warmth and comfort.

Oh but my new coat, she thought, I only just bought it. She kicked again.

Indifferent to acceptance or struggle, the river wrapped her in strong arms and pulled.

29

Dead Babies

//

L ight. Hard yellow light.
A little baby girl with springy black curls sat on the
end of the white bed. She wobbled because she'd only
just learned to sit up. Nita was afraid she'd topple and fall off. She
tried to reach out to save her but found she couldn't move.

The baby girl said, 'Not very nice, is it? When your family
tosses you out like so much rubbish? A girl can get quite
depressed, neh?' The soft baby fists waved in the air and a bubble
appeared between the rosy baby lips.

'Who are you?' But Nita's voice hardly dented the profound
silence.

'Depression's always been my problem,' the baby said.
'Unwanted and unloved since my very first scan. At least you
had an okay life till you went to college. But I must admit, your
family's quite the drama group, neh? Driving you into the river
like that? Wow! They know you can't swim.'

'You're a ghost,' Nita decided.

'The ghost of girlies past, present and future,' the baby
agreed, blowing another ghostly bubble. 'Deprived of the right
to bear arms and go shoe shopping.'

'Am I a ghost too?'

'Well I don't know. I'm only a baby. You've really got to
decide some things for yourself.' The baby let rip a ghost fart

and looked satisfied. 'All I can say is beware of depression and melancholia. And don't rub your eyes after chopping red chillis. That'll *really* make you cry.'

Nita blinked in surprise and the baby toppled and fell off the end of the bed.

'Why is it?' Nita asked, 'that the things I most fear always happen?' Her words never cleared her lips because there was no breath behind them.

Light. Dim yellow light.

A face hangs suspended like a paper moon about nine inches from her face. A child with a pogo-stick jumps up and down on her chest. It hurts.

Nita tries to smile at the craggy moon face. She says, 'Are you a ghost?'

The moon cracks open, showing yellow teeth, and says, with the booming voice of God, 'I am a taxi driver.'

God drives a taxi, Nita thought, without surprise. He's very hard to find on a rainy night. He takes you where you need to go in his own way, in his own sweet time. He knows everything. But no one listens.

She said, 'Please, sir, will you ask that kid to get off my chest?'

Light. Yellow light.

The nurse said, 'Blankets. We need more blankets here. This is hypothermia after immersion in water, isn't it? The river? Ooh blimey! That'll be a shed-load of antibiotics too. We haven't got a bed free so just leave her here.'

The ambulance man said, 'I'm putting your bag at the end of your trolley, flower. Don't kick it off.'

'What about God?' Nita asked. Her voice flaked like bark from a dead tree.

'If you mean that taxi driver who pulled you out of the river, he went home for a hot shower and a change of clothes. Brave man. I'm not sure you would've survived if you'd been waiting for *me* to jump into a manky cold river at night.'

'Who is he?'

'Dunno his name, flower, but he works for City Cabs. He said he'd come and see you tomorrow. If he ain't caught pneumonia. That was a frigging cold night to go swimming.'

'I didn't mean to.'

'I should effing well hope not. Rest now, and do what you're told. I got another call to go to.'

Light. White teeth, greying hair.

Harris Searle said, 'Of all the A&E departments in all the world you had to walk into mine. I couldn't believe it when I saw your name go up on the board. You just had to come and find me, didn't you? Couldn't stay away.'

Not a ghost or God this time—more a nightmare, Nita thought. Then she saw with horror that he was real.

'Nurse!' But trying to shout produced a nasty wet cough that almost made her vomit.

'Things are getting lively,' Harris said. 'There was a pub brawl. Everyone's busy. They've forgotten all about you. Except me, that is—I'll never forget you.'

'Help!'

Harris laid his hand quite gently but firmly over her mouth. He looked down at her with a smile that was almost kind. 'Now let's get you out of those wet clothes. We should find somewhere more private.'

He was wearing a short-sleeved nylon jacket in regulation green. The muscles of his arms boiled under pale skin and turned regulation green too. The trolley rocked with the motion of the river. He said, 'I can't believe they left you alone like this—out in a corridor.'

Nita rolled sideways and fell onto the hard floor. She vomited over Harris Searle's shoes.

'Oh you dirty little cow!' he said, jumping back.

Pollution, Nita thought. My father and Harris agree. She tried to get up but her legs were as weak and wet as over-cooked noodles.

He lifted her as easily as a father would lift a baby and set her back on the trolley. Blankets, wet clothes—nothing stopped him.

'No!' she said. But her voice, like the far off cry of a gull, didn't stop him either.

'Drunk,' he explained to someone she couldn't see. And while pushing the trolley he pulled up the safety bars to stop her rolling off again.

'No!' she cried again, unheard. No strength, no voice, she thought. I'm like a baby in a pram. I'm too weak to walk—I must go where I'm pushed. The baby girl trundles unwillingly towards her death. Her fate was written before birth, XX, on her chromosomes.

The trolley turned left, shook and rattled over something uneven, then stopped.

'Hey!' someone shouted from far away.

'Help!' Nita replied helplessly.

Again Harris Searle's hand descended over her mouth. She tried to bite him but he laughed and doors shut like a sigh. With a queasy lurch the lift dropped into a pit.

'This is a teaching hospital,' he said in a conversational tone. 'Even the morgue is a teaching facility. We have all sorts of interesting exhibits. Even a teacher can learn something here.'

The doors sighed again and the journey continued into a cold, cold place.

'Dead babies, for instance,' he went on. 'Those snotty little med students all go "ooh-aah" about the dead babies.'

Nita crashed, feet first, through two sets of swing doors into a shelved aisle.

'Sit up and look,' he ordered. He pulled away the dry blankets and the deep cold seeped through her wet clothes like probing fingers.

She obeyed, struggling up, and saw stacks of jars—pickles on a supermarket shelf.

'This is a foetus with Downs,' he said, taking a jar down and holding it in front of her face. 'And this is what Thalidomide looked like unborn.'

Milky mutant things suspended in watery graves passed before her eyes until she shut them.

'Not interested?' he said. 'Okay, what else have we got down here? Oh yes, I know what'll amuse you.' He shoved the trolley through another pair of doors, saying, 'Let's see if we can find what's left of her, shall we?'

'You've got it so wrong,' Nita whispered. 'The baby isn't mine.'

'Turning your back on your own.' His face was so close to hers she could feel his spittle freeze on her cheek.

'Don't you turn away from me,' he said. 'No one can be as goody-goody as you lot are supposed to be. You ain't none of you for real. You've all got your secrets buried deep. You aren't like our girls, parading their sex for all to see and enjoying the attention. What's the point of fucking someone who's giving it away? It's disgusting. But your lot—you're different. When you're fucked you stay fucked. It ain't something you do between ten sambucas and throwing up behind the sofa on a Saturday night. With you it's all a dirty, shameful secret. I like that.'

'You're sick,' she said. 'You know nothing about me. You don't even know who my "lot" are.' She tried to slide down the trolley, away from him, but her wet clothes stuck. Killed twice in one night by a coat, she thought.

'Look,' he said as if she hadn't spoken. He pointed to a small pile of plastic bags. 'That's your daughter—chopped up like dog meat and stored in evidence bags by a pathologist who didn't give a toss.'

Like a jointed chicken, she thought. Butchery and forensic science use the same knives. Alia, born in blood and water, stored in a freezer, is now wrapped in plastic bags and left out on a counter. Left out on a counter?

'You're lying,' she said. 'If that were evidence it wouldn't be sitting out on a counter in unmarked bags.'

'You're so clever,' he said, 'you and your superior education. I saw you when you first moved in to Guscott Road. You were a fat little thing—a pregnant thing. All them gossipy cows said so. You can't talk your way out of that.'

There was a sudden clash of steel on steel from behind her. She swung around to look, and there was Harris standing over her with a knife in his hand.

'A fat little thing' he said, 'But a little, shameful killer. Know what a turn-on that is?' He slashed the cold air twice then brought the knife point to her throat.

'Get your kit off,' he said. 'I want to see you as you really are.'

Was that the knife...? Nita could almost see the ghost of Alia's frozen blood on the blade.

She was shivering so violently she was afraid she'd fall against the point and stab herself. What a way to die, she thought—stripping, obeying a mad man. Then she thought, No. I won't do it. Death before dishonour.

'I sound just like my father,' she said out loud, shocking herself.

'What?' It seemed to be the last thing Harris expected to hear too.

'Is everything fated to happen twice tonight?' she said, staring straight into his once kindly grey eyes. 'You're the second deranged man to threaten me with a knife. Can't you do something original?' She couldn't get up so she lay down again with her arms crossed over her chest. She closed her eyes and thought, not about babbling brooks, sandy beaches or anything to do with water, but about going to sleep in clean dry warm sheets in her own bed.

He grabbed her arm to pull her up, wrenching her away from her warm clean bed. It hurt.

But from nowhere a loud voice said, 'Hey, what's going on here? What're you doing in a restricted area?'

The effect on Harris was instant. Nita heard the clash as he dropped the knife. In a voice that had lost its menace he said, 'Mr Winston, sir, this is the woman who... isn't she supposed to be identifying a body? A baby. That's what I was told anyway.' He sounded like sweet reason itself.

And then there was Toby, just out of sight, saying, 'That's a *lie*. A nurse saw you wheel a patient into a lift—unauthorised. She told Leo.'

'Mind your own business, fag.'

'That's enough, Searle,' said the voice of authority.

Leo came to her side and said, 'We saw your name on the list, Nita. We came as soon as we could. But there's been a big pub punch-up and we couldn't find anyone from Security.'

Toby said, 'Are you okay, Neets? Did he hurt you?'

The voice of authority, Mr Winston, said, 'You'd better come with me, Harris Searle, there's questions need answering.'

'Seriously, Mr Winston,' Harris said, 'a cop up in A&E told me to bring her down here.'

'He's lying.' Nita forced the words out through teeth almost fused together by cold. It was the last thing she remembered.

───✦───

Warm and dry, Nita thought. I went home. She struggled to open her eyes but her eyelids wouldn't cooperate.

Toby said, 'She's sleeping.'

'No I'm not,' Nita mumbled. Harsh institutional light crept into her fuzzy vision.

'Well, you should be,' Toby said.

'I'm afraid Harris Searle will come back.'

Leo said. 'He's locked in the security room till the police have time to deal with him.'

'They'll let him go,' Nita said. 'Then he'll find me.'

'No he won't.'

'Can't I go home? I'd feel safer at home.'

'It wouldn't be wise, darling,' Toby said. 'There are builders in and out all the time at the moment. And Leo and I are still staying with Pete and Mike so we won't be there to look after you.'

'You have a high fever,' Leo said flatly. 'You're going nowhere till they've brought that down.'

'Maybe they could transfer me to somewhere else?'

'Maybe,' Leo said, 'and maybe you can sleep now. We'll find a couple of chairs and stay for a while.'

It wasn't just Harris Searle. Nita had nightmare thoughts, grotesque half-dreams about him, her father and Nariman together, pushing her down narrow labyrinthine corridors to an underwater morgue and throwing her into foetid water, too dirty to see through. Dead rotting babies floated in the foul liquid. One of the babies was her brother Ash.

'Leo?' she said, swimming to the surface of the dream. 'Can you find Ash?'

'Go to sleep.'

'My brother, Ash, was hurt. Is he here too?'

'Is his surname Tehri?' Leo said. 'Of course I can find out. But only if you go to sleep. Now shut your mouth and shut your eyes.'

30

Learn to Swim

//

S ergeant Cutler sat on the chair next to Nita's bed. He glanced suspiciously at the five other patients in the room and said, 'This ain't a geriatric ward, is it? I ain't scared of much, but old ladies give me the flaming heebie-jeebies.'

Nita wanted to say something sarcastic like, Is there no end to your talent for being offensive? But she was too tired, although she discovered she had managed to sleep for six solid hours. Six hours unconscious in a public space she thought with a shudder. Drowning must be an exhausting pastime.

Cutler said, 'Well, you'll be happy to learn that there's a warrant out for your father and his brother and nephew.' He shifted his bulk uncomfortably on the hard chair. 'I expect you'll be even happier to find out that Eavers has been summoned to the third floor. She'll be out on her ear by the end of the frigging day.'

Nita dug up enough energy to say, 'No.'

'Whadaya mean "no"? She was right, you know. She said you'd never lay a charge against your family. Whatever they've done, she said, you'd let them get away with it.'

'No.' She struggled to sit up straighter. 'You've got it wrong again Sergeant Cutler. Eavers didn't tell my father where to find me. It was a neighbour, trying to be helpful.'

'Shit,' Cutler said, lumbering to his feet and searching his pockets for his phone. 'I'd better call my governor before he makes a complete prat of himself.'

A passing nurse sang out, 'No mobile phone calls on hospital premises.'

He put away his phone gracelessly, saying, 'I wouldn't want to bugger up anyone's pacemaker, now would I?'

'And no fucking swearing,' muttered the eighty-year-old in the bed next to Nita's, just loud enough for Cutler to hear.

Nita smiled at her tiredly. She wished she were eighty and could say what she liked to big policemen. She felt eighty. Why didn't she feel brave too?

'What about the rest?' he asked. 'Are you letting your dad off scot-free? Eavers said you'd get us all involved, waste a lot of time and energy, and then back down as soon as they put the least bit of pressure on you.'

'I don't know.' Nita turned her head away. She couldn't bear to think about it.

'Well, make your mind up. It's attempted murder we'll be charging them with. And you're the only witness.'

Except maybe for Ash, she thought after he'd gone away. Ash was a witness. He'd seen his father's knife, and yet he'd found the courage to warn her. His reward was a beating from Cousin Ardesar. But according to Leo, he wasn't in the hospital.

Ash defied his father. The little godling of the Tehri family, the only son, took sides with the shamed animal daughter against his father. What would happen to him now? Would it be worse than concussion? Or would the family find a way to forgive the only son? Was he even alive?

News of a sort came from the man she had believed was God. He was the City Cab driver who had saved her life. He brought grapes. 'I thought of chocolates,' he said, embarrassed. 'But I've seen you at the YMCA gym a couple of times so I thought you'd prefer fruit.'

'You're absolutely right,' Nita said. 'Thanks so much... for everything. It was freezing and filthy but you jumped in and got me out. I don't know what to say.'

'It's fantastic,' he said enthusiastically. 'It was nothing special, not even a long swim. But now I'm some sort of local hero. I did an interview this morning with that woman from City News—the blonde one—and I've never been on telly before. Then the Chronicle and the Standard sent photographers. My girlfriend thinks I'm quite a celeb.'

'You are to me too,' Nita said. 'I don't even know your name.'

'Danny. You've made me famous—or rather that kid in the car park did. I'd never have known you were in trouble if that kid hadn't told me.'

'What kid? Please—I really need to know if he's alright.'

'Calm down, it's okay. He looked as if he'd been in a fight, but he was on his mobile calling the police and ambulance when I left him. I expect that bunch of guys took him home, cos he wasn't there when I brought you out. I would've asked them to help but they didn't look as if they spoke English.'

'It's just as well,' Nita said. 'They were the ones who pushed me in.'

'No shit!' he said, fascinated. 'Don't tell me—it's one of those "honour killing" situations, isn't it? Wow! I thought you just fell in by mistake. Maybe that's why the police want to talk to me. What do you think?'

'Probably. Make sure you tell them about the kid who was on the phone. I would've drowned if he hadn't told you where to find me. He's my brother and he's on my side. He's a terrific kid.'

After he'd gone, Nita did her best to think about the unthinkable. She decided that she *would* testify against her father; she would not let him, Uncle Jag, Cousin Ardesar or Nariman get away with what they'd done. They'd left her no other choice. She couldn't defend herself against them so she would have to attack. And maybe it was the only way she could rescue Ash from them. If the police knew he'd tried to save her from attempted murder, if they knew he was in danger too, maybe they'd intervene. Maybe the whole sick incident would loosen the family's hold on him. Then Mina would hear of it and come home with the babies.

Nita found herself hoping that Mina's scan would reveal the presence of a girl child. If Mina couldn't find the courage to come home for her own benefit, she'd do it to protect a daughter. One forced abortion of a baby girl was surely one too many. Mina knew that. She'd said so and wept on the phone to Nita about it.

Nita, feverish in a hospital bed, silently swore an oath to herself, to her sister and her brother that, however long it took, she would look after Mina and the babies, and help Ash.

Ash, Mina and Nita had suffered enough for their parent's values. So they were the ones who should try to change them and stop passing cruelty and stupidity down through the family as if they were cherished heirlooms. Or indeed as if they were inheritable characteristics like brown eyes and black hair.

It was the heaviest decision Nita had ever made. Exhausted and sweating with fever she dropped into a shallow, uneasy sleep.

'Lunch,' a skinny woman said, nudging Nita's foot. 'Wake up or you'll miss it.'

'What is it?' Nita sat up to look at a pale wet mound on a white plate.

'Dunno,' the woman said. 'Could be chicken, but the pork looks pretty similar. And the fish. *And* the macaroni now I come to think of it. Give it a good sniff.' She rolled her trolley out of the ward. Nita was still too queasy and groggy to eat, so she pushed the tray away.

'It's better than nothing,' said the eighty-year-old in the next bed, chewing stoically.

Nita was too polite to say, 'No it isn't. I could do better than that with both arms tied behind my back. I'd never mistreat food or people like that. Food should nourish. It should be enjoyed. Not endured.'

Like life, she thought. And yet up until a week ago I was teaching in a school because I was too scared, too inhibited, to contemplate life outside an institution. Yes, I liked working with the children, but that wasn't why I chose teaching as a career. It was because I felt safe within school rules. I needed to be told what to do.

She stared at the unidentifiable lump congealing on its plate. Without fear, she thought, without those inhibitions that have been drummed into me since birth, I might be brave enough to do something I really enjoy. Like feeding people with food that makes them say, 'Wow!' and hold out their plates for more. I could take a risk—take a business course—learn to run my own catering business.

Suddenly she saw herself in a big warm kitchen. Behind her at a table, helping to chop tomatoes and coriander are Ash and Mina. They're laughing the way they used to when they were kids. Mina's children are under the kitchen table, scuffling and telling each other secrets.

This is what I want, Nita thinks. This is why I must become brave. Because you have to be very brave to take your own life into your own hands.

But first, she thinks tiredly, I must learn how to swim.

About the author

//

LIZA CODY is the award-winning author of many novels and short stories. Her Anna Lee series introduced the professional female private detective to British mystery fiction. It was adapted for television and broadcast in the UK and US. Cody's ground-breaking Bucket Nut Trilogy featured professional wrestler, Eva Wylie. Other novels include Rift, Gimme More and 2011's Ballad of a Dead Nobody. Her novels have been widely translated.

Cody's stories have been published in many magazines and anthologies. A collection of her first seventeen appeared in the widely praised Lucky Dip and other stories.

Liza Cody was born in London and most of her work is set there. Her career before she began writing was mostly in the visual arts. Currently she lives in Bath. Her informative website can be found at www.LizaCody.com and you can follow LizaCody on twitter.

Printed in Great Britain
by Amazon.co.uk, Ltd.,
Marston Gate.